# TEACHER'S PET

R.K. LILLEY

ISBN: 978-1-62878-062-8

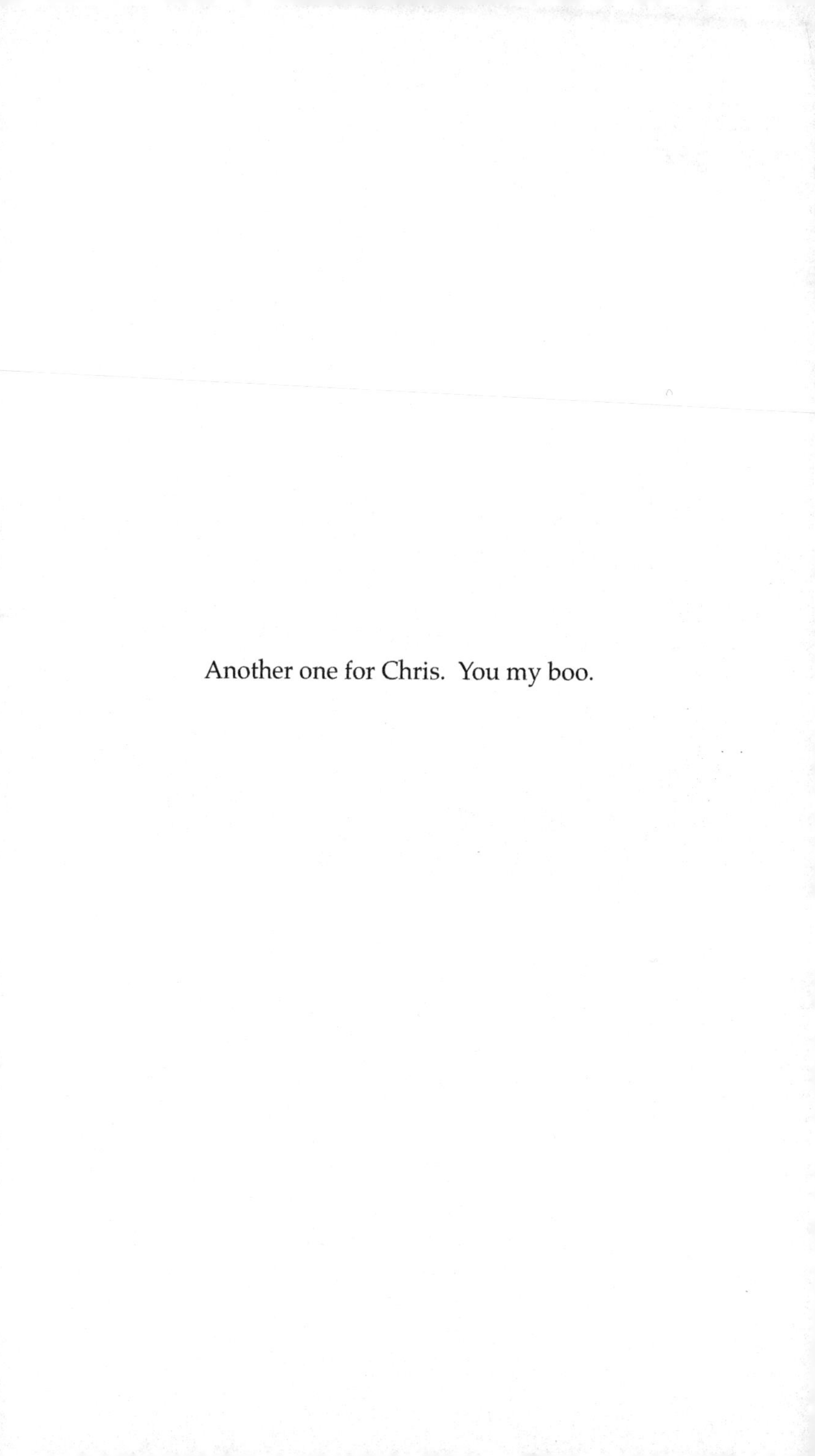

Another one for Chris. You my boo.

# CHAPTER 1

**CARTER**

**I want you to be my first.**

I stared for a moment at the strange text from an unknown number.

My response was quick and simple:

**Me: I think you have the wrong number**.

I shouldn't have even had my phone out. I usually had it locked away—trying to be a good example to my class that you didn't have to *live* on your phone.

I glanced up as my students started filing into my classroom.

Every single one of them was on their phones, and it would stay that way until the bell rang and I made them put them away. It was a given.

Even as I had the thought, my phone dinged another text at me, and I glanced down at the screen.

**No. I'm definitely talking to you, Carter.**
**I've never been fucked, and**
**I want my first time to be with you.**

*What in the ever-loving hell?* I thought, taking a seat behind my desk, never taking my eyes off my phone.

I texted back:

**Who is this?**

"Hello, Mr. North," a low, raspy female voice said from directly in front of my desk.

It wasn't a voice suited to a high school English classroom, and it certainly shouldn't have belonged to a girl that was barely legal.

I reluctantly looked up at my most vexatious student.

Nova Monroe beamed back at me. She was a problem. Head to toe, a problem. Her silky black hair. Her fuck me, Daddy lips. Her huge, real, *barely legal* tits. Her dusky golden, way too accessible flesh. Her long, thick lashes shading gorgeous, dark bedroom eyes. Her tiny waist that I could span with my hands.

Her career-ending ass.

They were all problems. Problems that I was determined couldn't and wouldn't be *my* problems.

"Hello, Miss Monroe," I said coldly, trying my best to sound impersonal and professional. Anything to compensate for the fact that my cock got hard at just the sound of her voice.

I made myself break eye contact with her. "Please take your seat," I told her.

She moved away to obey. Unfortunately, I glanced up as she did so. That career-ending ass was barely covered in a school uniform, pleated skirt that was definitely shorter than dress code. Shorter by a long shot. I had no clue how she even got away with it. I almost called her out on it, but stopped short. Pointing out that I was aware of it was not in my best interest or hers. Some other teacher would hopefully notice and put a stop to it. I needed to stay as uninvolved as possible with that landmine of a student.

The school I worked at had uniforms not because it was some posh private school. It was just the opposite. It was one of the worst schools in the county, and that was really saying something in Vegas. The uniforms had been implemented when gangs started openly recruiting on school property. It was one of many efforts the district had enacted to keep the students less distracted and more focused on education.

I had no idea if it did any of that, but it was a fact that on one student in particular that uniform was distracting the hell out of me.

Nova sat down slowly, unconsciously arching her back as she wiggled into the old-fashioned, wooden desk chair.

She always sat in the front row, closest to my desk. She often had a candy in her mouth, making those fuck me lips tantalizingly wet, making my mind go inevitably to *other* things I liked wet.

She lowered her eyes demurely as she ran her hands down her torso, presumably smoothing out wrinkles in her white, button down, uniform dress shirt. I didn't see any wrinkles in the fabric, but there were plenty of other things I couldn't keep my eyes off of.

Her perky tits with their perfect cherry nipples were so clearly outlined that it made my hands itch, and my cock twitch.

I wouldn't be standing up for any lectures today. Fuck my

life.

I'd been dodging jailbait without effort for years, but Nova Monroe was a special sort of challenge. My own personal hell, if I was honest.

She'd turned eighteen a few months ago. I knew that because she'd had the unmitigated gall to tell me she was legal the exact day it happened.

A day hadn't gone by since where that knowledge hadn't tormented me. She was a shameless, dauntless tease.

**NOVA**

Mr. North didn't fuck students. Everybody knew it because every girl in school was at least a little bit in love with him. Including me. He was perfect, and I'd been obsessed with him since I first laid eyes on him in 9th grade. I was a senior and eighteen now, and the obsession hadn't gone anywhere. Just the opposite. It had grown out of proportion until it felt too big for me to handle.

I was to the point where I didn't want to handle it. I'd been saving myself, but not anymore. I was ready.

I wanted Mr. North to have his way with me, whatever, however, wherever he wanted.

I shifted in my seat restlessly, drawing his eyes to my bare legs under my desk.

He tried to be good, I knew he did, but it was getting harder for him. He couldn't hide the heat in his eyes as they lingered on my bare, untouched flesh briefly before he tore them away.

I loved it when he looked at me like that. I loved it when he looked at me, period.

He was a big man, a former college football player that doubled as one of the high school coaches during football season.

Big and gorgeous.

His voice when he lectured was cold and stern, but his eyes were warm and intense with an interest he thought he hid better than he did. But I could read him better than most because I had been paying very close attention. I didn't have a choice. I could never take my eyes off him.

He was perfect; a large, fit man with broad shoulders, messy brown hair and a warm, irresistible smile. His face was handsome, with even features, melting chocolate brown eyes, and dominated by a jawline so defined it made me wet.

He even dressed the part of my perfect teacher daydream, wearing pristine white dress shirts and well-tailored slacks.

On some lucky days—today being one of them—he even went the extra mile with conservative wool blazers and perfectly folded ties. He looked like a studious professor, head to toe. No one could look at him and not crave his approval. Or maybe that was just me.

I wanted his approval. But above all, I wanted his attention.

I wanted to have all of his overwhelming masculine intensity focused only on me.

He started going over the day's lesson without standing up from his desk, his voice monotone, his eyes aimed down. This was unusual for him. Usually he moved when he taught. He paced, he spoke directly to students, he engaged.

Not today. Today he barely looked up. Instead he read directly from a textbook. He was phoning it in today, which I'd never seen him do.

He was more distant than usual. He was barely present, which was out of character.

His expression was perfectly composed. That was perfectly on brand for him.

He looked like a man who had never been ruffled by anything. I wanted to ruffle him. I wanted to affect him in any way at all.

I almost reached for my phone and barely stopped myself. Mr. North was very strict about us putting our phones away after the bell rang, and though I did want to get his attention, I didn't want to displease him.

It took all of my self-control, but I managed to wait to check my phone after the period was over and I'd left his classroom.

"Have a nice day, Mr. North," I told him quietly as I walked by his desk.

He didn't look up at me, but his shoulder twitched in a small movement that spoke of tension, and I knew he noticed me. "Goodbye, Miss Monroe," he returned, his voice dismissive.

As soon as I was out of his sight, I pulled out my phone, eyes scanning over the text conversation that dominated my thoughts, desperate to see if I'd gotten a response from the object of my obsession.

**I want you to be my first.**

**Mr. North: I think you have the wrong number.**

**No. I'm definitely talking to you, Carter.**
**I've never been fucked,**
**and I want my first time to be with you.**

**Mr. North: Who is this?**

My heart raced as I typed in my response.

**Me: Guess**

**Mr. North: I'm not playing this game.**

I went outside to escape the chaos of the bustling hallway and found a quiet spot to go through my phone. I didn't let nerves stop me as I found just the right picture and pressed send.

I knew I needed to act fast. I didn't have time for delays anymore. It was now or never. I wouldn't even *have* a phone in a matter of weeks, and I'd fantasized about this for years, so I had to take my shot.

**Me: Let me show you.**

**CARTER**

I nearly dropped my phone when I saw the picture that flashed across the closed screen and just managed to hide it in my pocket instead, keeping my eyes trained straight ahead.

It didn't matter. The image I'd barely glimpsed was burned into my memory.

Mrs. Green, the principal, droned on without a break in her week's agenda. I glanced around at the attendees of the routine faculty meeting. Not everyone was paying attention, but no one seemed to notice my reaction to what I'd seen on my phone, thank God.

I closed my eyes, rubbing at my temples.

That made it worse. My mystery texter had done a number on my brain. I couldn't stop thinking about what I'd seen.

It had been a lot of skin.

*Fuck.* Who was it? My mind flashed to Nova Monroe, but I didn't know if it was because that's how I pictured her naked, or because it was actually her.

*Fuck.* Did I *want* it to be her?

Some part of me clearly did, and I was not okay with that.

I'd always had contempt for the teachers that got off on bagging students. To take advantage of a young girl (even if she *was* legal) like that was reprehensible to me.

But I didn't want to take advantage of Nova. I wanted to

take *care* of her. In every way.

*Fuck.* This line of thought would lead to my personal and professional ruin, and still I couldn't get it out of my head.

It felt like it took forever before I could leave. It was only after I'd gotten into my car, driven a good five miles, and then pulled over into a near-empty parking lot before I pulled my phone out again and looked at the picture.

Getting nudes was hardly an anomaly so I could only figure it was the conversation and my own errant thoughts that had my heart pounding as I looked at my phone.

The picture got right to point, cropped to show me her body from shoulders to thighs. Every inch of it was perfect.

She was naked and had round, perky, natural breasts that were big enough to overfill my large hands. Her skin was golden and even-toned everywhere.

My mystery virgin was showing me plenty, but none of it was identifying her for sure. I couldn't even tell her hair color. Her sex was shaved, her legs parted just enough to show me.

But one thing I did clock right away; it certainly didn't rule out Nova.

I told myself I didn't want it to be her.

Only one of my heads agreed with that. I was hard as a rock, and looking at that gorgeous body only had me picturing one face to match it.

**Me: You don't look like a virgin.**

I immediately regretted sending the text, but even so, I watched for her response.

**I'd be happy to show you in person.**

**Me: This isn't funny.**

**Tell me who you are.**

She didn't bother to respond to that. I put my phone away and tried to forget the whole thing.

# CHAPTER 2

A few days later and I was driving home from work directly to my gym. It was just a few blocks away when I saw a lone figure walking on the side of the road.

I instantly knew who it was. She was carrying a full, oversized backpack, but I recognized those curves. The shape of them was permanently branded into my brain.

Fuck. *Why* was she walking on the side of the road?

I was still cursing as I pulled my car over onto the shoulder.

I rolled down the passenger window and watched her walk over and lean down. Nova's eyes were wary on me, but she smiled tentatively.

"Hello, Mr. North."

"Hello, Miss Monroe. Why are you walking on the side of the road?"

"I don't have a car," she explained in a small voice. "So I'm walking."

"Get in," I told her. "I'll take you home."

I helped her put her oversized backpack into the trunk, handed her into the front seat, and slid back behind the wheel. "Where to?" I asked her.

She looked down at her lap and started rubbing her hands together. She seemed nervous as she answered, "I'm not sure. My aunt and uncle kicked me out a few days ago. I've been staying at my friend Michelle's house but that wasn't working out, so I'm kind of between houses right now."

My heart twisted in my chest. "You're homeless?"

She shrugged, looking away. "Just for now. I'll figure out something."

I couldn't help myself. I reached over and touched her shoulder. "I'll take you home. You can stay with me until you figure out something more permanent."

"Are you sure you want me staying in your house? Wouldn't that look bad?"

I felt my face tensing up in something akin to annoyance. "Of course I won't let you be out on the street. There's plenty of room at my place. And it doesn't really matter how it looks, since what it *is* is perfectly innocent. And it will be no trouble for me. We don't need to get in each other's way."

She had a look on her face that made me think for a moment that she would argue with me, but after a brief pause, she nodded, looking forward without another word.

I knew it was dangerous to take her in like this, but I didn't see that I had another choice. I didn't have it in me to leave one of my students homeless and walking on the side of the road.

That being said, I knew right away that it was a mistake. I was walking a dangerous path here. If even one person at the school found out that I was letting Nova stay in my home, it could cost me my teaching career and my reputation. Add to that my own acute, inappropriate lust for her, and I'd just laid the groundwork for my own professional ruin.

Knowing all of this didn't seem to matter, though. I was involved, and I didn't see a way out that I could live with.

"You said your aunt and uncle kicked you out," I began, wanting to get the whole story from her. "What happened? And where are your parents?"

"My parents died four years ago. Car accident." She said it with such clipped stoicism that I could tell that she didn't like to talk about it, which was hardly surprising. "And my aunt and uncle got custody. They have a very small house, and my aunt's brother just lost his job and moved his entire family in. There simply wasn't any room."

"So they just kicked you out?" I couldn't help it, my tone was indignant. The very idea straight-up pissed me off.

She shrugged. "Yes. I'm eighteen, and I'll graduate in a couple of months. The idea was always for me to leave as soon as I was done with high school. They just decided I should do it a few months ahead of schedule. We were never close. My uncle is fine, he was my dad's brother, but his wife never liked me, and her brother and I . . . don't get along, so I wasn't really surprised. At least I have a job. I used to just waitress to pay for my phone and stuff, but I've been saving, and if I cancel my cellphone plan, I should be able to scrape together enough to put down on an apartment pretty soon."

I glanced over at her. Her voice had been blank, emotionless even, but her eyes showed me that she wasn't unaffected by her aunt and uncle's callous actions.

She tugged at the hem of her skirt, and I tore my gaze north. Our eyes caught for another electric moment before I managed to look away.

I opened my mouth to ask her how much cash she needed

to help her put down first and last month's rent on an apartment, but couldn't do it. I didn't want her staying in some crappy apartment in the sketchy part of town. If she stayed with me she could save her money, and I had plenty of room.

"We'll go to my house, get you settled in, and try to figure out what you need," I told her.

She fidgeted with the hem of her skirt. It drew my attention to her legs, which were nearly bare in the tiny, pleated skirt she was wearing. "I have everything I need," she assured me.

"Are all of your uniforms like that?" I asked in a carefully neutral tone.

Her clothes were a problem for me. If I was going to stick to my own rules, I needed her to cover up more. I wasn't proud of it, but it was a fact nonetheless.

She shrugged nonchalantly, but her eyes were glued to my face as she answered, "They don't take up much room. All my clothes fit in one bag."

No, they wouldn't, being that they consisted of hardly any material. "We'll talk about it later," I told her.

We were almost to my neighborhood before I thought to mention, "For obvious reasons, it would be better if you didn't tell anyone that you're staying with me."

I didn't even have to turn my head to see her rolling her eyes. "Do you think I would do that to you, Mr. North?"

"I just thought I should be clear. It *would* look bad, obviously."

"Obviously," she agreed, though there was a bite to the way she said it.

"No one would believe that you were just staying with me, and that it was completely innocent," I felt the need to explain, probably because I'd had a hard-on from the moment I'd seen her walking on the side of the road.

Of course no one would believe it. Even my own dick wasn't convinced.

We were silent for the rest of the drive, which didn't take very long. I pulled into my garage, shutting the door behind us before I got out of the car.

# CHAPTER 3

"Nice place," Nova said, looking around as I led her from the garage, through the mudroom, and into the kitchen.

It was a nice place. Too big for me, too much in general, but everything was top of the line, and my interior designer had made sure it all matched up, design-wise. Lots of cool tones, shiny surfaces, and rare flashes of vibrant color.

"You pay for all this on a teacher's salary? This and those cars?" she asked skeptically, referring to my second car that she'd obviously spotted in the garage.

I turned, leaning my hip against the large slice of white marble that made up my kitchen island. I folded my arms and glared at her. "That is a rude question, Miss Monroe."

"Sorry," she said, biting her lip and making very solid eye contact with me. Her eyes were almond shaped and dark and seductive enough to break my resolve.

I looked away first.

"I wasn't trying to be rude," she continued. "I'm just

curious. I've heard you're rich, but no one knows why."

I sighed. "If I tell you, will you keep it to yourself? I don't need everyone knowing my business."

"Of course. I'll never tell anyone any of our secrets, Mr. North. I swear it." Her voice now was breathy and low. She was messing with me. She was a sweet little thing, I knew, but clearly she had a naughty side.

I went back to glaring at her. "Knock it off. Don't make this situation between us sound dirty, okay?"

"Okay," she repeated back promptly, but she didn't look the least bit sincere or contrite.

"I'm an author. That's where I make my money. The teaching is a passion project, though sometimes it feels like more trouble than it's worth."

She blinked. I'd surprised her. It made me flush. Maybe I was interesting to her. Not just some boring teacher after all.

"That's really cool. What's your pen name?"

"I prefer not to say."

"What genre?" she asked.

"No more questions. Let me show you to your room."

I led her toward the back of the house, up the back set of stairs, and to a large, furnished bedroom that no one had ever used before. I waved her in, but stayed outside. "Make yourself at home. There's an attached bathroom that should have what you need, but make a list if there's anything else I can get you."

Without warning her soft body was pressed up against me, her arms snaking under my arms to hug my stomach. Her sweet little head fit perfectly under my chin, and her hair smelled like fresh oranges. I wanted to bury my face in it.

I wanted to grab her perfect ass in both hands and nail her straight to the door.

I wanted to fuck every hole on her body until she was dripping with cum, head to toe.

My breathing was harsh as I carefully moved my hips away from her. She was just hugging me. No need to make it filthy just because my body wanted it to be. My brain was the one in charge here, even if I had to remind myself of it constantly.

"Thank you so much, Mr. North," she said into my shirt, nuzzling her face softly between my pecs, in the center of my chest. "No one's ever been this nice to me. Not since my parents died."

I shut my eyes tightly as those words sank in.

I felt it then, the first raw, dizzy edge of new emotion.

Her helplessness should have lessened my ardor, but it seemed to have the opposite effect. It made me even more desperate to take care of her, in every way.

I'd been celibate for too long, I told myself. I had a very high sex drive, and I'd been too busy to get laid lately. That's all that was happening. I needed to go out and fuck someone more appropriate than this little angel/devil.

"It's no trouble," I said. My arms were stiff at my sides, my hands twitching to either push her away or grab handfuls of her with both hands. "I have plenty of room, and I'm happy to let you use it for as long as you need. You can even use my other car if you promise not to tell anyone who you're borrowing it from."

I barely got the words out as her lower body burrowed closer to mine until my rock hard dick was very obviously jabbed against her stomach.

She gasped or I gasped or we both did. "Mr. North," she moaned, rubbing against me.

Involuntarily my hips pumped against her, humping hard twice before I thrust her away.

I glared, but she wasn't looking at my eyes. Her gaze was aimed straight at my errant erection.

She licked her lips. "Let me help you with that."

My jaw clenched, and my left eye began to twitch in time to my aggravation. "Stop that."

"I'm eighteen," was her infuriating response.

"Well, I'm *thirty*, so that hardly matters."

"Twelve years isn't that big of an age gap."

I was still holding her away with both hands, and she was leaning with all of her slight weight toward me. "Stop that. Stop looking at it."

She ran her tongue over her teeth then bit her lip. She was intoxicating me, and I needed to get away, fast.

Still, I was frozen to the spot.

"It doesn't have to mean anything to you," she said quietly and soberly. "Just use my body as your own personal sex toy. You can do whatever you want with me. I'll never say no, and I'll never tell anyone. I know you don't care about me, but you want me, so take me however you want to. Any filthy thing you can think of. I want it. I want *you*."

My eyes were shut, and my hard-on was throbbing in time to my sped-up heartbeat. "Stop that. Stop talking. Everything you just said is wrong. I do care about you. I care deeply about your welfare. That's why this needs to stay impersonal. I'm your teacher and your roommate for as long as you need it. Nothing more. Okay?"

"Okay," she agreed, way too quickly.

Insincerely.

I tried to explain it to her, to stress the importance of it. "When I became a teacher, I was entrusted with the welfare of the kids I teach. It's a code I'm not supposed to break. Do you know what kind of a scumbag it would make me to violate it?" I paused. "To violate *you*." Fuck, I was making it worse. Just the thought had me *throbbing*.

She didn't answer. I don't think she even heard me. She was still staring at my pulsing, straining cock.

I backed away, and thank God she let me. "I need to go do

some work. Why don't you get yourself settled in? I'll be downstairs in my office if you need the keys to the car."

With that I made myself walk away.

Barely.

It was a worrisome start to our new living arrangements.

It was only about thirty minutes later when she appeared in the doorway of my office. I'd left the door open so she could find me if she needed anything.

I raised my brows at her expectantly, not saying a word about her too tight waitress dress and apron. "Need a car?" I asked.

She bit her lip and nodded.

"What are your hours?" I asked.

She shrugged, and my eyes moved to her perfect, perky tits.

"That work uniform seems a bit tight on you," I said in spite of my better judgment. I shouldn't have brought it up.

She ran her hands down her body, lingering at her heavy breasts. "It helps with the tips."

I felt myself flushing hotly with anger. "You shouldn't use your body as currency. You have more to offer than that."

"I shouldn't tell you then that I was thinking about starting an OnlyFans to help save up money."

I glared, more than half-tempted to take her over my knee. "Don't even joke about that. You're better than that."

"Even if it's just to pay for college?"

I wanted to shake her. "Listen, if you need money just ask *me* for it. I'll help you, and you don't have to do anything you'll regret later."

"You shouldn't tell a girl something like that, Mr. North. You're too trusting."

"I'm not telling *a* girl that, Miss Monroe. I'm telling you. If you need money for college, or anything else, I have it. Don't exploit yourself when you have other options."

"I've never had other options before." She gave me an impish smile, and she looked way too young when she smiled like that. "Sounds fun. Just remember you have other options, too. I'll be home late, but I'll leave my bedroom door open for you."

"Stop that," I warned softly.

She laughed like it had all been a joke.

"Don't tease me, Miss Monroe."

She winked at me, the little brat. "Never." Without another word, she left.

I stewed for hours. This was going to be a disaster.

She didn't get home until nearly two a.m.

And it was a school night.

I was unaccountably furious.

I was waiting when she walked in the door, still in her work uniform/porn fuel of a dress. She looked tired and dejected but still extremely fuckable. I had a vivid flash of what it would be like to fuck her when she was too tired to move, when she had no strength left, how soft and pliant she'd be, so malleable under my hands and around my cock. I'd work her tender flesh until she was a satiated puddle under me.

My own messed up thoughts made me even more furious.

"What are you even thinking working this late on a school night?" I wasn't shouting but my voice was low, stern, and mean enough that she stood up straight, looking like I'd slapped her.

"I need the hours. You think I was out having fun?"

I pulled out my wallet. "How much did you make? I'll pay you that much to stay home and do your homework.

I've noticed you've been falling farther and farther behind on your assignments and English used to be your best subject. I hate to see what your other grades look like."

She waved me off, moving past me. "You've already done too much, Mr. North. I can't take any more help from you."

Without any agreement from my brain, my hand shot out and grabbed her wrist, stopping her progress. "You need to stop talking back to me. Now that I know you need help, I'm going to have to insist on helping you. *I simply insist.* I'm all you've got. Just think of me as a kind of . . . foster parent . . . that's helping you get on your feet for the future."

She was suddenly in my personal space, looking up at me.

I'd always dated tall women because of my own towering height, but I suddenly found that I loved how petite she was, how she fit against me, how she had to look up, up, up to meet my eyes. "Foster father?" she asked softly, tracing her free hand up my chest. "So kinky, Mr. North. Should I call you Daddy?"

I pushed her away. "Go to bed," I ordered harshly.

Luckily, she obeyed.

# CHAPTER 4

**NOVA**

I parked Mr. North's 911 Porsche as far away as I could and walked the rest of the way to school. I didn't have an answer if anyone asked why dirt-poor me was suddenly driving around in a car like that. I'd have to think of one if this whole dreamlike experience continued.

I still couldn't believe he kept a car like that in his garage everyday while he took a baseline model 3 Tesla to school. Still a very nice car, but no Porsche 911. I'd looked it up.

I nodded and smiled at a few friendly faces in the hallways on the way to my first period. I sat in the back, dodging the eyes of a football player I'd dated for a minute and promptly avoided once he started pressuring me too much for sex. Even then I'd known I was saving it for Mr. North. And certainly no one else had any chance after yesterday when he'd morphed even more into my stern, caring, dream man. Imagine a guy like that, offering to solve all my problems. He was too perfect. Even more than I'd fantasized about.

Now I just needed to make him see me as more than a problem to solve. To see me as a woman.

Of course there was his errant, huge erection. He'd been sporting it from the second he'd picked me up. I was absolutely hung up on it. *Obsessed.* He didn't want to want me, but that didn't seem to matter.

I'd suspected I'd made him hard before, hell that was always my goal, but up until now he'd managed to hide it under his desk if that was the case. Yesterday he'd had nowhere to hide. From the drive to his house and even when he'd chewed me out for coming home too late, he'd been unmistakably and prominently hard as a rock and ready to go.

I wondered how it would work my first time, with him being so big. My friend Maddie had told me her boyfriend broke her hymen with his fingers, and I wondered if I should try to do that to make the first time easier. I looked at my small hands. My fingers weren't that big.

Mr. North had big hands. Thick, long fingers. Maybe he'd do it for me.

I sighed. Fat chance. He'd rejected me, and every inch of his body meant it except for one notable part.

I comforted myself with the knowledge that eventually that part might win over his common sense. It certainly looked formidable enough to make a difference.

English was my last period, and it was torture waiting for it. I was already way behind in all my classes, and I learned *nothing* that day, daydreaming instead about my favorite teacher.

When I'd found him in his home office before my shift yesterday, he'd been wearing reading glasses. I loved when he wore his reading glasses. I shuddered just thinking about it. He looked even more like a stern teacher in them. I wanted to eat him up with a spoon like that.

Mr. North studiously ignored me when I walked in and for the first half of class. He stayed behind his desk again, and I squirmed in my seat thinking about what that meant.

He told us we had a half hour to catch up on late work and started working on his computer. He put on his reading glasses and I shuddered.

That caught his eye. His gaze locked onto me and narrowed. "Get to work, Miss Monroe. You're too far behind to be sitting around daydreaming."

"Yes, sir," I told him.

He shut his eyes, one hand flying up to rub at his temple, then promptly ignored me for the rest of class.

I stayed behind when everyone else left, watching him until he looked my way again.

"Need something?" he asked me in a very unfriendly tone.

"I want to see you stand up from that desk," I said. I'd gotten bold, but waiting for him to make the first move was clearly not going to work.

"Go home," he said harshly. "And knock it off. This is my place of work."

I stood up, taking a deep sigh. His eyes went to my breasts as they moved with the motion and stayed there. I could tell he didn't know he was staring. He was that caught up.

I bit my lip and glanced at the door, dragging a hand up my body to finger my own nipple.

"Stop that," he said through his teeth.

I tweaked my nipple until they were both prominent and hard, clearly visible through my old, threadbare, washed a million times, uniform shirt.

He was panting and glaring at me.

"Just push your chair back," I said softly. "Let me see it and I'll leave."

He shook his head. He looked like he wanted to throttle

me.

I started to lift up my skirt and he snapped, abruptly pushing his chair back.

I stepped closer, feeling a rush of relief, desire, and power as I saw his stiff erection straining through his pants.

He pushed his chair back in and buried his face in his hands.

I felt bad for tormenting him. Just rotten. But I couldn't stop. I'd never wanted anything more.

"What's that in your mouth?" he asked, not looking up at me. "What is it you're always sucking on?"

I moved the sour candy around in my mouth before answering. "Lemon drops. Want one?"

He looked up at me, stood, and backed me into his desk without touching me directly. He held out his hand. "Give it to me."

I stuck out my tongue, showing him the half sucked candy in a taunt.

He took the bait better than I could have imagined. He took it out of my mouth with his fingers and put it in his own.

Instantly he backed away, but he kept sucking on my candy.

"I took my panties off right before class," I told him. "Did you notice?"

"You need to go." His tone was quiet but vehement enough that I obeyed right away.

I was digging through his fridge when he got home from school. He was a good hour behind me.

I'd changed into a thin stretchy white T-shirt that barely covered my butt and nothing else.

My aunt had thrown most of my clothes away before I could get them all so I really didn't have much to wear outside of my school and work uniforms.

Still, that didn't explain why I wasn't wearing a bra or panties.

He just stared for a beat, frozen in place, his eyes running down my bare legs then up again.

"We need to set some ground rules. You can't dress like that around this house. And you need new uniforms. Ones that actually fit you."

"I don't have anything, and I haven't had time to shop."

His eyes were on my chest. My nipples were sensitive and prominent and often showed through my clothes, but his gaze on them made them tighten up and point right at him.

I squeezed my thighs together. Of course he noticed.

He swallowed hard, his Adam's apple bobbing with the motion.

The shirt was very thin, and he stared for a while. "Are you out of underwear, as well?"

I was so turned on that I thought I might do something drastic. My hands went to the hem of my shirt. "Wanna see?" I teased him, knowing he'd turn me down.

He was breathing hard, staring and staring. His hands were twitching like he wanted to grab something, either me or his dick, I figured.

"I'll order you some things." He paused, then reached for his wallet. He took out a credit card, placing it on the counter. "Use that for whatever you need. I mean it. Just shop online. It shouldn't take you that long."

I eyed the credit card, feeling uncomfortable. I didn't want his money, but could hardly turn the offer down. I was destitute. "You keep offering me money but refuse to fuck me. You're a strange man, Mr. North."

He let out a half choked laugh. "And you are incorrigible. Go put on some underwear or I'll start lecturing you until you're sick of the sound of my voice."

I shuddered in pleasure and he noticed with narrowed

eyes. "I love your lecturing voice. I've recorded some of your classroom lectures to masturbate too."

He pointed to the stairs, his nostrils flaring. "You don't know when to stop."

"When your big dick isn't pointing straight at me, I might take your rejections more seriously," was my parting shot.

# CHAPTER 5

**CARTER**

I made her tell me all of her clothing and shoe sizes before she left for work and spent the afternoon buying her more appropriate clothing instead of grading assignments or working on my fast approaching writing deadline.

I even went to the school website and bought her new school uniforms in the right sizes.

I figured I had to buy her some sexy little Mary Jane shoes to go with the uniform.

I knew I was obsessing when I caught myself buying her a fifth pair of shoes. They'd gotten progressively less useful as I shopped. Where would she even wear that? I asked myself, even as I clicked to buy a pair of fuck-me stilettos.

My phone dinged a text at me. It was just a picture at first, quickly followed by some infuriating words.

**In case you deleted the picture**

The picture in question was the one my mystery virgin had sent before. The one that showed her naked tits and bare pussy.

I would not respond. My fingers were twitching to, but I *would not.* I wanted badly to ask her for one with her touching herself, *but I would not.*

That was small consolation as I found myself, phone in hand, picture on screen, cock out, furiously beating off at my desk.

Looking at her, I came so fast it would have been embarrassing if anyone was there with me. And worse, I had the urge to send her a pic of my still spurting dick when it was over. No sanity in sight even after I came. This was lunacy.

The worst of it all was that I was almost completely convinced my mystery texts were coming from my new housemate.

I made an unaccountably unpleasant but necessary decision. This was getting out of hand.

The next day Nova stayed after class again, sitting at her desk and watching me.

I was ready for her this time. "Move along. I'm in a hurry. I have plans tonight."

She took the bait immediately. "What plans?"

"I have a date."

She didn't bother to hide how much that crushed her. I could hardly stand it. "I didn't know you were seeing anybody."

"It's nothing serious. I obviously just need to get laid." I was purposely lewd and to the point. Cruelly so.

She was clearly upset but still relentless. "You can get laid at home any time you want."

"That's not possible. And besides, I prefer grown, experienced women. Now *move along*."

I felt like an absolute wretch as I watched her walk away, her posture more dejected than I'd ever seen it.

I didn't see her when I came home and changed. It was for the better, I told myself, but still somehow I was worried about her.

The date was a disaster. Nice enough lady, but I could barely pay attention to a word that came out of her mouth. We'd met on an app. It was a clear-cut DTF situation. We were just politely having dinner first. Before the F part. I wasn't even looking forward to it, but I was so pent-up I knew I'd have no problem performing stud duty to this nice, age-appropriate lady.

I wondered about my little non-age-appropriate problem at home. Was she working tonight? How late? How badly had I hurt her feelings? Did she hate me now?

I had a horrible thought then. Was she so upset she'd run away? I'd have no idea where to look for her if she left.

I considered getting up and leaving right then.

"You're hotter than your picture," my date said, trying to draw my attention back to the present.

I smiled. "So are you," I returned politely. It wasn't entirely true. I'd barely noticed. I'd barely glanced at her. I was being a real asshole.

The pervasive thoughts won. "I'm so sorry," I told my date, interrupting her mid-sentence. "I have an emergency. At home. I have to go. I'll get the bill. Again, I'm so sorry."

The poor woman was still trying to figure out what happened while I settled up and took off like the place was on fire.

Nova wasn't at home and I was losing it. I didn't even know where she worked.

I checked her room. She hadn't taken her stuff. I sat on her bed, relieved beyond belief. I had to keep her at arm's length, but I couldn't bear to drive her away. She needed me, and I *needed* to be the one to take care of her.

I was still sitting on her bed when I got another text from my mystery virgin that confirmed everything I'd feared/ fantasized about. It was just a picture, but it was enough.

It was similar to the first picture but expanded to encompass more. Also her hair was down in this one, which was a dead giveaway of her identity for me.

She'd obviously taken it in front of a large mirror, and she'd cropped the top half of her face out of the picture, but I'd know those fuck-me lips anywhere.

Her black hair fell around her naked body, falling nearly to her hips, but she made sure it didn't cover the big, perky tits that I'd fantasized about more times than I cared to admit to.

One of her hands held the camera, but the other was busy elsewhere, and my eyes tracked it when I finally managed to tear my eyes off her oh-so fuckable breasts.

I stared at the hand barely covering her young, bald pussy and tried to scrape my jaw off the floor. I looked closer. I had to know if her fingers were inside. No. Just barely covering herself.

What the hell was I supposed to do with this?

As though the little vixen read my mind, new words appeared on the screen of my phone.

**Nova: Do you know who it is now?**
**Do you want to be the first to fuck me, Mr. North?**

I typed three responses and promptly erased them. I could not do this. This was *wrong.*

**Me: This is highly inappropriate.**

**Do not text me anything like this again.**

There. That should take care of it. I erased the entire conversation, put my phone away.

Another text arrived, and I couldn't seem to stop myself. I looked.

**Nova: Please don't fuck her**

I ignored that.

**Me: Where are you?**

**Nova: Work**

**Me: Where are you taking these pictures?**

**Nova: I took them all weeks ago. You like? Want another?**

Another picture popped up before I could answer.

It was similar to the first one, but this time her fingers were inside, like she'd read my fucking mind.

I was suddenly furious. With jealousy.

**Carter: Who else have you sent them to?**

**Nova: Just you. Want the video? It will prove all the pictures were for you but you have to ask me nicely for it.**

I couldn't help it. I took the bait.

**Carter: Please**

**Nova: Please what?**

**Carter: Please send the video**

In less than a minute, it came through. It was short, but it was enough. It was clearly taken in the same place and time as the two pictures, everything was the same except her fingers were moving in and out of her pussy and in the background was the sound of my voice droning on about Shakespeare.

She'd recorded one of my lessons and listened to it as she got off.

She hadn't been kidding, the impossible little brat.

On top of that, she was moaning like she was about to come.

I watched it on repeat.

It was unforgivable, just beastly, but I pulled my dick out and jacked off on her bed. Real dirtbag stuff. I hated myself even as I humped her pillow.

**Nova: Did you like it?**
**Say something nice**

It was an hour later, and I was surprised it'd taken her that long to ask. I fought with myself for another hour.

**Carter: I didn't fuck her.**
**I left dinner early.**
**I was worried about you.**

**Nova: Just for that you get a longer video**

It showed up even as I was reading her last text. A full two minutes of her either coming or making a very convincing show of it.

What was I going to do? I was so fucked.

**Nova: Well?**

I closed my eyes and counted to ten. And lost the battle once again.

**Carter: I jacked off on your bed,**
**but that's the closest we can get to fucking.**
**Okay?**

**Nora: I'm so wet.**
**I'm soaking wet while I serve**
**people dinner and it's your fault**

I thought for one crazy moment, *God, I love this girl,* followed quickly with, *I'm losing my mind.*

**Nova: I won't wear any**
**panties when I'm sleeping.**
**Feel free to join me tonight or any night**

**Carter: You know I can't and I won't**

**Nova: You're no fun**

**Carter: Tell that to your bed**

**Nova: Don't clean up after yourself.**

**I want to smell you there**

I was hard again. Stroking myself again.

**Nova: Dick pic???**
**Please? R U hard?**

I had a nearly overwhelming urge to indulge her. Was it really worse than watching her masturbate and painting her bed with my cum?

I was positioning myself and taking the picture as I had the thought. I was already headed straight for hell, so why not?

The picture was a good angle, my cock thick and long and hard, my hand fisting myself. I sent it and started jacking off again as I thought about her receiving it.

**K: Cum shot? Please?**
**Video? Pretty please**

It took some dexterity and positioning, but I gave her what she wanted. I was fisting myself and spurting onto her pillow, phone in my free hand. It was insanity.

Her response was quick.

**K: I'll do anything.**
**Fuck me please please please**

As it sometimes happened, with release came a sliver of sanity.

**Carter: That's the end of it.**
**Delete all these texts and**
**don't speak of it again.**

I cleaned up, went to my bedroom, and locked the door. I didn't trust her. I didn't trust either of us.

# CHAPTER 6

**NOVA**

I couldn't concentrate. Mr. North was lecturing the class from the seat behind his desk, a new pattern these days, and I wanted to touch myself there and then. His lessons had become an acute sexual trigger for me.

Instead I sucked on lemon drops and ate his sitting figure with my eyes in huge, hungry gulps. It was an easy way to pass the time.

The classroom emptied, and I didn't even think about leaving, though I did stand up.

Mr. North seemed to be ignoring me completely, eyes on his computer. A new tactic, but a sound one. If I wasn't so determined, it might have worked.

I walked around his desk, standing by him and looking at his screen. He was actually working. I bumped him with my hip.

"Don't start. I'm busy," he said grumpily.

"Do I smell like you today? I could smell you in my bed

last night."

"I cleaned up after myself. Go away."

"I found a pillowcase in the dirty laundry. I know your scent now. I want more."

He was breathing hard, and he wasn't telling me to go away now.

"I'm not wearing panties. I took them off before class for you again."

"Stop." I saw him mouth the word but no real sound came out.

"Touch me and I'll leave."

"That's crossing an even more serious line." He paused. "Are you sucking on lemon drops again?"

"Yes," I said, rolling the candy around in my mouth.

"Hand it over," he said gruffly, but didn't reach out a hand this time.

There was a small, silent standoff before I took the lemon drop out of my mouth.

I held it out to him. He tilted his head the smallest bit to aim his eyes from his computer screen and at me. Slowly, he stuck out his tongue.

I stared stupidly for a beat before setting the candy there.

His tongue curled around my fingers as he took the candy, licking and sucking for a prolonged moment before he pushed them out of his mouth.

I was panting.

"Are you hard?" I asked unsteadily. I felt so close to getting what I wanted, what I'd wanted for *so* long, that I was a bit lightheaded with it. "Let me see."

Without warning his hand was under my skirt. He was still facing his computer, eyes aimed straight ahead now, as though nothing unusual were happening, but he was fingering me and cursing under his breath as he did it.

"Did you think I was lying about being bare for you?" I

asked huskily.

He closed his eyes, letting out a heavy breath. "You're wet." He said it like that discovery had put him in agony.

"I—," I stopped talking as he pushed a big finger into me.

"God, you're so small. You really are a virgin." He moved his finger around and I moaned. He pulled it out slightly, I protested, and he pushed it back in, once, twice, then again.

"Deeper," I gasped.

He pressed a little deeper this time, and the pressure was intense. "I'll do permanent damage if I go deeper than this." He pushed a little as though to test it.

"Do it," I begged.

Abruptly his finger was gone, and he was looking directly up at me as he sucked it clean.

"That's the hottest thing I've ever seen," I told him.

He didn't answer, just went back to his work, clearly trying to ignore me again.

"Let me get under your desk and suck you off."

His eyes snapped back to me, and he looked angry now. He turned in his seat, squaring his shoulders to face me as he studied me and asked, "Have you done a lot of that? Sucking guys off?"

I shook my head. "No. I saved it all for you. I've been obsessed with you since freshman year."

"What have you done? I want to hear every sexual act you've performed with those boys I've seen you cuddling up to."

I thought about it. "Making out. Brett Stevens felt me up. Over the bra. And Jake—"

"That dumb jock?"

I smiled. "Yeah. He fingered me over my panties, and I touched his dick over his jeans, and he came instantly in his pants so . . . almost a hand job? That's about it."

"Stay away from Jake. He's practically a cave man."

"I haven't gone near him for quite a while."

"Are you dating anyone now?"

"No. Not for like a year. I gave up trying to be interested in anyone but you."

His gaze was intense. I ate it up. He opened his mouth to say something when the classroom door swung open.

I almost jumped away from him, but we weren't doing anything wrong just then so I stayed where I was, standing a little too close to his sitting figure but nothing scandalous.

Ms. Malone, one of the school's APs, smiled warmly at Mr. North, raising her brows at my presence.

"Carter. Can you come see me before you leave? Finish what you're doing. It's no rush."

He nodded and she smiled again and left.

She was around his age and attractive enough that I found myself getting insanely jealous right away.

"Are you two fucking?" I asked him point-blank.

He swiveled his chair and gave me his sternest look. I squirmed where I stood. "That's a crass question. And I don't date co-workers, so the answer is no. I need to finish this. Go home."

I was waiting for him when he got home, in my thin T-shirt again.

He was coming into the house through the garage door, and he froze in the doorway when he saw me standing in the kitchen.

His eyes raked over my body. "You're wearing that shirt again."

"I haven't had time to get anything else."

"And you're bare underneath," he added.

It wasn't quite a question.

My hands went to the hem of my shirt.

"Show me," he said gruffly.

I hadn't been expecting that, but I was thrilled nonetheless.

My whole body warmed with pleasure.

I dragged the shirt up slowly, not stopping until it hit my naval.

"You're completely shaved," he remarked almost absently. He dragged a hand through his hair, looking a little lost but never taking his eyes away. "Show me the rest," he said, voice deeper even than normal.

I wasn't quite sure if he wanted me to open my legs or lift my shirt, but I opted for the latter because it was a little less embarrassing.

I showed him my breasts, and I could tell it got to him. "Anything you want," I told him, grabbing my own flesh, pinching my nipples between my fingers. "Make a mess of me. Treat me how you treated my bed last night. I want your cum all over me."

It was overkill, unfortunately. Enough so that it brought him back to his right mind.

He closed his eyes, waving a hand as though to ward me off. "Stop. I'm sorry. Cover up. I'm so sorry."

I let my shirt drop, thoroughly bummed that he'd stopped there. Still, it was something. A little participation was vastly better than none at all.

He opened his eyes and gave me a very serious look. "I apologize. You're a beautiful young woman, and I'm sorry I took advantage there. Now, for the love of God, please go cover up."

# CHAPTER 7

**CARTER**

Against my better judgment and all sense of self-preservation, I sought her out in her room less than an hour later.

She was, at least, wearing shorts and a bra now, so she'd actually listened to me for once.

She was sitting in her bed, her hair in a messy bun, school laptop propped in front of her.

"Come downstairs," I told her gruffly. "I'm going to start helping you catch up on your schoolwork."

We sat side by side at the kitchen table, and I went through her assignments, one by one. Ironically we didn't touch on my class or the work she owed me.

It was unethical, but I knew I wasn't going to fail her, no matter what. I couldn't say the same for her other teachers.

She'd had a rough few years, and the more I looked into it

the more unlikely it seemed she'd be going directly to a university for the next school year.

"I'll keep looking into it," I reassured her. "I'll see what I can do, but there's also nothing wrong with community college, of course."

She was unresponsive when I spoke about anything after high school. She still wasn't comfortable with me paying for college, or with the idea that money wasn't a problem for her anymore in general. I figured she'd adjust to it with time.

"For now, though," I told her, "getting you to pass all your classes for the semester so you can graduate is the priority."

That she was more responsive to, and we worked on her schoolwork for hours, making an encouraging amount of progress.

There were more than a few tense moments as we sat side by side our heads canted toward each other as we looked at her laptop together, both of us sharing one small screen out of necessity.

I had my arm around her chair to squeeze in closer as I helped her with geometry. Our thighs were pressed together and more than once her hand found its way to resting on my knee.

I glanced at her, and she seemed absorbed in her work, unconscious of what she was doing.

I didn't want to pull her off task, and I honestly wasn't sure if she was messing with me, if she even knew that she was doing it.

We'd been at it for a long time when she started rubbing her temples.

I couldn't help it. I took over, digging my hands in her silky hair to rub her scalp. I was massaging her head with one hand, the other rubbing the nape of her neck when she leaned forward, resting her forehead on the hard table with a soft thump.

I winced in sympathy and pushed my chair back. "You need a break," I told her firmly.

I rose, pulling her with me. "Let's go sit on the couch for a minute and I'll rub your head."

It was a bad idea, but I couldn't help it. She was so tense and stressed, and I just needed to make her feel better. Simply had to.

I sat on the sofa and pulled her between my legs, rubbing her shoulders.

She was very responsive to even a simple touch, and that was more than I needed to know. I massaged every tense part of her from the middle of her back to the top her head. She went boneless under my hands.

She was so relaxed. She was leaning back against me, no longer holding her own weight.

I let her, even pulling her flush against me, arms wrapping around her to rub her taut abs.

I was hard, of course, but she didn't comment on the discomfort of my erection stabbing into her as she was trying to relax, and I appreciated that.

Eventually she began to writhe restlessly against me. "Do you want me to stop?" I asked her, a rasp into her ear. My hands were massaging her abs, getting dangerously lower because I was only human.

"Never," was her soft response.

It was enough. It was too much. I did what I'd wanted to do for ages. I pulled her shirt up and rubbed her soft tits, rolling them against my palms.

She moaned. It wasn't helpful, and it didn't make me stop stepping all the fucking way out of line.

I rolled her nipples between my fingers until they were erect and trembling. One hand snaked down into her shorts and she gasped. I groaned and started rubbing her clit.

Her writhing continued, and my hips churned against her

restlessly.

"How does that feel, pet?" I breathed into her ear as I rubbed her clit and a nipple softly between my fingers, setting up a gentle, tandem rhythm with it. My hips were pumping with that rhythm, rubbing my dick on her shamelessly through our clothes.

"So good," she panted.

I bit her neck and got her off like that. It was so fucking out of line.

More out of line was me holding her in a secure clinch against me as she cried out with her release, feeling every bit of her pleasure as her body trembled against me. I pushed her back with my hand, humping my dick into the softness of her ass.

For the first time in my life, I came in my pants.

It was humiliating and demoralizing, and the only small consolation for it was she had no idea, as she busy was going through something similar herself.

I straightened her clothing and pushed her gently off me.

I was already up and walking away as I said, with deepest remorse, "I'm very sorry. I should not have done that. It was *completely* my fault, and it will not happen again."

I showered, changed, and went to my office to work. I had a strong urge to find her and set her back to task on her homework, but I didn't. Mostly because that wasn't the strongest urge I had.

The strongest urge I had was to do something else altogether, something I would not, could not do. I'd already fucked up enough for one day.

Ignoring the urge didn't make it go away, of course. And sometimes the urge came to you.

It wasn't long before Nova found me.

She hovered in the doorway of my office, looking uncertain.

The look on her face, her posture, as though she wasn't sure if she was welcome, had something tender and fierce unfurling inside of me.

"Come in, pet," I told her gently. "Can I help you with anything?"

"Do you mind if I work on my homework in here with you?"

"Not at all. Make yourself at home."

"I'll go get my laptop." She moved to leave, but my bookshelves caught her eye.

Ah, that. Well, it was only a matter of time. Might as well get it over with.

She was running her hands along the spines of a collection of books, all written by the same author. "You like romance novels?" she asked, plucking one off the shelf and paging through it.

I smirked. I couldn't help it. "I do," I answered.

"Me too," she told me. "They're my favorite."

She looked at me. Stared at me then at all of the book shelves.

I saw her mind working. There was a definite theme going in the room, and I saw her catching on.

Multiple copies of the same books, stacks of them, all the same genre, all the same pen name.

"You *write* romance," she said with wonder.

She was living here. It was inevitable she'd figure it out, so I told her, "I do. Don't let it get out, please. *Any* of the author stuff, I mean."

"Of course I won't. I would never do that. I won't tell anyone *anything* about you. *Ever*. I swear it."

Of course she didn't drop it. This sort of thing was just too interesting to people.

She was looking at the inside of a book when she said, "Holy shit. You've written *twenty* romance novels?"

"To be fair, I started when I was twenty-one, so it's not as hard as it sounds."

"Are they the kind with sex?"

"Of course they are. What's even the point of a love story without sex? It would be like baking a cake with no sugar. Is that even a cake? At that point it's just inferior bread."

"I agree," she said enthusiastically. She paused. "Is it awkward, though, writing sex like that?"

"Not at all," I answered easily. "I love sex. To be honest, it's my favorite thing to write about. Sex is beautiful and wonderful. And it's easy to write about anything that's on your mind that consistently."

"I've never read you, but I'm going to read every *single* one of these."

That was a troubling development, but there wasn't exactly anything I could do about it. I sighed. "Just don't let the reading get in the way of your homework."

**NOVA**

The next few weeks passed by in an easy blur of school, work, catching up on assignments, and reading Carter's books.

I lost a lot of sleep, but there was no question it was worth the exhaustion. I couldn't have stopped if I'd tried. I was obsessed with Carter's novels in a way I'd never been with anything aside from the man himself.

They weren't just sexy books, though they were *emphatically* that.

They were also passionate and warm, and each one had its own pulsing heart and soul. They gave me such a glimpse into how he felt about love, what he'd be like if he gave his heart to someone, and it was staggering how much I wanted not just the man himself now, but the picture he'd painted of what romance could and should be.

His writing was succinct but lush with the precise details to hook you.

His characters were the best part. They felt like real people and what he put them through, he dragged the reader along for, no matter if it was wonderful or tragic.

Every book was unique to the other, but they were all addictive and beautiful.

I'd loved reading for a long time, but became so infatuated with it then that by the end of his fifth book I'd decided I wanted to become an author someday myself.

It took courage, but I shared my impossible little dream with him. My biggest fear in the sharing was that he'd shoot the idea down somehow, find me lacking to follow his same path.

But of course he didn't do that. He did the opposite. He encouraged me, guided me, praised the idea. He was just too good and too perfect. He was the only person I'd ever met that just got better the deeper you dug.

He made me feel like becoming an author was realistic and attainable instead of a pipe dream, even helping me, aiming me in a direction to start.

"You can do it," he told me. "It's the best job in the world. And you have me. I'll always be here for you, to guide you when you get stuck, as all writers do."

"If I wrote something would you read it and tell me if it's any good?"

His eyes were shining at me, his smile beatific. "Of course. In a heartbeat. Perhaps, when you find your stride, we can write something together."

"I'd love that," I told him shyly.

"I love the way you write women," I told him when I was on his tenth book.

"How's that?"

"Like we're people, not just coveted objects or plot devices. You'd be surprised how many male authors don't."

"You read a lot, then?"

"As much as I possibly can, every chance I get. I've read just about every piece of fiction in the school library."

"I shouldn't be surprised. You're very well spoken, particularly for someone your age, and you were always a good student in my class."

"Not lately."

"That's hardly your fault," he told me gently. "And before that, you were exemplary. And don't worry about a thing. We'll get you back on track, okay?"

I couldn't get enough of him like this. Doing this exact thing, the thing he was *always* doing, in one form or another.

Giving me attention. Reassuring me. Tending to me. Taking care of me.

I could feel my eyes devouring him, could feel his reaction to it in his soft eyes.

I'd been in love with him. Now it had grown beyond all proportion. I was in love with him *and* his biggest fan.

"Does it distract you that I stay up late reading your novels every night?" I asked him.

We were working in his office again. It was a rare slice of productive time between my school and work, and he was helping me plow through more homework.

I was trying not to be preoccupied with what else I wanted him to plow.

"Everything about you distracts me," he said, not looking at me directly.

"I need to start getting ready for work," I told him, shutting my laptop.

But I didn't move. We were sitting side by side. I touched his knee.

He stood abruptly, moving to sit at his desk. He tapped his

mouse, looking at his computer.

I went and stood next to his chair.

He looked up at me, raising his brows. "Aren't you in a hurry?"

I put a hand on his shoulder, and he didn't pull away. I leaned forward, pushing my breasts against his face, and he didn't pull away.

I rubbed my hands over his head, pressing him against me.

His hands gripped my butt in both hands, and suddenly I was straddling him in his chair. He was pressing me hard against him, his hips churning under me, our loins flush.

He was just so deliciously huge. His shoulders. His hands. His raging hard-on. Everywhere.

A hot, drenching rush of sensation swept over me.

Our eyes were locked, and I felt like I was under a spell, like we both were.

He cupped my face in his hands, and for the first time, he pressed his lips to mine. And it was perfect.

His mouth was tender on mine, gentle but commanding. It was the first time I'd kissed someone that knew what they were doing. It was heaven. I never wanted to stop.

I rocked against him in the chair, rubbing my breasts into his chest, but he never took his hands from my face as he showed me what it meant to express your desire perfectly through a simple kiss.

It was beautiful and full of magic, and somehow I fell even more deeply in love.

# CHAPTER 8

**CARTER**

I found out in a roundabout way—asking her questions here and there so she wasn't too on guard about it, she didn't like those kinds of questions—that her worthless relatives still had her social security card and birth certificate.

Their address and names were easier to access, so I didn't even have to ask her for those and clue Nova in to my intentions.

I paid them a visit for multiple reasons, not the least of which that I felt the need to give them at least a small piece of my mind. They deserved much more, but I tried to come at it as her teacher, not her lover.

Her aunt answered the door, eyeing me up in a curious way, though the twist to her mouth was so unpleasant that it made you think it was frozen in that shape.

She was a frumpy middle-aged white woman with

nondescript brown hair. Nondescript everything, really. I caught on instantly why she'd taken such exception to an exceptional girl like Nova.

I was dressed in teacher business casual, my expression blank and professional as I asked, "Are you Laura Monroe?"

Her brows raised. "I am. And who are you?"

"I'm Carter North. I'm one of Nova's teachers. May I come in?"

She didn't look pleased about it, but she moved aside and said, "I guess, if you insist. You know, she doesn't even live here anymore. She ran off again. Not our fault."

I felt my blank expression slip as contempt filled me. "Is your husband around?"

She sneered. "He's unemployed, as usual, so yeah, he's usually around. I'll go get him. He should handle this. She's not even my blood."

She disappeared and I hoped that was the last I ever saw of her because I wasn't sure I could be civil to that awful woman for even one more second.

She was gone for a while, which was curious because their rundown house was tiny. She couldn't have had a hard time finding him.

As I waited, sounds drifted to me. It sounded like there were at least a few small children in one of the three closed doors.

A man in a dirty white tank with a beer belly hanging out stumbled out of that room at one point.

I eyed him up. Something about him set me off immediately. Somehow I instantly knew this was not her uncle. Perhaps he was just too disgusting to be a blood relative to her, perhaps it was him coming out of the room with the crying children, but somehow I knew.

He almost flinched when he caught sight of me, and I didn't like that either. He felt instantly threatened by me, and he should have.

"Who are you?" I asked him bluntly.

"Erm, I'm Laura's brother. Who are you?"

"I'm Carter North, one of Nova's teachers." His flinch at her name made my fists clench.

"Is she in trouble?" he asked.

"Not at all. This is a welfare check. I'm here to see why her relatives put her out on the streets when she's still in high school."

"She's eighteen," he said defensively. "And it was her idea to leave. You know she just took off one day without a word."

I stared at him until he started fidgeting and looked away. "And why, I suppose, would she do something like that?" It was an accusation. Every instinct I had told me this creep had something to do with her feeling the need to leave. "Where did she sleep while she was here?" I asked him.

He wouldn't look at me now. "On the sofa. My family has the spare room. Listen, I've got to go. You looking for Ed? I'll go get him."

He took off but went right back into the same bedroom so I knew he was just avoiding me now.

I couldn't seem to help myself. I was knocking hard on that door before I even made a conscious decision.

He opened it, looking more scared than ever. I grabbed him by the collar, gripping it into a handle, and shutting the door behind him so his family wouldn't see.

He wasn't a small man, but he was small enough, and I had him up against the wall, my face close to his, without even a struggle.

"If I find out," I gritted out at him slowly, making deadly eye contact the entire time, "that you laid one fucking finger on her, I will make you pay for it, do you understand?"

He was so terrified, he was drooling, and I knew I'd hit a

target square on. My instincts had been screaming at me since the second I set eyes on him. "And if you ever think of so much as glancing in her direction in the future, it will be considerably worse than that. Are we clear?"

He managed to nod.

I let him go, and he sagged against the wall. "Stay the fuck away from her," I snarled at him. "And get out of my sight."

He had some sense because he disappeared with impressive speed.

I was still clenching my fists, over and over, when another man stepped out of the other closed door.

There was no real family resemblance, but I figured the fairly normal looking guy that stepped out was her uncle just by process of elimination.

"Ed Monroe?" I asked him, voice cold as a grave.

He nodded, swallowing. I was intimidating on a good day, when I wasn't feeling murderous. I knew I was on another level just then, and anyone with a drop of sense would feel it.

"I'm her teacher, Carter North," I introduced myself. "You know you've done a less than dismal job taking care of your brother's daughter," I told him almost conversationally. I knew that if he was capable of feeling guilt, that one should be a punch to the gut.

He was. He'd been hunched over in shame from the moment he stepped out of his room, but he bent farther at that.

"It's bad enough you put her out on the streets, but if I find out she's been further abused in this house, every adult that lives here is going to face consequences. Know that. But I'm here for her documents. Her birth certificate, her social security card."

He looked stumped. "I have no idea where any of that is."

"Figure it out," I gritted out. I sat down on the stained sofa that I couldn't believe they'd made my Nova sleep on, staring him down. "I'll wait."

"I-I'll, um, ask Laura," he stammered. "She might know."

"You do that," I bit out.

It did the trick. They managed to find what I asked for within a half hour. I more than half suspected Laura had kept it all from Nova out of spite.

Either way, I managed to leave without punching anyone. Considering how I felt about every single adult in that house, I thought it was a rather impressive feat of self-control on my part.

I set up a bank account for Nova that same day. She was uncomfortable with taking any money from me at all, so I didn't tell her I put fifty grand in it. It just made me feel better to know that she had means.

I was working in my office and just about to turn in for bed. Nova was in the house somewhere. She was off work for the night, and though I'd been working on some schoolwork with her earlier, I had no clue what she'd been up to since then.

It was a sweet sort of torture to have her around so constantly. She lingered in my mouth. She was the grit in my teeth. But not grit like sand, more like strawberry seeds; a pleasant abrasion.

Though I'd crossed some serious lines with her, I hadn't fucked up nearly as badly as I wanted to. She'd been living with me for weeks now and though I hadn't taken her, it felt impossible that it wasn't heading in that direction inevitably.

She'd be graduating in a few short months. If I could only wait that long, it would at least be something. But a few months felt like forever when every minute of your day your mind was consumed with one thing.

God, I wanted her.

As though my thoughts had conjured her, she appeared in my doorway.

She was wearing one of the soft little pajama shorts sets I'd gotten her. Online it had looked fairly modest and appropriate, but Nova's body had other ideas. The little shorts were showing off most of her legs, and they were loose enough that all I could picture was what I could fit up there.

Easy access. I shivered.

The top was possibly worse. It was made of thin jersey and should have covered everything, but it buttoned up, and Nova wasn't a fan of buttons. Also, she wasn't wearing a bra.

She held up a copy of one of my books, she had it open and was waving it around enough to distract me from her body and to focus on what she was saying.

"I want you to do this to me. Exactly what you wrote right here."

I never remembered every detail of the books I'd written, but some things certainly stood out. The one she was holding was by far my most erotic title, and it had been a bit controversial. It had a lot of degradation kink in it, which wasn't for everyone.

The fact that she'd singled out that book in particular made me feel a bit lightheaded and unhinged.

I wanted to know every *single* thing in that book that had gotten her attention.

"Stop that," I told her instead in my sternest teacher voice. "You shouldn't talk to me that way. We're not doing this."

She shivered. I'd known she would.

Even my rejections were foreplay for us at this point. The sterner the better.

"I'm not a kid," she said stubbornly. "I'm eighteen, and you want me. I don't understand the hold up."

"I think you should go to bed before this gets out of hand," I told her. I knew that was what would be best, even if I didn't *feel* it.

She approached me, got close enough to grab, and I knew I

was in trouble. "At least give me a kiss goodnight."

Goddammit.

I did it. I had her straddling me in my chair, shirt open to fondle her as I kissed her and kissed her, letting my mouth show her what I wanted to do to every part of her. Cajole. Seduce. Invade. Dominate.

I pulled back to look at her gorgeous tits, fondling them, rolling them in my hands, sucking on them. They were big enough to bask in, and I savored them to my heart's content.

I pulled back from sucking on a sensitive nipple and gasped out, "I'm so obsessed with your tits. It's been a problem for longer than I'd like to admit."

I was dry humping her, thrusting up at her, her body jerking, breasts bouncing with each measured jolt. I cupped them, completely enraptured at the sight of her like that, her earnest eyes on me, her body ripe and ready.

Against my better judgment and quite frankly a loss of my self-control, I said to her, "Tell me what you're fantasizing about. Why did you bring me *that book* in particular? What you do you want me to do to you *exactly*?"

"Do you really want to know my fantasies or are you just saying that because you're hoping they're the same as yours?" she asked. She was turned on and a bit out of it, but her tone still had a note of coy teasing in it.

"Both. Above all, I want you to be honest."

She took a deep breath, licked her lips and said, "I want you to pull my hair. Spit on me. Cum on my face. I want you to call me your little slut. I want you to fuck me so hard it hurts, and then I want you to keep going. I want you to use me like I'm your favorite sex toy."

"Jesus, Nova, you've watched too much porn," I said without meaning to sound quite so judgmental. I'd been expecting something similar to come out of her mouth. It was her bluntness I think that caught me off guard.

"Maybe," she said, more defiant than defensive. "So what? I want you to fuck me like you hate me, and then I want you to choke me, berate me, make me crawl. Call me any nasty names you can think of. I want you to be bad for me and *only* me, and when you're done I want you to take care of me like you love me, to pamper me, and make me feel cherished. I want you to give me a bath and wash my hair and hold me. I want *all* of your attention, your worst side and your best."

I studied her carefully, wondering how much of this she really wanted, and how much of it was curiosity.

"Do you hate the idea?" she eventually ventured to ask. "Does it turn you off?"

"I don't think I'm capable of being turned off by you at this point," I said, being honest without answering right off the bat. "But I probably won't spit on you. I'm also not sure I should indulge you with the rest of it. I'm not sure it's what's best for you."

"Please," she begged. "Don't tell me it's bad, that *I'm* bad, just be bad with me. And then be very, very good."

I continued to study her, torn. I'd have no problem giving her what she wanted. The problem was that I wanted to give it to her like that *too much.*

"You're the perfect person to do this to me," she said, like the little vixen could read my mind. "You don't need it, so I'll have no problem telling you if it's too much, and you won't hesitate to listen."

She was the most irresistible enticement for me, but I managed not to give her a straight answer just then, instead kissing her and fondling her, distracting her off the topic so I could step back and think about it without my dick completely taking over the decision.

We got carried away, and I almost came in my pants again.

Instead, panting, I pushed her off me.

She looked like her brain was too addled with lust to form

a coherent thought.

Also, she was topless and looking at me with her heart in her eyes.

I'd never been so tempted by anything in my life.

She was gorgeous and so utterly fuckable, I was gritting my teeth.

"Put your top back on and go to bed, pet," I told her.

She obeyed half of that, walking away topless, her shirt still on the floor at my feet.

It took all I had not to follow her.

Instead I dragged myself away to my own bedroom. I have no idea how I did it.

Moreover, I had no earthly clue how I could possibly resist next time.

Every encounter between us was building the tension until I knew it was only a matter of time before I snapped.

I calculated the days to her graduation. It wasn't looking good.

She was pulling me in, deeper by the touch, captured more with every sensation. And we hadn't even fucked.

The problem was that what she was making me feel was more than physical. This wasn't just about hot sex.

More substantial things were building the fire inside me.

Physical touch might be the kindling, but emotion was the spark.

The next day at school I was rifling through the supply closet nearest my classroom. It was during fourth period, my free class.

I don't know how she knew I was there just then, or what the fuck she was doing out of class.

Also, the second I saw her, I couldn't even remember what I'd been looking for.

The instant our eyes met, it felt like a planned assignation. I couldn't have defended it to save my life, because I didn't even hesitate.

She stepped inside, I shut the door, locked it, and I pinned her against it.

I took her mouth roughly.

Kissing her was drugging. I couldn't get enough of it. If nothing else was on the table, in some strange way I thought I could be content with that alone.

Of course my dick didn't agree, and *everything* was on the table, as she was more than happy to remind me every day.

I had her ass in my hands, my hard-on trying to nail her to the heavy wooden door, stamping my frustration against her soft body in dry, hard humps.

"You're going to fuck up my whole life, aren't you, pet?" I rasped out.

I didn't let her answer, taking her mouth before she could.

Her legs were wrapped around my waist, and I straightened, holding her to me by the hips, thrusting against her, showing her just how I would fuck her standing up.

I was about a second away from coming when I tore my mouth away from hers.

"We *have* to stop," I panted. "We can't do this here.

"Where then?"

"We need to settle this at home, so I don't take it out on you at school."

"Now?" she sounded hopeful.

"After school." It was torture to say it, torture to think I had to wait that many hours. "After school," I repeated more firmly this time, "go straight home and wait for me."

# CHAPTER 9

**NOVA**

I barely made it through the rest of my classes.

In fact, I left before my last period.

I was too agitated to stay for his class and behave myself, so I did the opposite.

I ditched and decided to go for extra credit instead.

I went home and set about finding his bedroom. It took a minute. He'd never shown me where it was, the house was huge, and there were a lot of rooms.

When I found it, I set up my phone to take a video of the bed and hit record. I stripped out of my top and bra but left the skirt on. I buried my face in his pillow, bare ass facing the camera. I started rubbing my clit, taking in his scent.

I didn't hold back, every moan and gasp a heartfelt performance for my favorite teacher. I rubbed my clit against his pillow, working myself up nice and hot.

I got myself off, rolling around in his bed like I was marking my territory.

Afterward I hit send and went downstairs to search for food.

He got home just as I was taking a bite out of a sandwich.

I hadn't bothered to get fully dressed. Barefoot, bra gone, shirt unbuttoned and hanging open. I still had my skirt on, but underwear was a distant memory.

"You keep telling me to make myself at home," I told him with a smile and took another bite.

He didn't respond. His eyes were on my body, and it was intoxicating how he caressed me with his gaze.

"Did you get my text?" I asked him cheerfully.

"I saw it was a video," he said almost absently. "I didn't watch it."

I lifted myself to sit on the counter, letting my legs swing. "Watch it now." I took another bite.

With a deep breath, he took out his phone and watched it.

I don't think he even knew he was doing it, but as he watched he drifted closer until he was standing nearly between my legs. I spread them wider, and he moved to fill the empty space, still watching his phone.

I set the sandwich down behind me. I took his free hand and put it between my legs until his fingers were brushing the lips of my sex. He rubbed me gently then withdrew.

I was disappointed for a second, but then he grabbed my hand and guided it to touch his hard dick.

Tentatively I rubbed my hand over his length, feeling him through his pants. He made a harsh male noise as I slid my hand up and down his shaft.

He was still watching the video as I clumsily undid his belt, button, and zipper. I pulled his straining cock out. It jerked in my hands.

"It's like it has a life of its own," I murmured, feeling it thoroughly.

"Sometimes it feels that way to me too," he returned

unsteadily.

I loved the feel of it, and I gripped him with both hands, pumping at the smooth flesh.

He moaned loudly, his eyes falling closed. "Careful, you'll make me come."

My eyes widened in wonder. I pumped harder. "Really? Just from this? This fast?"

He stopped my hand with his, sending me an unfriendly look that made me *shiver*. "Not usually, but you've got me in a bad state. *Tease*."

"It's not teasing if you mean it."

His hand fell away and I started stroking again. "What if I want you to come? I want to see it. I haven't done any of this before."

He stopped my hand again, put his phone down, and faced me squarely. "You want to jerk me off? With just your hand?"

I didn't hesitate. "Yes." I pulled his now free hand under my skirt. "Can't we do that?"

With a curse he moved in, bending his head down to touch his forehead to mine, his big finger pushing into me. "You first," he said roughly.

I let go of him, falling back to brace myself on my hands. My shirt fell open wider, my heavy breasts completely bared to him.

"Are hands enough?" I asked him in a pant. "We can do anything you want."

He shook his head and cursed. "More than enough. It's *too much*. Just hands is a good start. *You're* too much. I'm not sure I could handle all of you." As he spoke, his finger was making steady progress, pushing deeper as I squirmed. He bent down and tongued a nipple, moaned, and started sucking. He was tender at first, but he sucked harder the deeper his invading finger went.

He pulled his head back with a gasp, our eyes locking. "You're so beautiful," he told me roughly. "I love the feel of you."

His finger was moving in and out in shallow motions, making it hard to answer but I managed. "What else? Tell me more nice things," I panted. "What else do you like about me?"

He laughed, but it was a pained sound. He leaned his face close to mine. "Everything. Your personality, your body, your boldness, the sound of your voice, your face. I like absolutely everything about you, especially the stuff that drives me *crazy*."

"Now tell me something less nice," I said, a plea in the words. I was a bit embarrassed by what I was asking, but I knew from his books and our conversation the night before that he'd get it.

He didn't hesitate. In fact, he exceeded my expectations, and they'd been high. "I'm going to stamp you into my very own fuck toy. You're going to become my personal cum pet, you little brat."

As he spoke, his finger was busy inside me. I cried out roughly.

"Repeat it back," he said sternly.

It was just perfect. His nice guy persona was taking a break. In its place was someone nearly mean and a bit aloof.

Stern teacher goodness squared.

"I'm your cum pet," I panted.

"And?" he asked coldly. "Were you even paying attention? Or were you being a bad student again?" His most disappointed professor voice was out to play.

I could have come just listening to that tone from him. "And your fuck toy."

And?"

I had to think and my brain wasn't working that fast.

"And a little brat."

He started kissing me, and it got out of control pretty quickly. I found myself sucking on his tongue while his finger pumped in and out.

"Deeper," I said against his mouth.

He pulled back. "Deeper and it's going to hurt. You understand?"

I did. He was going to break my hymen. I met his eyes earnestly. "Please please please," I chanted, our panting breaths mingling together.

He pulled back and bit his lip, looking down at his hand, which had gone still, finger half inside me. "I'm finding it almost impossible not to break it with my dick."

My eyes flew down to his quivering length, and I whimpered. "Please," I asked. "I want it so bad."

"Hands only," he said as though he was convincing himself.

"Just put it in once," I tried. "You can take it right back out."

He looked at me like he was hoping I had a point. "I'll just stretch you out a bit, then get you off with my fingers. I won't come in you. Okay?"

My whole body was shaking. I couldn't even speak I wanted it so bad.

He pushed my legs wider, cursed, and took off my skirt. He pushed his hips between my thighs, his cock bumping against my belly.

Panting, he angled it down, hooking it against my wet entrance. He leaned down, sucking hard at my nipple as he started pushing in. The pain in my nipple helped distract me somewhat from the pain and pressure of his thick cock stretching me.

"I could come right now," he panted against my skin and went back to sucking.

Suddenly and shockingly, he shoved himself deep.

It hurt and I cried out, hands moving to grip his shoulders as though to hold him back.

He stilled, lifting his head to watch my face. "Too much?" he asked.

I answered, "No," even as I nodded my head yes.

His eyes were tender, but he didn't relent, pushing deeper. His hands were firm on my shoulders, holding me still while his lower body invaded mine slowly but relentlessly.

"I've never been inside a woman without a condom before," he panted, thrilling me. I would take any of his firsts I could get and gladly give him all of mine.

"Does it still hurt?" he asked as he was pushing deeper still.

I wanted to answer no, but I looked down and saw that he wasn't even halfway in. So much of his heavy shaft was still visible, little trails of blood sliding down the thick veins of it.

"You're just too big," I told him.

For some reason that made him smile wide, a handsome, hot smile, and he looked more pleased than I'd ever seen him. "Not so bold now, are you?" he asked, voice thick with satisfaction. "Worried you bit off more than you could chew? Don't worry, pet. I'll fit."

He followed my eyes down, and we both watched him push in deeper. He rubbed my clit and I squirmed, which made the pressure almost unbearable. I went completely still. "You're wet enough to take me," he panted. "I just need to stretch you out a bit."

"A bit?" I asked disbelievingly, eyes still on his heavy shaft.

"I've never had a virgin," he said, shoving deeper as he fed me that little piece of heaven.

"Really?" I asked. I loved that, another first for me.

"Really," he answered archly. He used my distraction to shove in a few inches all at once.

I couldn't help it. I let out a little half-stifled shout.

"It's too much," I sobbed. There were tears trailing down my face, and he started kissing and licking them away. He wasn't pushing deeper, and I tried to look down to see how much was left.

He smiled at me, and it was so loving that I almost melted. "Don't look down. Look at me. We're almost home, okay?"

I licked my lips and tasted my tears. He started kissing me passionately. "You feel so good. I can't believe how good you feel," he panted between kisses.

I tore my mouth away to speak. "You said you were just gonna break it and pull out. You already broke it. I saw the blood."

He was kissing my cheeks again, licking away the tears. "I know, pet. Can I just push all the way in? I won't fuck you. I won't come in you. I just want to feel you grip my whole cock, then I'll pull out, okay? It's so good, baby girl."

His tone was so soft, so cajoling. It was impossible for me to refuse him when he was being so tender with me. "You can do anything you want to me," I told him, only crying a little bit now. "I love you."

He moaned loudly, gripped my hair roughly with one hand, the other hard on my hip, and shoved home, bottoming out inside me. It hurt, but I loved the finality of it. I wasn't a virgin anymore.

He looked down, using his hard grip in my hair to angle my head for the same view. He was all the way in, our groins flush, his whole huge length completely swallowed into my trembling sex.

"Fuck," he shouted, wrenching all the way out suddenly. White, thick cum was spurting out of his engorged tip. He shoved it against my belly, grabbing my hand to grip around his shaft. He kept coming on me, rubbing against me as he clutched his hand over mine to stroke him.

He pushed me down and forward by the shoulder roughly, pumping cum on my tits, humping his dick against the soft globes hard enough to leave marks. "Fucking take it," he said roughly.

He gripped my hair tighter, pushing my mouth down to take some of it, still pumping.

I opened my mouth to lick him, and he shoved his tip between my lips forcefully.

"Suck it," he said roughly. *"Fucking suck it."* He'd lost all control and I loved it.

Clumsily I started sucking on his tip, trying to look up at his face as I did it. I couldn't quite manage, but he saw what I was attempting and groaned, fisting my hair to pull me up to his mouth. He kissed me passionately for a long time, eventually peeling my hand away from his dick.

He kept kissing me, his hand rubbing my clit, a finger pushing in now, and he was right, it went in much easier.

He pulled back a little to ask, "Can I eat you out?" he panted.

I pulled his face back to mine. "Next time. This time I want you to kiss me while you touch me."

He groaned and started kissing me again, his finger getting more insistent, deeper, rougher, his thumb rubbing my clit just so, the pressure so perfect I knew he must have done it a thousand times.

Abruptly he shoved a second finger in, and I whimpered into his mouth. He kept finger fucking me as he whispered the sweetest little things to me between kisses. "I love your lips. I've been dreaming about this. Did you know what you were doing to me?"

He pulled back to look into my eyes. He smiled tenderly. "You did, you little brat."

I started sucking his tongue as I got closer, and he seemed to know it, pumping his fingers in as deep as they could go, other hand pinching and stroking my clit with the exact right pressure.

My head fell back as I came, and he continued to soothe me with his hands and kiss my neck. Soon he was sucking at my nipples like he couldn't get enough. I ran my hands covetously through his hair as he nuzzled against me. I had dreamed of this too.

"Are you seeing anybody else?" I eventually asked him.

He straightened at that, studying my face. I could tell by his eyes that I had broken the spell. "It can't be like that with us. You know we can't . . . well, we can't really date or anything."

I was crushed, but I recovered quickly. "So we'll just live together and fuck then?"

He started kissing me again. I ran my hands over his back only then realizing he hadn't even undressed.

I pulled back, momentarily distracted when I saw that his cock was still out and hard again.

He put his hand over it, flushing in embarrassment. He started to shove himself back into his pants, and I tried to stop him. He stepped back and turned away.

"Can you come again?" I asked. This I hadn't known.

"Yes, but I'm not going to." He sounded regretful already. "I need to show some self-control. We did enough damage today." He paused and I felt him pulling farther from me with each second. "I knew you were going to fuck up my life."

That had me sitting up. I put my legs together and got down from the counter. I held my blouse closed over my chest, and started to move away, intending to go to my bedroom and sulk and probably cry my eyes out.

He stopped me by hugging me from behind and kissing my neck. He fondled me lightly as he said into my ear, "That sounded harsher than I meant it to. None of this was your doing. And that was . . . so amazing. Unbelievable. You were perfect. I'll never forget it, but that doesn't mean it was a good idea. I just need to take a step back and get my head on straight, okay? I've never lost it like that in my life. I'm sorry. This was all my fault."

He was confusing me, his words contradictory, his touch at odds with it all, giving me hope and taking it away all at once. It was hurtful and bewildering.

"I need to shower," I told him, reluctantly pulling away.

"Are you okay?" he called to my back.

"I'm fine," I lied.

# CHAPTER 10

**CARTER**

I watched her walk away feeling a little shell-shocked. She was barely covering anything with her blouse, her skirt still on the floor.

What had I just done?

Lost my fucking mind is what.

I thought about picking the skirt up and handing it to her, but I didn't trust myself to do even that much. If I followed her it wouldn't stop there. I was still somehow on the verge of taking her and doing God only knows what to her this time. Watching her in the shower. *Yes, that.* Joining her there. *Oh, yes.* Shoving my cock down her throat. *Yes, that.* Eating her out. *Yes, that.* Spreading her wide and fucking her raw. Fucking her mindless. Filling her to dripping with my cum. As many times and as much of it as I possibly could. Owning her cunt so completely that neither of us could walk tomorrow. *Yes, especially that.*

So I made myself watch her go and hated it.

I'd never fucked up this bad in my life, and I was still so punch drunk giddy from it that I wasn't even sorry for it yet, not truly, but I knew that was coming.

I locked myself in my bedroom, sincerely frightened at what I'd do if she joined me there. The look on her face, her sweet brown eyes, the tears pouring down those baby angel cheeks as I'd pushed into her would haunt me for the rest of my life, I was sure. She'd been so tender and soft, so innocent as she met my eyes and took every huge inch of me. I'd been ruthless about it once I started. Patient but relentless. And it had been too much for her, but she'd let me in to the hilt. I'd never forget it.

And then there was the other part, the things she'd wanted me to say to her. I'd thought about that stuff before but had never felt comfortable enough with a partner to do it, had never been willing to shut off the nice guy in my head and indulge in something a touch more sinister.

I was still so consumed with it that I started jerking myself off in the shower thinking about it, the sight of traces of her blood still on me perversely stirring me.

I stopped myself short.

It had been just perfect, beyond all expectations and fantasies, and I hadn't even fucked her for real yet. We'd barely scratched the surface of all the things I wanted to do to her.

I was still trying to convince myself that I could never touch her again with my upper brain.

My lower brain had other ideas. I didn't even want to jack off because I wanted to save every drop of cum in my future for her personally. It was *so* fucked up. And so intoxicating.

I wanted to go to her now, to kiss her and hold her, but I didn't trust myself for one second not to take it further.

But even with all my inner conflict and indecision, my own

sense of right and wrong that hadn't changed, hadn't budged an inch, I just couldn't picture a future where I didn't eventually get to break her in completely and fuck her proper. Certainly no one else could do it. She was mine now.

I was beating off again before I realized it and made myself stop.

I was disgusted with myself, but I knew then that I was saving it for her. Every drop of my seed would go on her and in her. Anything else was a waste.

I was so fucked.

I tossed and turned for most of the night and woke up at five a.m. feeling a strange kind of panic.

I went straight to her room. I was wearing boxer briefs and nothing else, but I didn't consider taking the time to get dressed. The panic wasn't going away; it was growing with every step.

If she's in there sleeping I'm going to fuck her awake, I thought, then castigated myself for the thought.

But, as some part of me had known by the panic in my gut, she was gone, her backpack with her.

I tore down to the garage. The cars were both there.

She was on foot. When did she leave? How far could she have gone?

I called her, but it went straight to voicemail repeatedly.

I threw on a T-shirt and jeans and starting looking for her, driving slowly block by block, wishing I had some clue which direction she could have gone in, or when she had left.

I was a mess when I finally gave up and went to work. I was late and I looked terrible. Every co-worker I saw asked if I was okay. I was an absolute wreck, but somehow I got through the day.

Nova was absent, and I wanted to howl with worry. Was

she okay? Where had she gone? How much of the night had she been out on her own, and would she come back?

I told my last class that I had a personal emergency and left them, telling them to study but knowing they'd just play on their phones.

I drove around looking for her again, but I didn't even know where to start. I went into three diners to see what the waitresses were wearing to sleuth out her place of work, but it was a dead end.

Another day went by like that, worse because my worry was growing with every hour she was out on her own. She needed me and I'd failed her. It crushed me as nothing ever had before. I vowed not to fail her again, but I didn't know how that was possible when what she wanted from me was destructive to her well-being in general.

The third day she showed up in class with Jake's arm thrown over her shoulder like they were a couple again.

I thought steam might come out of my ears.

She sat down at the back of the class, next to Jake, but she didn't seem to be paying him any mind.

He kept touching her, though, the illiterate fuckwad. I thought I might kill him. I wanted to tear him apart, limb from limb.

"Hands to yourself, Mr. Hawkins," I finally snapped.

And she didn't once look at me.

As I was taking attendance I said, "Miss Monroe, you have two unexcused absences this week. Care to explain?"

She still didn't look at me, head tilted down. She looked sad and forlorn and so fuckable, I had to sit down.

A succinct, "No," was her only answer. Little brat.

I told her to stay after class for a word, and I was surprised when she did.

I stayed behind my desk. "Come here," I told her gruffly.

She surprised me again by obeying.

I had an awful thought. "You better be wearing panties today, sitting that close to fucking Jake." Before I knew it, I was up and shoving her against my desk, hand up her skirt. When I felt her underwear I backed away, horrified by what I'd done and *where* I'd done it. It was out of line not to mention someone could have easily walked in on that.

She finally looked up at me and glared. "At least *someone* wants me."

I couldn't fathom what she meant. "You think I don't *want* you?"

"You hated that we did what we did. You regretted it right after. I don't want to cause you anymore hassle. I found another place to stay while I figure things out."

I saw red again. "Where? With *fucking Jake*?"

She had the nerve to roll her eyes. "No. At a shelter. It's fine."

It felt like someone had slugged me in the gut and taken the rug out from under me, all at once. I had to sit down. I thought I might actually cry for the first time in years. *A shelter?* I took a few bracing breaths before I tried to speak calmly. "Please come back home with me. I'm sorry. I made a mess of things. I'll try to do better. Okay?"

She studied me for a long time. "I don't know. I'll have to think about it. You said I was fucking up your life, Carter, and that's the last thing I want to do."

I took a few more bracing breaths, gaze locked steadily to hers. "I don't know what's happening. I'm lost here, I can't deny it. I feel like the worst kind of scum. I've taken advantage of you when I only wanted to take care of you. But I can tell you right now that I'd rather ruin every part of my life and career than see you out on the streets by yourself. The thought is *unbearable* to me. Please, *please,* come home with me."

She somehow looked less convinced than ever. "I won't as

long as you keep saying you're taking advantage of me. I can't bear *that*."

"Okay. I won't say that again."

She studied me for a long time, then eventually asked, "We'll drive home together?"

"Absolutely," I said, feeling so relieved at her capitulation that I was *weak* with it.

"On one condition."

"Anything."

"I get to go down on you while you drive."

Lord, have mercy. It was checkmate. Not only did I want that, I felt like I couldn't refuse.

I was so relieved that I barely gave a thought to anyone seeing us walk out and get into my car together.

Teachers can drive students home, I told myself. Luckily no one got close enough to see that I was hard as a rock the entire walk from the classroom to the parking lot.

We were driving and a few blocks away from the school before I spoke. "This maybe isn't the ideal place to give your first blowjob. It's going to be an awkward angle."

"You can't back out on the deal when I'm already in the car, Mr. North," she said like a little brat as she grabbed for my belt.

With a sigh I pulled over, taking my dick out for her. She unbuckled and leaned over the console, and I started driving again.

"This is unsafe," I told her gruffly as she tongued my tip. "Can you wait until we get to the house? I'll park and you can suck me off safely."

She completely ignored me, ringing her plush lips around me teasingly. It was too much. I snapped, grabbed her hair, and shoved her down roughly.

*That* was too much too fast, and she gagged a bit before I let up. She kept at it, trying to take me as deep as she could. It was a valiant, distracting effort.

"If you don't want me coming in your mouth, tell me now," I told her. I was going to lose all coherent thought soon, I could tell.

I put my Tesla in self-drive for the first time. I'd never even tried it before, I didn't trust it completely, but it was either that or crash.

"Use your hands," I told her, burying both of mine in her hair roughly. I pulled it, tugging her up and down. I gagged her again and wasn't even sorry. She'd asked for it. I showed her how to stroke the lower base of my cock while she sucked at the tip. "Deep throating is overrated," I told her unsteadily. "A real good blowjob takes both hands too." In spite of what I'd just said I pushed myself deeper down her throat. She didn't gag that time, actually took it pretty well, and I started fucking into her mouth with a purpose.

"Ever heard of a skull fuck?" I asked her, but of course she couldn't answer. I just kept talking and fucking her face, my dick getting deeper down her throat each time. I didn't know if I was trying to scare her off or what, but I couldn't stop saying crazy shit to her. "It's when you fuck someone's face with a purpose. Like a rough fuck to the throat with no breaks. Breathe through your nose. You've got this. Fuck, I'm gonna come. You're going to swallow every drop. I want you to gulp it like you love it. Take my cum. Fucking take it." The tip of my dick was pounding down her throat, and it was so out of line and I still couldn't stop. I pushed deeper than I knew she could handle and started coming. She was gagging even as she tried to take it all down her throat.

*I think I'm in love,* I thought to myself, but of course I wasn't stupid enough to say it out loud.

I was still gripping her hair, pulling it, being a bit of a

bastard. "Clean it all up, little cum pet," I told her in my best stern teacher tone. "Every drop that dripped out when you gagged. I want you to lick it clean." She was moaning she was so turned on the more I talked. "There's still some coming out. Suck the tip until it's finished," I told her raggedly.

Like a perfect dream girl, she did it.

I prayed I hadn't soured her on blowjobs forever. I'd lost my fucking mind back there.

I took over control of the car with one hand, the other still in her silky hair. She started to sit up, but I pushed her back down. "I didn't tell you you could stop sucking. Keep at it." I thought I said that just to see if she'd do it. "This mess is your fault," I told her harshly. "Clean it all up." Angel that she was, she did it.

I praised her the rest of the way home, stroking her hair and keeping her face in my lap, her cheek against my softening cock. "Well, what do you think of blowjobs? Probably not quite what you pictured."

Her hand was stroking my thigh like she couldn't stop touching me no matter what I did to her. "I like it," she said decisively and I laughed.

She sat up and smiled at me. "Did you like it? Was I okay?"

I almost melted and almost attacked her again right there. I stroked her cheek with my free hand. "You were so good. Best blowjob of my life."

She blushed and narrowed her eyes. "You're lying. Don't make fun."

"I swear. The way you did it, the way you took it down your throat and tried your best was the hottest thing I've ever seen. I didn't go easy on you. I should have, but I lost it and you handled it so well, baby girl."

She was flushed with pleasure now. "I loved it. I didn't

want you to go easy on me. I wanted you to show me how you liked it. I'll get used to it and be better at taking you down my throat next time."

I could barely stand it. It was a struggle to make myself stop touching her to put my dick away.

"How many times can you come in a day?" she asked suddenly and I about ran off the road.

"I don't know. I've never kept track. Five? Maybe six if I pace myself?"

"I wanna break your highest record."

"A man can only handle so much. How about we break *your* record? I'm going to make you feel real good when we get home, okay? I can't believe I didn't make you take your tits out for that. When I fantasize about you sucking me off, your tits are always out."

She beamed at me. "You fantasized about that?

"Endlessly."

"Tits out next time?" she asked.

I patted her hand, feeling more deliriously happy than I could ever remember. "Next time," I assured her.

# CHAPTER 11

**NOVA**

When we got home, he followed me into the bathroom attached to my bedroom.

We stripped together without speaking.

I'd rarely seen him without his shirt buttoned up to his throat and here he was showing me every inch of skin all at once.

I was deliciously overwhelmed by him.

He was more than fit and big everywhere. He was muscular and tan and more tantalizing even than my dreams.

He started the shower, adjusted the temperature, and nudged me in and under the spray, turning my back to him.

He soaped up my torso, reaching around to cup my breasts, slickly twisting my nipples until I was squeezing my thighs together.

He was hard, and his naked, rigid hard-on kept bumping against me from behind.

I reached back to stroke him, but he shooed my hands away.

"Leave it alone. Stop. Bad girl. I mean it. Don't touch it. It's your turn," he said and started sucking on my neck.

One of his hands stayed squeezing and stroking at a tit while the other snaked down and started massaging my clit.

I reached up, digging my hands into his thick hair, grabbing it by the handful. He pushed two fingers into me. I was slick, and he shoved them all the way in smoothly and started pumping, hard and fast.

His dick was digging into my back again, and I wasn't sure if he didn't notice or couldn't help it, but I leaned into it.

He withdrew it, working me hard with his hands.

"Rub your dick on me," I panted. "It's getting me off faster. Please."

With a curse, he started humping his big cock between my legs, not entering, just stroking along my flesh with firm pressure. He pinched my clit right as his fingers inside of me moved just so and I came, back arched, sobbing.

One of his hands dragged up my body, lingering over my breasts, then up to my face, turning it to kiss him deeply. He withdrew his hard cock and busy hand, turning me to face him.

He just kissed me for a long time, backing me up against the shower wall and pressing his huge self against me.

I hiked a thigh up, trying to draw his hips between my legs, but he resisted.

He dragged his mouth from my lips to my neck and lower, painting a trail of heat down my body as he went.

The huge muscles of his back bulged under my hands as he used his mouth on me tenderly, tirelessly.

He took his time making his way down, and by the time he drove his tongue into my cunt, I was primed. He feasted on me and it was better than anything my mind had ever come up with in my wildest fantasies.

I came again, and I don't even remember drying off or going to the bed, but we were there, tangled up and naked, and he was eating me out again. He sucked my clit hard enough to make my back arch off the bed as I came again. He didn't even slow, still sucking, his fingers drilling into me purposefully.

I begged him to fuck me. Instead he worked me over thoroughly in every other way, got me off until I either fell asleep or passed out cold, I wasn't coherent enough to figure out which.

I woke up alone and with the feeling that I was late for something important.

Oh shit. Work! I was going to be late, and my boss would not be happy. I was already on his shit list from all the shifts I'd missed amidst the fallout of my aunt kicking me out and me scrabbling to find a place to sleep a few weeks ago.

I changed into my work uniform in a hurry, noting with some wonder that the closet in the room I was using was even more filled with clothes I knew Carter had bought for me. It was overwhelming to have such thoughtful treatment after so many years of neglect from all of the people that were supposed to care for me.

But I couldn't linger on that now. I rushed downstairs.

I slowed as I caught sight of a shirtless Carter in the kitchen cooking something delicious by the smell of it. My stomach growled, but I ignored it. My sex clenched, a visceral reaction to the sight of him after all he'd done to me, and I ignored that too.

Carter caught sight of me and eyed me the way I imagined I was doing to him.

He approached me, bending for a quick, hot kiss.

I started to hurry to the garage to leave, but he stopped me by grabbing my arm. "I keep meaning to ask. Where do you work? I'd like to know where you are in case I need to reach you."

"The little diner on Harmon and Tropicana. Close to the university."

He nodded. "I know where that is. Thank you."

I tried to tug my arm loose to leave, but he didn't let me, pulling me close. He started kissing me, wet, drugging draws at my lips, his hands buried in my hair, using it to pull my head back for deeper angles against his mouth.

"Don't go," he said in the most convincing tone he could conjure. "Stay home and let me feed you dinner and fuck you as many times as you can take."

I was so tempted I trembled with it, but it was impossible.

"I need this job," I told him, my tone almost pleading with him. "What happens when you don't want me around anymore? Then I'll be homeless *and* jobless."

His kiss this time was almost painful. Punishing. He drew back and glared at me. "That's not what's happening here. Even if I never lay another finger on you, this is your home. And if you need money I'll provide you with it; whatever you need."

The concept was so foreign to my experiences that I just couldn't see how it was real or moreover, that it could last for any length of time.

I pulled away, and he let me go, though he looked pissed, nostrils flared. "I'll be back late."

He looked like he wanted to break something, but he let me leave.

My shift wasn't over for another hour and a bunch of obnoxious college boys were making my life hell. I was exhausted and fed up.

Usually it wasn't this bad, the students from UNLV came in to study and drank too much coffee at all hours, but this crowd was especially rowdy.

It was only Thursday, but for some reason the place was full to capacity. On the weekends, we got the crowds after they left the bars and needed to carb up before stumbling back home, but it was unexpected, if not unheard of, on a Thursday.

One table in particular was getting loud and making crude comments that they had to know weren't out of my earshot.

You couldn't be meek with men like that or they walked all over you. With a suggestive laugh one asked me, "What time do you get off?"

I shot back, "Never," and they roared with laughter but laid off me for a while after that.

I'd been working here since I was sixteen so I knew how to read customers by now. The types that were real assholes never tipped well, if at all. If you aren't afraid to show someone what an asshole you are, you certainly don't care if they think you're a bad tipper. Hell, I thought some of them were probably proud of it.

So with that, when I clocked an asshole, I served them but didn't even try chat them up.

I was staying away from that table as much as I could, but it was fifteen minutes until closing now and they showed no signs of moving even as the rest of the patrons had made their way out.

I sighed. I was going to have to kick them out myself, I just knew it. My manager was never good with that kind of thing, always put the burden on someone else, and it never turned out well for me.

I heard the bell ding that sounded when someone came in. I opened my mouth to tell them we were closing, then shut it abruptly. I smiled bemusedly, forgetting everything but the man walking in.

Mr. North had arrived to check up on me. I was suddenly less tired, more filled with cheerful energy.

He was dressed casually in a T-shirt, sweatpants, and sneakers, his hair messed up, his expression grumpy as hell.

"Have a seat anywhere," I told him as I approached, grinning up at him. "We're closing in fifteen minutes, but I can get you whatever you want if you order quickly."

He looked around like the entire place had offended him personally.

Just then one of the guys from the rowdy table called loudly for me by name. I needed to start wearing a fake name tag at work, I decided on the spot.

"I'll be right back to get your order," I told Carter, walking over to their table.

I felt Carter following behind me, and I wondered why for a brief second before I was distracted.

"Give us your number," one of the guys told me. It wasn't a question. It was an order, and his tone was gross. "What's your Insta?" another guy asked, his tone slightly less offensive. "We're having the party of the year at our frat tomorrow, and you're *coming*." They all laughed at that like it was really clever.

I rolled my eyes and opened my mouth to say something sassy back, but Carter beat me to it.

"Elliot Brown, is that you?" Mr. North's deep voice boomed from behind me. It was his sternest professor voice ,and I shivered a little.

One of the guy's eyes bulged open comically. "Mr. North?" he asked, sounding way different than he had all night. More meek.

"Ah, you remember me," Mr. North rumbled out darkly, glaring at him. "For the rest of you, I was his high school English teacher a few years ago. The same high school this young lady *still* goes to." He paused, smiled grimly at their reactions. "That's right, she's in high school. I hope you're ashamed of yourselves for hitting on an underage girl. How about you avoid this place from now on?"

He hadn't even finished speaking when they started to get up and leave. One of them finally handed me a credit card and I settled them up.

I grinned at Carter when they were gone. "Would you come here every weekend and do that? I'm not half so effective when people won't leave."

He sat down at the closest table, rubbing a hand over his tired face.

"Sure, baby girl, whatever you need."

"I was kidding."

"I wasn't. I wasn't kidding about paying you to be a student instead of working yourself to the bone, either."

"I'm not comfortable with that."

"How about I pay you to do other things?"

I felt my cheeks heat. "Like sex?"

He looked like he wanted to choke me silly. "Of course not. Like office work. Something that takes less of your time so you can get your grades back on track. I'm very serious about this. If there's anything you wanted from me, anything at all, I would do it if you would do that for me."

The way he said it, so grave and steady, like he'd given it a lot of serious thought, had me pausing and considering instead of immediately refusing. "I'll think about it," I told him finally.

"Another thing. If you ever leave again because you're angry with me, please don't go to a shelter. There's enough money in your bank account that you can at least get a hotel room."

"I don't want to waste money. You know I'm still saving up."

"Trust me, there's enough money in there that you don't have to worry about getting a hotel room if you need it."

"How much is in there?" I asked, feeling a bit odd, conflicted. I was touched by his generosity but ashamed at my need for it.

"Enough," he said curtly, rising. "It's late. I'll see you at home."

# CHAPTER 12

**CARTER**

When we got home, I sent her to bed, going the opposite way to my own bedroom. "Think about it and give me your answer as soon as you know," I told her as I walked away.

She didn't want my money or my help. It was infuriating. I needed something to bribe her with so that, at the very least, I could make sure she graduated from high school.

The next day I woke up early to find her gone. I tore down to the garage to find my Porsche gone, as well. I breathed a little easier. She was coming back.

I was edgy all day as I waited for my last class.

My heart pounded when she finally walked in. She didn't even say hi, just sat in her seat, and plopped a piece of candy in her mouth. She sucked on it and stared at me like she wanted to eat me alive. Great. Another class where I'd be lecturing from my seat. It was becoming a habit.

I didn't have to ask her to stay after class.

"Well?" I asked her after everyone else left.

"Well what?" she shot back without rising from her seat.

"Don't toy with me, pet. Do you have an answer for me?"

She chewed on her lip. "I have to *quit* quit, or can I just cut down hours?"

"Quit. That place is a dump, and I don't like the area. You never get to go back."

"And for that you'll give me a job helping *you*, and grant me one request?"

"Correct."

"Okay. I want you to fuck me for real."

I closed my eyes and licked my lips. I was really going through it. I needed to be inside of her so bad my teeth ached with it, but my voice was steady enough, "That's it? Done."

"Right here?" she teased me.

My eyes snapped open, but I was having a hard focusing on anything but the very near future when I was balls deep inside of her. "No. At home. After I make you dinner."

"Before dinner," she pressed.

I took an unsteady breath. "I have a meeting in five minutes. I'm not sure I'll survive."

She grinned and stood up. "I'll be at home waiting for you."

I rose, moved to her, and pushed my fingers into her mouth, plucking the candy out.

I put it on my tongue, never breaking eye contact with her. I pushed my fingers back in her mouth, making her suck them until they were clean of the sticky lemon drop.

"Naked," I said roughly, stepping decisively and excruciatingly away from her, when what I wanted to do was crawl inside of her that instant. "In your bed with your legs spread wide," I said firmly. "Wet and ready for me."

She saluted me and winked. "Yes, sir."

I shut my eyes and shuddered. I was in a bad state. "Just go, you little brat," I ordered.

Now how was I going to make it through the next hour?

I found her exactly how I'd instructed. Naked on top of her sheets, bedspread flung from the bed. Her legs were spread wide, her eyes on me.

Her body was perfect everywhere, skin dusky and flushed, body lithe and firm with curves for days, and I took the sight of her in devouring bites. I didn't quite know where to begin. I wanted to do so many things to her that I shivered deliciously in anticipation.

"Show me your pussy. Use your fingers to open for me."

She blushed but didn't hesitate. She bit her lip and obeyed, opening herself delicately with her dainty hands. Her perfect little cunt was wet and swollen even from feet away.

My cock ached so bad I felt it deep in my gut.

I stripped quickly, her eyes on me.

I'd pictured myself taking it slow the first time with her, but it was hopeless. I was too profoundly worked up. I needed what I needed and I needed it *now.*

"I can't wait. I'm sorry. Do you mind? I'm coming in." I was panting. *"I need inside of you now."*

She bit her lip and parted her thighs wider with gratifying enthusiasm.

I climbed on top of her, settling between her legs. I kissed her coaxingly as I pressed my hips down. My cock was so hard, it was pulsing between us.

I guided my thick tip to her entrance. I pushed in excruciatingly slowly. She was sopping wet but so tight I was gritting my teeth. I reached down, using my fingers to pull her wider as I bore deeper.

She didn't speak, but she wasn't quiet, gasping, moaning and crying out as I stuffed my heavy cock into her slick, taut flesh inch by inch. It was exquisite. It took all I had not to cram her full in one go. Just the thought of that almost made me shoot my load halfway in.

I reined in the thought and kept pushing in with shallow plunges now, making more progress with each thrust.

She was gasping, her breasts heaving with it, and I couldn't take it anymore I started thrusting for real, lunging in and out with much less restraint.

I pumped in and out of her forcefully but slowly, and it was so good.

Her eyes were shut, her head thrown back. She was panting, and I couldn't tell if it was from pleasure or pain. She was still so tight but I couldn't stop moving even to give her time to adjust. I had to have it just how it was, deep and complete and *now*. I'd never needed anything so badly in my life.

"Are you okay?" I panted at her. "Is it too much?"

"It's . . . overwhelming," she said.

It wasn't exactly a clear answer. I could have used a yes or no, but then again I didn't want to stop, didn't know if I could.

And I didn't, fucking her with heavy thrusts, squeezing my dick in and dragging it out, over and over.

Eventually I snapped, I pushed her legs wide and rammed in until I found the end of her.

I jarred against her cervix and stayed there, rutting in short humps that jolted her whole body. "It's so good. Does it hurt like this?" I asked, but I didn't stop pumping in and out, not for a second. Her whole body was quivering, her big tits bouncing with every movement.

"I don't care. Don't stop. Finish me." Her tone was heartfelt, her wet, dark angel eyes looking deeply into mine.

That effectively took me off my leash. I let loose on her, fucking how I craved, not holding back, giving it to her good, ramming in and out *long* and *hard* and *fast* now. I was big, and it was a rough ride, and she took it all in spite of her inexperience.

I didn't last a minute like that, pinning her legs open wide and arching into her as my top blew off, my cum jetting deep into her womb. I kissed her, humping into her, feeding her cunt every last drop. "Fucking." Thrust. "Take." Thrust. "It," I grunted out as I finished.

"Once you get used to me, it'll feel better," I told her when we eventually came up for air. It had taken me a long while to become coherent again. I was still inside of her and had no urge to pull out. "We just need to break you in."

Just the thought of it had me turned on, and I was getting hard again inside of her.

"It felt good," she eventually said softly. "It was a lot of pressure, but I was starting to adjust to it when you . . ."

"Lost my mind?" I asked tenderly, stroking her hair out of her face.

She smiled tremulously at me. "I liked it. I just need to learn to get there when you do."

"It's *my* job to get you there." I said, "I just lost control. I'm normally better than that, I swear. Here, I'll show you." I was propped on my elbows, hands moving over her soft breasts, cupping and kneading at her pliant flesh. Her deep pink nipples were exquisitely responsive. I sucked, pinched, and tormented them until she was crying out and writhing on my cock.

I moved inside of her and she stilled. "See? You're already getting used to me."

I dragged my cock out of her cunt with no little reluctance and moved down her body. I nuzzled into her sex, obsessed with the fact that she was filled with my seed. My fingers dragged at the trails of it running down her thighs, rubbing it back into her seeping entrance. "I'm going to stuff you so full of my cum. I'm going to permanently mark you with it." I was more than a little mortified by my own words, but I just couldn't stop talking. "So much and so often you won't know what it's like to be without it. You're my creature now. My perfect little sex pet. You're going to walk around with my cum seeping out of you every day and everywhere you go from now on."

"I can't wait," she breathed.

I rewarded her with the tip of my tongue vibrating against her clit. I got her worked up thoroughly this time before I mounted her again.

I pushed deep, holding her hips and working all the way in, her soft flesh giving in deliciously to my relentless descent.

I loved watching her gorgeous, expressive face when I was inside of her but I felt an overwhelming urge to break her in properly. With a groan I pulled out, turned her over onto her hands and knees. Abruptly I shoved in from behind. I worked myself in deep, then dragged out, once, twice, slow but steady. I was bent over her, one hand working her clit, the other fondling a bouncy tit.

I started plunging with faster, steadier, heavier thrusts. Her flesh was giving way easier, going soft and pliant as I worked it, keeping at it until I felt a vibration starting around my submerged shaft. With a low groan, I started pumping hard and fast. She was coming and I was more than ready to meet her there.

She was moaning and squeezing me and I let loose for real, thrusting until her knees collapsed. I had to hold her by the hips as I finished with brutal purpose, screwing deep and coming so hard I might've blacked out a little, coming to with my heavy weight pinning her down, my spurting dick still buried to the hilt.

I kissed her neck and lifted my weight up onto my elbows, which incidentally thrust my dick harder into her. I groaned and thrust again, her cunt milking me. "Take it, cum slut," I growled at her, grinding hard and slapping her ass. I barely recognized my own voice it was so low and harsh. I'd turned into an animal.

She moaned and writhed under me. She didn't seem to mind.

I groaned and kissed the back of her head. "I don't want to pull out. I'm spent, but you feel so good I can't bear to leave you."

She said something, a sleepy mumble that I thought was, "Me neither."

It set me off a bit, her soft, satiated state. "My dick belongs here. It's my territory now."

She moaned.

It wasn't good enough. I pulled her hair. "Say it," I ordered, tone firm, commanding.

"Your dick belongs inside me," she mumbled into the sheets.

"Inside your cunt," I corrected. "And say it all. Just how I said it. Were you paying attention? Or were you being a bad student again?"

"Your dick belongs inside me. My cunt is your territory now."

I hummed with pleasure. "That's right, pet. Your lovely cunt and all the rest of you, too." I smacked her ass again. "Don't you forget it."

Eventually I did pull out, turning her over.

She sprawled out, boneless, her eyes closed. I kissed her and she smiled without opening them.

"Dinner, pet?" I asked her.

"Sleep," she responded, turning away and burrowing into her pillow.

I smacked her bare ass again, but more lightly this time, then rubbed her plush, firm flesh. I was more than half tempted to fuck her again, awake or not, but instead I tucked her in tenderly and tore myself away.

# CHAPTER 13

**NOVA**

I woke up alone, which was disappointing. He'd fucked me for real then left me. What a bummer. I'd always pictured him staying with me and holding me all night after he took me.

It was a Saturday so I tried out one of the new outfits in my closet, a very nice white button up blouse and pleated gray skirt. Not far off from my school uniform, though much higher quality. He liked me schoolgirl proper. So kinky. I shivered with pleasure. He even had knee socks and platform Mary Janes to finish off the look.

I braided my hair into two neat braids to get it just right.

I went downstairs and found Carter dressed in his usual professor getup and cooking breakfast.

He turned his head and gave me the tender smile I was already addicted to. "Aren't you a sight for sore eyes? You must've been tired. You slept for over twelve hours."

I rubbed my eyes. "I haven't gotten a good night's sleep in

a long time, so I guess that makes sense." I smiled at him tentatively. "Was it—I mean—did you—um, well, was I any good?" I finally got out then started blushing profusely.

He left the stove still sizzling and approached me with a soul-melting smile. He cupped my face in both hands and touched his forehead to mine. "You were spectacular. Mind-blowing. I won't forget last night for the rest of my life. How about me? Was I any good?"

I was warm and blushing and so happy I felt tears welling up. It was just hot sex for him, but it meant so much to me that I could barely express myself. "You were the best," I said simply.

He moaned as though he couldn't keep the noise in and it was so hot. "And the only," he said softly and firmly.

"And the only," I repeated, sure it meant something different to him than to me, but just then I didn't care. I was so content that I didn't want to look ahead at what this would probably never be, instead I wanted to enjoy whatever it was in the now.

His hand snaked down and grabbed my sex. His touch was tender, but his voice was gruff. "And this is my territory."

I knew just what he wanted. I ate him with my eyes as I repeated back softly, "And my cunt is your territory."

He rewarded me with a kiss, both his hands moving to cup my face gently.

Eventually he pulled away to finish making breakfast.

"Can I help?" I asked.

"Just sit down and let me feed you. You must be starving."

I was. I couldn't remember the last time anyone had made me breakfast. He and I rarely ran into each other in the morning.

"French toast or pancakes?" he asked. "I made both. Along with the usual. Eggs, bacon, hash browns."

I thought about it. "French toast, please."

I was sitting at the table, knees together, hands folded on top, on my best behavior.

He noticed and shook his head at me. "You look so much like a well-behaved schoolgirl right now that I can barely take it. I can't even look at you. Eat your breakfast and behave," he finished, setting a heaping plate in front of me.

His hip was near my shoulder and I couldn't help myself. I rubbed his dick through his pants.

He cursed and jerked away, glaring. "Eat," he said, tugging at one of my braids before moving away.

I ate like I hadn't eaten in probably a year.

He watched me at first, as though to make sure I liked what he'd made me.

No one but him had ever taken care of me like this, no one but him ever made me food, no one had given a damn whether I starved for longer than I cared to consider. I loved the attention, and particularly who it was coming from.

Eventually Carter sat across from me and ate just as ravenously.

"Any plans today?" I asked him when we finished.

He was flushing and avoiding my gaze, and I suddenly had a sick feeling in my gut. "About that . . ." He began stiltedly. "Can you wear something less . . .provocative? I love how you look right now, but I can't be around you looking like that unless we're spending the day fucking like animals."

I beamed at him though he didn't see it. "Let's do that. Your bed or mine?"

He sighed like it pained him, still not looking at me. "I wish, but not today. I totally forgot until I saw a message this morning. I have a . . . friend coming to stay for a few nights, and I promised I'd pick her up from the airport. The plans were made months ago. Like I said, I'd completely forgotten until this morning."

I felt something inside of me slipping away, like I was losing something precious that I'd have liked to hold onto. "A friend?" I asked in a small voice.

He looked at me then, and I could tell I wasn't going to like his answer. "She's my ex-girlfriend actually, but we're still close."

I felt just sick.

He seemed to read my mind, and he looked concerned. He reached his hand toward me like he wanted to touch me across the table, but stopped himself. "She's an interior designer, and there's a big convention in town that she always attends. Happens once a year, and she just stays here because it's convenient and we get to catch up."

I nodded, trying to be mature about it. "But you're just friends now?" I asked, and my tone sounded small and childish just how I hadn't wanted it to.

He grimaced but nodded. "Just friends. I'll introduce you to her. She's only here for two days so there's no need for us to explain ourselves. I'll tell her you're my student and you needed a place to stay, which is the truth. Let's keep the rest to ourselves, yeah?"

I nodded. "Of course," I said, my heart breaking a bit. "I'll stay out of your way, I promise."

He looked suddenly like he wanted to throttle me.

I squirmed.

"That's not what I said," he stated in his firm teacher voice. "This is your home. You don't need to stay out of anyone's way. And she'll be gone in just a couple of days."

I nodded. "How long ago did you date her?" just sort of slipped out.

He looked as uncomfortable as I'd ever seen him. "A long time. More than six years. Let's not do this, okay?"

"How long were you together?"

He stared at me, nostrils flaring, trying to will me, I thought, to stop asking such personal questions. "Three years."

I was a bit devastated by that. Three years meant they'd definitely been in love. How much of that was left? I couldn't imagine it all just going away, especially if she still visited.

Just friends, I told myself. He'd said just friends.

I could be mature about this.

"Can I sleep in your room with you while she's here?" Okay, maybe I couldn't.

He gave me a stern look. "I don't think that's a good idea."

"Where will she be sleeping?"

He sighed. "A guest room."

"Where? Close to your room?"

"No. I'll put her next to you if it makes you feel better."

He'd read my mind. I wanted to keep track of where she slept while she was here. I wanted to see with my own eyes that she wasn't sleeping with *him*.

I had a million other questions, but I didn't know if I could handle the answers just then so I fell silent.

"Are you okay?" he asked me gently.

I nodded, looking down at my lap. "When do you have to leave to pick her up?"

"Soon. I meant it about you changing out of that. I seriously can't handle it. And the braids . . . please make this easier for me."

I looked up hopefully. "We could be quick—"

"No, we couldn't. If I take you to bed right now I'm not going to be able to stop anytime soon. You're lucky I even let you sleep last night. Like I said, she'll only be here for a couple of days. We can last that long." He sounded like he was trying to convince himself.

"Of course. I was thinking I could start helping you with

the office stuff today. Can you point me in a direction to get started?"

He chewed on his lip. "I don't have time to show you the ropes, and I'll be gone for several hours."

"Several hours?" I asked.

He studied me, looking worried. "I'm going to pick her up, and we're going to lunch and then we'll probably walk around on the strip and catch up a bit. Don't look at me like that, pet. This doesn't change anything between us, I swear. Hey, stop that."

I was mortified that tears were rolling down my cheeks, and I waved him off. "It's fine. I get it. Sorry, I'm just a baby."

He got up, came over, pulled me up, sat down, and then set me down on his lap.

I buried my face in his chest and cried. "Was that—were we a one-time thing?" I asked, and hated myself for being such a needy child.

His breath was unsteady, and for some reason I found that comforting.

His hand was stroking restlessly over my hair and fingering my braid. "Not by a long shot," he finally got out. "Please don't cry. I can't take tears, and I honestly can't stand it that I made you cry. I *hate* myself right now. What do you want me to do? I'll do anything you say if you'll stop crying."

I pushed away and got up, wiping my face. His pity was the last thing I wanted. I couldn't even look at him. "I'm sorry I'm here and being such a nuisance and getting in the way of your plans. I can go somewhere else for a few days. It's really not a big deal. I don't mind."

He grabbed me roughly and by the look on his face I thought he wanted to shake me, but he just stared right down to my soul. "Don't you dare," he said through his teeth.

"Would you like to come with me to pick her up? Would that make you feel better?"

It would, and it made me feel world's better that he'd offered, but I refused. I knew he didn't really want me to come.

"But you'll stay here?" he asked worriedly.

"I'll stay here," I said. I honestly couldn't stand the idea of he and his ex alone in this house together.

"Because this is your home," he said firmly.

I nodded and he kept staring until I repeated the words back, "Because this is my home."

He yanked me against him for a long hug, kissing the top of my head and murmuring sweet things until it was time for him to leave.

I watched him drive away, wondering how I could make the next few hours pass by quicker. I just kept picturing them out together, eating together, even holding hands. They're going on a date, I thought, and couldn't see it another way.

He couldn't do any of that with me. Go out for a meal or a walk or anywhere at all. He'd claimed my body, but he couldn't claim me in public, not even for something as normal as a date. Ours was strictly a relationship for behind closed doors.

A dirty secret.

I'd always known that, but it still stung.

# CHAPTER 14

I had plenty of homework to catch up on, but I was too unsettled to sit down for one second, let alone concentrate long enough to get something done.

I finally texted my friend Michelle, though we hadn't talked much lately.

I'd stayed at her place a few times since I was kicked out, but I could tell she and her parents were worried I'd overstay my welcome or make them adopt my problems.

Most of my friends were harder for me to be around lately. It was difficult to hear them complain about really trivial things all the time when my world was falling apart, so I'd withdrawn quite a bit.

Everyone had let me. Again, no one wanted to adopt my very real problems.

Except for Mr. North.

I'd barely sent off a text when my phone started ringing, Michelle's face flashing on the screen.

"Hey!" I said brightly when I answered. I'd learned to

hide my feelings from normal kids my own age years ago. No one I knew could relate too much of what I was going through.

"Hi!" she returned cheerfully. "Can you hang out? There's a party tonight, and I don't want to go with just Maddie. You know how she is. She'll ditch me the second we get there and some football player smiles at her."

I paused, really torn about it. I didn't want to go, but I *really* didn't want to stay home. "Sure," I said finally.

"You're the best! I can pick you up. Are you still at that . . . shelter place or whatever it is?"

I had to smile. We were worlds apart, but it was nice to pretend in her world sometimes, where homeless shelters were an afterthought. "I'm staying with a friend," I told her.

"Who?" She sounded almost jealous though she clearly hadn't wanted me to stay with *her*.

"You don't know them. It's temporary, but anyway, I can meet you somewhere. What time?"

"Well, about that. I need an outfit. Want to go to the mall right now? I can . . . like buy you something or whatever."

I felt a little sick at her tone, sort of patronizing and almost smug, and I felt another strong wave of gratitude for Carter and his endless generosity. "That's really nice," I told her, "but I have a little money right now. I can buy myself an outfit, too."

"Oh yeah?" she sounded relieved. "Nice. Okay. Meet up in thirty?"

"Works for me," I said instantly. No more agonizing free time while I waited for Carter to come home from his date. Yippee.

I didn't change as Carter had requested. He wasn't around to see me so what did it matter? I did unbraid my hair, leaving it loose and wavy down my back instead.

I parked at the food court entrance of the mall, hoping to

avoid Michelle seeing the Porsche, but she'd parked there too and unfortunately spotted me getting out of it.

She looked at me oddly as I approached her.

"Whose ride is that?" she asked. The look on her face . . . it was like she thought I'd stolen it or something.

"It's my friend's car," I said vaguely and defensively. "I'm just borrowing it for the day."

"Wow. Nice. Where'd you meet this friend?"

I sighed. I really wished she hadn't seen it. "Long story. Let's shop. What kind of outfit are you looking for?"

We shopped for hours and Michelle bought at least five dresses. I just bought one outfit to wear that night. It was a fitted beige crop top and a low-slung beige and pink plaid, pleated skirt. It was cute, and it would drive Carter mad when he saw me come home in it. Childish but satisfying.

"That's so hot," Michelle told me when I tried it on. "Who are you trying to impress?"

I rolled my eyes. "No one at this party," I said cryptically.

"Your shoes even work with it," she pointed out.

I looked down. The Mary Janes *were* just right.

"You're really into the pleated skirt look right now, huh? You'd think you'd get enough of that with the school uniforms every day, but it *does* look good on you. Want to get ready at my house?"

That was my favorite thing about Michelle. No matter what mood I was in she never picked up on it and she talked endlessly through every awkward silence. It made me feel almost like a normal teenager for a minute. "I'd love that," I told her.

When I was paying I could tell she was checking out the card I was using, but she didn't openly ask and I wasn't going to volunteer any information about why I suddenly wasn't so short on funds.

We took her old Honda Civic to her house instead of my

Porsche, and she said she'd drop me off back at the Porsche after the party.

"Whose credit card are you using?" she asked me about five minutes into the drive.

I sighed. "It's not a credit card. It's a bank card. I opened up an account."

She was quiet for a bit. "Where's the money coming from? Do you have a sugar daddy or something?"

I laughed and she laughed with me, but when I thought about it, really, she wasn't that far off.

We did each other's makeup, heavy liner, too much glitter, and dark, dark red lips, Michelle chatting all the while, catching me up on the gossip I'd never asked for.

We did our hair in messy space buns. Mine was too thick, so we left the back half down in a waterfall against my back, buns in front.

Michelle had thin, light brown hair so I captured all of it easily into two small buns.

She fussed over mine, telling me she wished she had my hair.

"I wish I had yours," I returned. "I can't even put all of mine up. It's too thick."

She rolled her eyes. "I'm so sad for you. Let's get dressed."

I changed in her bathroom and came back out. Michelle was on her phone, frowning.

"It's only five," she said sullenly, "and I guess no one's at the party yet. We should wait. We don't want to get there first."

I shrugged. "I don't care either way."

She was still looking at her phone and suddenly brightened. "Maddie and Kris want to meet for dinner first. Let's go."

That worked. I didn't care if we never made it to the party.

Not thinking about what Carter was doing, instead dressing up and acting like a teenager for the day, had been good enough for me.

We met up with Maddie and Kris at a local pizza place. They both seemed surprised but happy to see me.

Maddie sized me up with a smile. "That's quite the hot getup. Who are you trying to hook tonight? I bet whoever it is, he'll bite."

I didn't have to answer because Michelle butted in with, "What about me? Don't you think *my* outfit's hot?"

Everyone had to reassure her that it was, effectively taking the attention away from me.

I made a note to keep her close to me at the party. She was a very good distraction. She made it easy for me to keep the focus off of myself.

The instant we walked into the house party, it felt like a mistake. It was crowded and loud, and I just wanted to know what Carter was doing with his ex right then.

Were they home yet? How long had she hugged him when he picked her up? Was he still attracted to her? I didn't wonder if she was still attracted to him. He wasn't the kind of guy you got over.

Did she want him back? Who wouldn't?

Maybe the party wasn't such a terrible idea, I thought, and set about distracting myself.

I just wanted to hang out with my girlfriends but it was a party and soon some football players were surrounding us, handing us drinks.

I wasn't surprised to find Jake's arm slung over my shoulder.

He grinned at me, leaning in close. He was drunk. The

times I'd gone out with him I'd noticed he liked to drink too much and didn't control himself very well when he did.

"You look hot," he yelled into my ear. He reeked of beer and weed.

I leaned away. "I miss you," he added. He was so loud everyone was staring at us.

I shut my eyes, embarrassed.

"Let's go upstairs," he continued.

I took a firm step away, giving him a dirty look. As if. We hadn't dated for over a year, had obviously never had sex, and he thought I'd just walk upstairs with him? It was ridiculous and insulting.

"No, thank you," I told him stiffly.

The way it came out was a bit colder and ruder than I'd intended, and everyone laughed. I smiled, trying to play it off, but Jake had the opposite reaction.

"Maybe if you weren't such a stuck-up bitch, you wouldn't be living in a homeless shelter," he said, his voice carrying.

The crowd laughed loudest of all at that.

I kept smiling and excused myself.

The bathroom had a line outside of it and I waited there, eyes pointed straight ahead, wishing I could be alone for just five minutes.

Michelle hugged me from behind, speaking into my ear. "Are you okay? Jake is just upset cause you dumped him last year and he's, like, totally still hung up on you, ya know?"

"I know," I said tonelessly. "I'm fine. I just need to use the restroom."

She came around to study me, seemed satisfied, and changed the subject as though nothing had happened.

She tapped my full cup of beer. "Drink up. It's a party."

I pretended to take a drink but intended to dump it as soon as I could without being noticed. No way was I drinking in a place like this. I didn't trust anybody here.

I didn't trust anybody anywhere.

Well, maybe one person, but I didn't want to think about him for even a second just then.

I didn't drink, but I did dance with my friends for a few hours. I turned down a few drunken offers, too.

Maddie and Kris accepted a few, disappearing with some football players as Michelle had known they would.

Michelle was solid in that if she came with you she left with you, but she never wanted to leave early.

I finally convinced her to go around midnight, but she grumbled for most of the drive to my car.

"Let's hang out again soon, okay?" she called as I got into the Porsche.

I waved and agreed, starting the car. I was backing out when a phone call flashed on the car screen on the dash of the car. My phone paired automatically with it from previous uses.

Oh, shit. Carter was calling.

I put the car in park and started looking for my phone, answering from the touchscreen as I did so.

"Hello," I called out, checking the floor.

"Where the *hell* are you?" a terse voice spoke quietly and furiously.

I found my phone just under the seat. Ah, *so that's where it went.* I was stressed out all night that I'd left it somewhere at the mall. "On my way home," I said, straightening and buckling up again.

"Where have you *been*?" his voice was trembling with rage. "I've been worried *sick*."

I felt bad, because I'd been more than half hoping this would be his reaction. Any attention from him at all, even the bad kind, was addictive to me.

I wanted him to miss me even though I knew it was immature and selfish. "I was giving you guys some space. I went out with my friends."

He didn't speak for so long that I wondered if he was still on the line. "How far away are you?"

I calculated. "Twenty minutes, maybe? Around that. Did you guys have fun today? What are you up to now?"

Another long pause. "It was fine," he said, his tone glacial. "We went to the shark reef, and now we're watching some movies here. I've been calling you for hours and hours. Were you ignoring me?"

"I left my phone in the car by accident," I said cheerfully. "I just now found it. I'm so relieved. I thought I lost it somewhere. It was bothering me all day." As I said this I saw that I had missed a dozen calls and several texts from him. "I'm sorry I worried you. I figured you wouldn't notice if I left since you were so busy today."

Another long pause. "Well, you figured wrong," he finally said, his tone odd, like he was trying not to lose it.

I could tell he was more pissed than I'd ever seen him, and I wondered how I should deal with it. Maybe if I ignored it for long enough he'd forget about it? Yeah, I decided to do that. "I'll be home soon," I told him. "Will you guys still be up?"

"Yes," he bit out.

"What are you watching?"

He ignored that question. "What were you doing with your friends?" he asked.

"We went to the mall, and I found an outfit for this party," I babbled as though he wasn't going out of his mind on the other end. "I bought it, but I shopped at H&M so I only spent like forty dollars."

He didn't respond, so I continued, "I can pay you back." It was all his money in the account he'd started for me. My own small stash of cash was still in the account my aunt had started for me. "Sorry if I overstepped my—"

"Shut up," he growled at me. Oh, he was really losing it. I wondered where his friend was and if she was wondering what was wrong with him. He sounded like he was about to rip off his shirt and howl at the moon. "I don't care what you buy or how much you spend," he continued in the same awful tone. "I've been worried *sick* about you for *hours*."

"I told you I left my phone behind by accident," I explained again calmly.

The bastard hung up on me.

# CHAPTER 15

**CARTER**

I was having a hard time putting on a good face for Amy as I joined her back on the sofa.

"Everything okay?" she asked.

I'd been stepping outside to call Nova, over and over, since we'd gotten back to my place so it was no wonder she asked, but I just answered with a neutral, "Yeah, sorry, let's get back to the movie."

I was sitting a few feet away from her, but she moved closer as the movie started up again, leaning her head against me. It was friendly enough, could even be innocent, but even I wasn't sure if she was making a move on me.

About fifteen minutes later, I saw lights flash across the window and knew Nova was finally home.

"Is that your teenager?" Amy asked innocently.

My teenager . . . I almost laughed. I had told her I had a student staying here, giving her only the bare facts and none of the incriminating ones. "Yeah, that's Nova. I guess she went to a party. She didn't tell me." I tried to make my tone as neutral as possible, like that information hadn't wrecked my night and made me livid even now.

She patted my thigh and gave me a very alarming smile. *Did she still have a thing for me?* I honestly didn't know.

"That's so sweet," she said. "You're such a good teacher."

Nova walked in while Amy's hand was still (innocently?) on my thigh, and I could tell she noticed right away.

Meanwhile I was taking in her barely there outfit, her heavy makeup, her wild hair, and trying to keep my shit together. It was an effort not to start yelling at her straightaway, a very strange thing for me. I wasn't known for having any kind of a temper.

Amy broke the awkward silence. "I'm Amy," she said with a smile at Nova. "Carter told me about your situation. I'm happy he could help you. Isn't he the best?"

Nova smiled back, but it looked a little off, her gorgeous face stiff, her eyes dark and fathomless with all that makeup.

I couldn't take my eyes off her. She looked so different, like a wild teenager seductress, and I wondered who she'd dressed like this for.

She noticed me staring and stared insolently back. "Nice to meet you," she said to Amy, sounding cheerful enough if you didn't see the look she was giving me.

Amy noticed the awkwardness. "Um, so want to join us? We're watching the newest John Wick movie. I forget which number it is. I just watch for Keanu."

Nova took her time answering and I almost called her to task for rudeness when she said, "Sure," and threw herself down on a nearby loveseat.

Her skirt was so short that I could see up it with the way she was sitting. I squinted. *Was she wearing panties?* She fucking better be.

Her shirt was a beige color that made you glance twice thinking it was skin. It was tight, and I could see the shape of her erect nipples through it. And then there was the rest of her, all of that perfect, golden skin showing. Her legs were bare from her ankles all the way up to that barely there skirt and her stomach was bare from ribs to hips. It was flat and toned, and I wanted to bury my face there. I wanted to lick her top to bottom. Her body was to die for and it was killing me.

I couldn't believe she'd worn that out. To a party. *Who was she dressing like that for?*

I felt positively violent.

She only stayed for about five minutes before she bounced up and left, mumbling something about popcorn.

Amy chuckled like something was funny.

I sent her a baffled look. She laughed harder. "Teenagers," she said as if that explained it.

"Excuse me," I said, getting up to follow Nova because I simply couldn't stop myself.

She was in the walk-in kitchen pantry, and she looked up as I shut myself inside with her.

"I'm looking for popcorn," she explained.

I put my hand over her mouth and pinned her front against the wall with my chest against her back. I was so angry I couldn't even speak at first. I was afraid of what I'd say to her. My free hand went under her skirt.

At least she was wearing panties. I let out one heavy, relieved breath. "Who are you dressing like this for?" I asked her, and my voice was as mean as I felt.

She tried to say something, but my hand was still covering her mouth.

I shut my eyes, setting my forehead on the wall beside her and pushed a finger past her panties and into her warmth.

She squirmed and I pressed my hard-on against her hip.

She tried to say something again.

"Shh," I said into her ear and took my hand away from her mouth to fondle her.

"She's going to catch us," she whispered at me infuriatingly. "You should go back before she sees what you're doing to me."

She was right and in answer I pushed my finger in deeper. "You didn't answer my question," I said and started finger fucking her, my dick humping against her impatiently through my pants.

She didn't answer, so I pinched her nipple so hard that she cried out. I cursed and covered her mouth again, my other hand still drilling into her.

I got her off and left her panting against the wall. I washed my hands and made popcorn without looking at her when she finally walked out of the pantry. If I so much as glanced her way, I was going to either put her over my knee or fuck her like a dog on all fours on the kitchen floor. I put the popcorn into two bowls, holding the larger one in front of me. "I'll share this one with Amy," I told her tersely, waving toward the other bowl. "That one's yours."

I left, keeping the bowl strategically placed even after I sat down next to Amy again.

Nova came back in with her popcorn awhile later, looking more sullen than ever. She threw herself down; it was indecent, her skirt riding even higher than before. I could see her panties clearly this time and I stared and stared. She caught me at it and stuck out her tongue.

Amy was luckily oblivious, watching the movie like it was more fascinating than the show Nova was putting on for me.

Nova pointed at the coffee table in front of us. There were two glasses of red wine I'd forgotten I'd poured earlier. I'd barely touched mine.

"Where's mine?" Nova asked impertinently.

Amy laughed gamely. "Let her have a sip of yours, Carter. It won't hurt to give her a little, and you haven't touched it."

As though that settled it, Nova got up and sat on the other side of me. Looking at me the whole time she grabbed my glass and took a deep drink of it.

Amy's eyes were back on the movie and I glared at Nova.

She grinned and took another drink. "That's enough," I told her sternly when she kept drinking.

She finished the glass and set it down, looking at me the entire time.

Amy giggled. She'd apparently had a few too many glasses herself. "Your teenager is sassy," she told me. "I think she's had wine before."

"I haven't," Nova said quietly, then got up and left.

I was trembling with the urge to follow her. I wanted to have it out, to rage at her, really give it to her good.

I wanted to pin her down and fuck her until she agreed to behave herself.

Amy eventually fell asleep on the sofa, and I covered her in a blanket and left her to it. She knew her way around the place.

I should have gone straight to my own room but I didn't. I went to *hers*.

She wasn't there.

My heart was pounding as I strode through the house to my bedroom. The door was shut and I thrust it open.

Nova was on my bed, leaning back on her elbows, watching me calmly. She'd taken off her shoes and bra, I could see, and left on her tiny top and skirt.

I shut the door softly behind me and locked it. I approached her, grabbed her bare foot, and dragged her roughly to the edge of the bed. I flipped her skirt up. She was bare. I was panting.

"You little brat," I told her, voice mean.

My dick was out, and I was on top of her in a flash, pushing her legs apart, shoving into her slick entrance. I held her hips up and drove into her.

Her shirt slipped up, baring her breasts. "Cup your breasts for me," I told her. I couldn't reach her with my hands holding her at this angle. I pumped harder.

She cried out and I stopped. It was a big house but I had no idea how much sound traveled through it. I wasn't used to this much company at once.

I pulled out of her and set her on the bed. I arranged her to my liking, cupped her hands over her own breasts. I sucked them until they were both erect and sensitized, covering her mouth the whole time.

I spread her wide, kept my hand over her mouth and guided my cock back to her entrance. I drove home hard and she whimpered into my palm.

"Shh, pet, shh," I crooned into her ear, fucking her in earnest now. "I'm." Thrust. "Gonna." Thrust. "Come." Thrust. "So hard." Thrust, thrust, thrust.

I pushed up with one hand. The other slid down from her mouth and covered her throat, squeezing carefully. "You like to be choked? This will have to do for now until I can choke you with my cock again."

I covered her lips with mine, fist braced at her shoulder, the other still gripping her neck, applying just enough pressure to have her gasping and squirming on my dick, and pounded away.

With some effort and luck, I got her off before I followed, rooting deep and filling her with cum.

"Did you let anyone touch you?" I growled into her ear when I got my breath back. My hand was still at her throat, rubbing more than squeezing now.

She stiffened under me. I pushed up to look at her face.

She glared at me. "Did anyone touch *you*? I saw her hand

on your thigh when I walked in. Did I interrupt something?"

I pulled out of her, looking down to watch as I did it. "Answer me," I bit out.

"I don't think I will," she said sullenly and I lost it. I pinned her to the bed, chest to chest, putting enough weight on her to make her breath unsteady. "Answer me," I said again, unraveling more by the second.

"You. First," she gasped out.

I flipped her around and pinned her to the bed with my chest against her back, her arms pulled high above her head. It took a few minutes for me to answer her calmly. "That was innocent. She was just asking me a question, and she does that sometimes. Now you."

She took so long to answer that I was hard and ready to go again as she spoke, "No one touched me."

I pushed her legs apart and worked into her from behind, my hand going around, grabbing her crudely. "And who does this belong to?" I asked, rubbing her with my palm.

"You."

"Whose exclusive territory is this?" I prodded, pushing deeper.

"All yours," she gasped.

"That's right," I growled into her ear. "Mine. Now who were you dressing up for?" I asked

I didn't think she'd answer and I stopped moving.

"You," she finally said, and I shoved home.

I fucked her rougher than I should have, but she didn't complain and I needed it like that, needed to get the rage out somehow or I thought I'd burst apart at the seams. I was panting, spent again, lying on her back, in her cunt, when I whispered into her ear, "I missed you. Please don't do that again. I need to know where you are. I worry about you."

She didn't answer and I pulled out, lay down beside her, and pulled her face first into my chest.

I drifted off like that, all wrapped around her, both of us still covered in sex, without another word.

# CHAPTER 16

I woke up alone the next morning, and I was disappointed when I should have been relieved.

I showered. As I cleaned myself, the mess still on me made me remember in visceral detail how I'd gotten that way. I needed to fuck Nova again. *Needed* it, and no way was I jacking off when she was on hand.

If only she'd stayed with me all night, I could've gotten my dick wet the second I was conscious. That's how I should've woken up, how I wanted to wake up every day going forward.

I found Amy in the kitchen cheerfully cooking breakfast. She was a tall, model-thin blond with no curves to speak of. I'd always found her very beautiful, especially when she smiled and laughed, but just then she didn't move me at all. The attraction was gone completely.

We'd always been better as friends, hence the easy breakup.

She was a bad but enthusiastic cook, and I'd always found

her efforts charming, but right then all I wanted was her gone. I needed to find Nova, see what she was doing, how she was feeling, what she was thinking.

"Can I help?" I asked Amy instead.

"Just have a seat. I haven't gotten to feed you in a while."

I didn't care for her tone or her wording but couldn't exactly take exception to it. We'd been broken up for a long time, it was firmly over between us romantically, but sometimes when she visited and we were both unattached, we hooked up. It was nothing. Just casual sexual relief with someone who knew the right buttons to push.

Or it hadn't been, but I was feeling almost gross about it suddenly, like we had done something wrong that I should regret, something that could be held against me, could possibly be taken in such a way that it would hurt Nova if she found out.

Amy was humming under her breath and smiling at me in a familiar way. "Will your teenager sleep in, do you think? I was hoping for a morning romp. I didn't mean to pass out on the sofa last night. It's been *ages* since I've gotten laid." She grinned. "I miss your dick."

I opened my mouth to speak when Nova walked in. "Oops," she said flatly. "Did I interrupt?" She turned around and left. The look on her face would haunt me.

Amy looked mortified. "Oh, God. She heard me. How embarrassing! You know I was just messing around. Mostly."

I buried my face in my hands.

"Should I go talk to her?" Amy asked.

I shook my head. "I'll do it."

"Oh, God. How awful for you."

She had no idea.

I excused myself and went after Nova.

It was as bad as I was expecting. She was crying and

packing up her stuff. I shut the door softly behind me and approached her.

She shook her head, warding me off with her hands as she backed into the closet. I cornered her there, holding her when she tried to move past me.

"I'll scream," she said into my ear. "Let me leave or I'll scream."

"Calm down," I began. I should have known better, but it just sort of slipped out. I was wise enough to know that you couldn't tell a woman to calm down as you broke her heart.

It was, obviously, the wrong thing to say. She started thrashing against me, and I dragged her to the floor and pinned her down with my whole body until she couldn't move.

"I don't care if you scream," I told her nastily. "I don't care what you do or say or what Amy sees, I'm not letting you leave like this." I took a deep breath. "Now let me explain."

She started fighting me again. It got her nowhere except pinned harder to the ground. "I don't care," she sobbed. "I don't care what you say, I want to leave."

I kissed her face tenderly, wanting to cry myself. Seeing her hurt like this tore me up.

"Please, baby girl" I told her gently, licking her tears. "Please let me explain."

She was still sobbing, quietly now, but she said, "Fine."

"That wasn't what you think. We weren't planning to hook up, okay? I was about to tell her no when you walked in. I swear it."

She was silent, her eyes closed. Eventually she asked. "She was talking like you hook up all the time, like it was assumed you'd have sex. I thought you were broken up."

"We are. *Very* broken up."

"But you still have sex?"

"Not for a long time."

"How long?"

I counted. "Almost two years, I think." It could have been true. I honestly couldn't remember. "We hooked up occasionally after the breakup, yes, but it was nothing."

She started crying again without making a sound, and it broke my heart.

"You're still in love with her," she finally gasped out.

I wasn't expecting it so it took me too long to respond, and she started fighting me again.

"I'm not! Not even a little bit. I'm not sure I ever was."

She went still. "You still have feelings for her though," she said.

"Friend feelings. I swear."

"But you kept sleeping with her for *years* after you broke up?"

She was such an earnest, innocent young thing that it was hard to explain to her how casual of an act sex could become even to someone you used to care for. I didn't want to explain it to her, couldn't do it, in fact. I didn't want to ruin that part of her innocence. I wanted to keep it intact forever. The act of love was sacred to her, and with her it was for me too, but I didn't know if she'd believe that if she were to tally up the casualness of my past experiences.

"It was nothing," I finally said. "And I never felt for her the way I feel about you. Not even close. Okay?"

"You promise?" she asked, her voice small and tremulous, but hopeful.

"I promise. And I'll tell her I'm seeing someone. I intended to all along, it just hadn't come up before then. I'll even tell her it's you if that's what you want."

"I don't want that. I don't want to get you in trouble."

"Telling her won't get me in trouble. You're legally an adult, and it's not like she works for the school district. It'll just make her mad and she'll probably try to rescue you from me, to be honest. She's a very good person. I really think you two will like each other once all this settles."

She shook her head furiously back and forth, looking adorable and grumpy. "No. Don't tell her about us. Just tell her you're seeing someone, but not me. I don't want you to mess up your friendship."

"Whatever you want," I told her, kissing her nose.

I carried her to the bed and tucked her in. "What are your plans today?"

"I have schoolwork," she said but her eyes were closed and I thought she was falling asleep.

I kissed her cheek, her forehead, her other cheek, feeling a wave of deep tenderness for her that was unlike anything I'd ever experienced. "Rest, baby girl," I told her gently.

She didn't stir.

"I'm going to talk to Amy, okay?" I spoke quietly. "And she'll be gone for most of the day and into the evening. She has that convention. I'm not going anywhere so come get me if you need anything. I'll either be working in my office or working out in my home gym."

She just nodded, not opening her eyes.

I kissed her cheeks again, then her forehead, then her mouth. I licked her lips, my tongue sweeping in to stroke against hers, and even then she didn't stir. She'd already drifted off.

I left her reluctantly.

Amy was still in the kitchen fidgeting with her burnt food.

We sat down and ate it together.

"Is she okay? Did I traumatize her?" Amy finally asked me.

I sighed. How to go about this? "She's fine. Just embarrassed."

"Oh, good. Me too."

I met her eyes. She was smiling at me pleasantly. I was

hoping she would make this easy. "About what you were saying earlier, before Nova overheard. I'm seeing someone. I meant to tell you yesterday but it never came up, ya know?"

She looked surprised but not upset. "I wish you'd said something. You know I'd never . . . if you were with someone. Is it serious?"

I didn't answer directly. "It's new but definitely exclusive."

She studied me. "I think it's very serious. I hope she likes me. She and I will need to be friends. I don't want to get booted out of your life for good. When do I get to meet her?"

I searched for the words. "Like I said, it's new, but . . . powerful. I've never felt this way before."

Instead of being jealous she looked intrigued. I was unutterably relieved. We'd been buddies and confidants for a long time. We'd grown up a bit together. Ours had been a young, practice relationship, where we'd modeled what it was to be with someone seriously more than feeling it for each other, exactly. I could easily picture never hooking up with her again, but losing her friendship would suck.

"I'm happy for you," she said simply. "I hope it works out and you invite me to the wedding."

I didn't respond to that, didn't begin to know what to say.

She changed the subject to something less awkward and I was thankful to her.

She left before noon for a day of conventions and networking, telling me not to wait up for her.

When I was finally alone in the house with Nova it hit me hard. It took all of my self-control not to go to her room and wake her up with my dick, but I resisted. It was a close thing, but I had work to do and I knew for a fact that she needed sleep and to do her homework more than she needed my cock shoved as far into her in as many places as it could possibly go.

I was working in my office sometime later when she finally appeared.

She was wearing an oversized T-shirt over bare legs, no bra. I couldn't tell about the panties.

"Do you want to show me the office work you were talking about?" she asked. "I'm ready to help."

"Not yet. Catch up on more of your homework first."

She chewed her lip. "Can I work on it in here with you?"

"At your own peril."

She dimpled adorably at me, and I wanted to hold her down, bite her neck and fuck her right there.

She didn't seem to notice, waving at the low sofa at the opposite end of the room from me. "I'll stay out of your way."

"I'd rather you didn't," just sort of slipped out.

She smiled innocently like she didn't believe me and left to get her stuff.

She settled on the couch with her school laptop, and I was effectively distracted, my mind lost to absolute filth. There was so much I wanted to do to her, I didn't even know where to start.

I lasted maybe ten minutes before I asked, "Are you wearing panties?"

She bit her lip. "Guess."

My brain short-circuited. "Show me."

She did it like the thought of refusing or even hesitating never occurred to her.

She lifted her shirt all the way up to her collarbone, and she was bare, and I was on her without even a thought. I didn't undress, just took my dick out and screwed her right there on the sofa.

She was soft, she'd just come, and I was holding her on my lap, her back against my chest, her shirt pulled up to her neck.

I squeezed a plump tit and fingered her.

"Are you sore?" I asked her, biting her earlobe.

"I don't care," was her answer, and it was enough for me.

I made her rise to her knees so she straddled me facing forward, positioned my dick and lowered her over it, pushing in. She was slick and tight, and I shoved in and started fucking her. "I'm going to do absolutely everything to you. I'll break you in so good. I'll teach you everything you need to know about working this dick. Your insides are going to form to the size and shape and feel of me. How would you like that, pet?"

"Yes, Mr. North," she panted and it got me going, fucking harder and deeper, all attempts at taking it slow gone.

Her legs were shaking when I shoved her to the ground, staying inside of her, on her back now humping into her relentlessly, a good hard ride, her cunt taking me and squeezing like it was made just for me. I pounded rigorously in and out of her, over and over, and shot my load deep inside of her womb.

I tried to be considerate after that, cleaning her up, and pulling her shirt back down and telling her to get to work on her homework with a little pat on her bare ass that almost had me shoving her back to the ground for another round, but I resisted, if only just.

Instead, I sat down beside her and made her go over each missing assignment she needed to finish from each class. We'd been making progress, but she still had a lot to work on.

Without her shifts at the diner every night after school she should be able to manage it.

Maybe an hour later she got up to go to the bathroom and when she came back, I pushed her against my desk and fucked her again.

"I want to pull out and come on your tits this time, but I'm too addicted to coming in your pussy," I panted into her ear as I pumped in and out in big, slick strokes. "I want to stuff you full. Fucking take it."

"It's new to me," I got out as I thrusted in and out almost leisurely, "riding bareback and shooting my load inside of *my* territory." I couldn't keep one filthy, wild, misfired thought in my head around her. They all just spilled out as soon as I got my dick inside. "It feels so much better than anything I can remember. I don't think I can stop. You're going to be milking my cum into your pussy every minute we can spare of every day. It's your job now. Being my sex pet. My filthy little fuck toy. How do you like that?"

"I love it, Carter," she moaned. She was close to coming. "I love *you*."

I turned her around and put both of her hands on the desk, grabbing her tits in both hands and shoving into her from behind. She was still tight as ever, but I forced my heavy length in with one long, relentless stroke.

I gripped her hips and rode her hard like she wasn't new to this, taking my pleasure with heavy slams of my hips against her ass. She was so pliant, so sweet and submissive that it made me go a little mad. I just couldn't get enough. I came so hard and deep and lost inside of her that my vision went fuzzy and my legs nearly gave out.

I watched as I dragged my wet cock out of her. She was sopping, from herself and my cum. I loved it. I could have taken her again right there. It was an effort not to start all over again, but I made myself hold onto one tiny bit of sanity. She wasn't actually a toy for me to stick my dick in constantly, much as that very thought got us both off.

She was also my student, and I needed to help her stay on track to graduate.

I was weak, though, and I showered with her first. I cleaned us both, managing not to get too far off track through sheer force of will. I dried her myself, not letting her lift a finger, even putting her into a clean T-shirt, panties, and cheer shorts myself.

I tugged her back to my office, kissed her on the forehead, then ordered her to get back to her homework.

Perhaps I did have some sense left. The verdict was out.

# CHAPTER 17

**NOVA**

I was getting strange looks at school on Monday, and I knew something was up by my first class.

No one was talking to me right away, but I could tell that they were talking *about* me.

It wasn't until lunch when my friend Maddie clued me in. "There's some nasty rumor going around that you have a sugar daddy," she told me. My mind went back immediately to when Michelle had seen the Porsche and said something similar. I instantly had a sick feeling she'd started the rumor.

She was one of my oldest, closest friends though, so I knew I'd give her the benefit of the doubt before I jumped to any conclusions.

"Everyone's talking about it," Maddie continued. "People keep asking me about it, but I've been telling them it's ridiculous." She studied me. "It is ridiculous, right?"

"Of course," I said but it wasn't even convincing to my own ears. Like most rumors, it did hold some of the truth. I did have an older man taking care of me now. I was sleeping with him, and he was supporting me financially. "Thanks for defending me."

"Of course. Um, there's also a rumor you're driving around in some Porsche that's worth like a hundred grand. Crazy, right?"

Again I had the sick feeling it was Michelle, but hoped I was wrong. I'd been parking far away from the school but that didn't mean someone else hadn't spotted me with it. "Totally crazy," I agreed weakly.

I thought things were bad enough, but as the day went on when I walked through the crowded halls I kept hearing snide little remarks that I knew were aimed my way, people talking about me loud enough for me to hear on purpose. They *wanted* me to hear. They thought I was trash, and I should know it and feel it.

I was even bumped hard by some girl I didn't know and when I said, "Excuse me," to her out of habit she shot back, "Watch it, baby hooker."

She said it so loudly it got a good laugh out of several people in the crowd.

I wanted to cry, but I'd learned to keep my feelings hidden from other teenagers a long time ago.

And, of course, just my luck, the worst was yet to come.

Jake cornered me at my locker before my last period, a wall of football players with him. They were crowding me, Jake in my personal space and glaring at me like I'd personally offended him, which I supposed I had by turning him down at the party and quite a few times before that. "Heard you're a homeless prostitute now," he said, and I didn't even recognize him his face was so twisted up with loathing. I hadn't thought he was the best guy before, but the way he was acting now was downright ugly.

His friends laughed and that was ugly too. It felt so

hateful when I'd never done anything to any of them that I thought should warrant this level of spite.

"Will you let me pass?" I asked quietly, looking through him. I was trying my best to check out of the whole thing mentally, a skill I'd learned a long time ago.

"Not until you tell us how much you charge. What's the going rate for a desperate teenage whore? And is there a group discount? I'm pretty sure we can all scrounge up enough change from our pockets to rent you out for the night."

I tried to push past him, but he didn't budge at first, breathing into my face. I shoved harder and he chest bumped me. I was already off balance from shoving against his immoveable form and it caught me wrong and sent me back hard, the back of my head hitting the bottom corner of an open top locker. I got a brief glimpse of Jake's shocked face before I blacked out.

I woke up held against a hard chest I somehow recognized right away. Carter was carrying me.

"You shouldn't have moved her," a worried female voice was telling him. The school nurse. "But since you already did, set her down here."

"The back of her head is bleeding, and she was out cold."

His voice was awful, choked up and emotional, and as he laid me down gently on the nurse's table I saw his expression. He looked like he was going to break down. I wanted to tell him to put on a better game face. This was not the place to be showing he was more than a teacher to me.

He saw my eyes were open. "Are you okay? What happened?"

The nurse shooed him away until he took a few steps back and started checking my head with soothing hands.

Eventually he asked again. "What happened? Someone said you were being harassed and got shoved, but no one would tell me who it was." There was violence in his tone and I knew right away that I could never tell him what had really happened. He would lose it and do something crazy, and the last thing I'd ever do is contribute to getting him in trouble.

"It was nothing that dramatic. Someone accidentally bumped me, I don't know who, and I fell against a locker and I hit my head."

If anything his expression got worse. He knew I was lying and he wasn't taking it well. Now he felt both angry *and* helpless.

The questions were mercifully put on hold as paramedics showed up and I went quietly through another series of check-ups.

I begged them not to take me to a hospital, I was terrified of the bill, and they fussed over me a bit more but relented, giving me an ibuprofen, bandaging my head. They gave me wound care instructions and asked if I had a ride home.

"I'll take her," Carter said.

"You're such a dear, Mr. North," the nurse said, beaming at him.

Wasn't he just?

The ride home was tense and awkward. I knew he was mad at me for covering for the person who'd shoved me, but he was also too worried about me to give me a hard time about it at the moment.

At home he babied me to an extreme extent, and I let him because I thought it might make him feel better and I liked the attention.

He arranged me on the living room couch like an invalid and brought everything he could think of to occupy me and make me feel better.

I asked for my school laptop.

"Are you sure? They told you to rest."

"Rest but not sleep, right? And it's hardly going to make me feel better to get even farther behind on my schoolwork."

He relented, bringing both his laptop and my own to the sofa so we could work side by side.

"Do you need anything?" he asked me for the dozenth time, at least.

I looked at him, love swelling up inside me. No one had ever cared for me like this before. It felt like no one had ever cared for me in my whole life before Carter. "I could use a kiss," I told him.

He leaned over and gave me a sweet peck on the cheek.

"I want a real kiss."

He gave me a stern look, and I felt an instant improvement in my mood. "Not until you're better. You know we'd never stop at one kiss."

"Can I at least sleep in your bed tonight?"

He looked torn. "Yes, but no sex until you're better."

"How will we know when I'm better? I feel fine now."

"I'll ask the school nurse."

"You'll ask her when it's okay to have sex with me again? Do you think that's wise?"

He smiled at me fondly. "I'll ask her about your recovery, you little brat."

"What about a hand job? I don't see how jerking you off will affect my head wound."

"Stop," he said, a warning in his voice.

I didn't, harassing him for the rest of the day and at bedtime until he finally relented, letting me stroke him under the covers.

"I want to see it," I told him.

He sighed and acted very put upon as he turned on the

light and sat up, removing the cover from his lap, but his dick was hard and straining up against his naval the whole time.

I took off my clothes and he protested that too but not for long. I sat cross-legged beside him and fisted his hot length with both hands.

He fondled me, his breath ragged. "I'm coming on your tits," he told me, pinching my nipple.

He let me play with him for a time before squirting some lotion into my palms. He showed me how to jack him off with both hands, one of his helping, the other kneading at my breasts.

I watched his cock as I worked at it, noticing the way his balls tensed up and his length grew and became impossibly hard right before he came.

He pushed me gently onto my back a moment before he started coming, thick warm liquid spurting out of his tip and onto my tits. My hands fell away as I watched him and he kept jerking his cock, shooting his load up higher, over my collarbone and onto my face. I closed my eyes and licked my lips, tasting him. He didn't stop until he'd milked out every drop.

When he was done he rubbed my breasts, making a real mess of it. One of his fingers traced my lips, coating them with cum, and I sucked on his finger until he groaned and pulled away.

I opened my eyes and watched him watching me. He had the most tender, grave expression on his face, and for the first time I let myself hope that he might feel for me even a fraction of what I felt for him.

He pushed my breasts together. "When you're better, I'll fuck these. Your tits are perfect. They were made for it."

"You could try it now. I'll let you know if my head starts bothering me."

"Stop that. You're incorrigible."

He took me into his shower and washed me tenderly, head to toe.

He held me until I fell asleep and when I woke up I was still being cradled tenderly in his arms.

I thought the head injury was a small price to pay if it led to that.

When I checked my phone the next day, I had way more texts than normal.

Some were from Michelle, asking if I was okay, asking if I'd heard about the rumors and then telling me she hadn't started them.

I didn't believe her, but I wanted to badly enough that I just let it go, reassuring her that I wasn't upset.

More surprising was a text chain from Jake. He was apologizing profusely and swearing he hadn't meant to actually hurt me.

I let that go too, reassuring him that I wouldn't tell as long as he left me alone from now on.

I knew if I got him in trouble it would only make things worse for me. He was very popular and his friends would find some awful way to retaliate. There was no winning in situations like these for a girl like me.

Knowing that Carter wanted to and would have defended me helped though. It made me feel stronger and less like a victim. I'd never felt like someone was in my corner like that before, to the point where I knew he'd throw everything away to stand up for me.

I took a few days off and so did Carter. I dearly hoped no one made the connection.

When we finally went back, it wasn't as bad as before. The rumors seemed to have calmed themselves at least to the point where I wasn't being directly confronted anymore. At least not until Carter came home that night, bursting into the house, wrath in his eyes.

"Why didn't you tell me?" was the first thing out of his mouth.

"Tell you what?"

"All the awful things they're saying about you at school. It came up during the staff meeting. The school is cracking down on it on social media."

I shrugged. "I don't even check my social media. Besides that, what could you do about it?"

He hugged me, being very careful with my head. "It's my fault! I told you to drive that stupid car around and someone must have seen it."

"My friend Michelle did," I told him.

"Your *friend* started those rumors?"

I shrugged again. "I can't be completely sure, she denies it, but I think so."

"I'll get you something more sensible to drive tonight. I'd trade the Tesla with you but too many people have seen me driving that. What kind of car do you want?"

I waved him off. "No. Stop. You can't buy me a car. It's bad enough I'm borrowing one you already had. Just forget it. The damage is done."

"I'm so sorry," he said, kissing the top of my head. "I saw some of the comments online, and I can't stand that they're talking like that about you. And in case you need to hear it, it's all bullshit. You aren't any of those things they call you. You're an absolute angel and I would know, okay? Now what do you want me to do?"

I raised my face to him. "Fuck me. I'm better. Please fuck me."

# CHAPTER 18

**CARTER**

Against my better judgment and my own conscience, I obliged her.

I sat at the kitchen table and took my dick out. I had her naked and straddling me. I strained to work my thick cock in at that angle. She couldn't take me without some urgent pressure. She struggled to let me in deeper, but I bore down hard, biting the tendon between her neck and shoulder and dragging her down until she took my full length with trembling gasps.

I taught her how to ride me with my hands on her hips, and she squeezed up and down my thickness with some effort. It was too good like that, with her squeezing my cock so hard, her little moans killing me, and I didn't last long. Even after I kept her there, kissing her deeply, still buried to the hilt. I kneaded at her breasts and played with her nipples as she milked me with her cunt. The orgasm kept going, little tremors that started at the base of my shaft and rocked us both. Even sated, I couldn't pull out of her, or stop touching her, teasing her.

"I love you," she said quietly. I watched her earnest face as she said it, heard the deep emotion in her voice. I kissed her for a long time, stroking my hands over her, soothing now.

I didn't tell her that she couldn't give it all away like that, her whole body, her whole soul, that she needed to hold some of herself back, or I was liable to take it all.

"It's prom next weekend," she said sometime later.

My face was buried in her neck. I was sucking and kissing her lazily, my hands rubbing lightly up and down from her shoulders to her hips.

I pulled back far enough to stare at her.

"I want to go."

"Do you already have a date?" I asked slowly. The very thought deeply disturbed me. It made me feel a little dizzy and off. I didn't know what I'd do if she went out with someone else.

"I'm just going to go with Michelle."

"The awful girl that started those rumors about you?"

"It's fine. I don't blame her. I really don't think she meant for it to be that nasty of a rumor. Sometimes the things people say get away from them."

I felt my hackles rising. The urge to protect her was nearly overwhelming for me, but how could I protect her from her own friends? It was beyond frustrating. "You're an angel for being so benevolent about it," I told her gently, "but you shouldn't put up with someone treating you like that. You deserve better."

She just looked down and shrugged like she didn't agree. "That's just how girls my age are. It's really not that big of a deal."

"Would you have done that to her?" I asked pointedly.

That got her, and her face scrunched up like I'd landed a blow. "Of course not," she said quietly.

She was still naked, still straddling me, and I squeezed her closer, kneading her shoulders and kissing the top of her head. I wanted to comfort her, but also I couldn't keep my hands off her. It was a problem.

"Listen, I just want to go to the prom," she said. "I want the dress and the pictures and stuff."

"Okay, baby girl," I said, hugging her close. "Did you not go last year?"

"No. I couldn't afford a dress."

That shut me up for a minute. Of course she'd get her way. I'd buy her all the dresses she wanted, that was a given.

"Just be careful," I murmured to her. "I don't trust that girl."

She was nuzzling into my chest and it was starting to distract me. "I don't trust anyone," she remarked casually. "Will you be there? At the prom?"

"Yes," I said, but something she'd said had gotten to me. "You don't trust *anyone*? You don't trust *me*?"

She looked up and there were tears in her eyes. "I do, but you're the only one, so what will I do if you turn on me, too?"

It broke my heart a bit and I hugged her close, squeezing her breathless. "I would never do that. I'm not capable of it."

"Nothing lasts forever."

I didn't know what to say to that. Clearly I wasn't in a position to make her any promises even if I wanted to. I was already taking advantage of her, and it would be too selfish to tie her down like that at this point of her life. She was just too young.

"I wish we could go together," she said quietly, changing the subject and letting me off the hook like the angel she was. "To prom, I mean."

I tilted her chin up until she looked into my eyes. "I wish

that too," I said sincerely and kissed her.

It drove me a little crazy but over the next week she was gone a lot more, on the hunt for the perfect prom dress even on school nights. I missed her, but she still had a lot of schoolwork to do, and it was infuriating that she was just getting farther behind.

I wondered if I could ground her until she got her grades in order but immediately dismissed the idea. She rarely listened to me even when I wasn't being unreasonable.

"What color car do you prefer?" I asked her one day as she was leaving again to shop.

Her eyes narrowed at me. "You can't be thinking of buying me a car," she stated in disbelief.

I shrugged, smiling blandly. "I'm just curious. Can't I be curious?"

"It was just such a random question. I guess I like black cars."

When she was gone I took the opportunity and found her a less flashy ride, one that she could keep. It was a brand new black Toyota. It was a sensible car and I figured no matter what she would have reliable transportation for at least the next decade.

She cried when I gave it to her. Just broke down. I had to hold her for a long time and reassure her, in fact *insist*, that she take it. That it was hers to keep.

I didn't want her to leave, loved having her around, but my conscience dictated that I had to help her become more independent, had to open more doors for her instead of closing her in with me for my own enjoyment, my own contentment.

Finally she told me she'd found the right dress, but she wouldn't show it to me.

"What will *you* wear to prom?" she asked.

I shrugged. "Black suit, white shirt, black tie probably.

Why?"

"Will you wear a peach colored tie? To match my dress?"

It seemed a bit brazen, all things considered, but the look on her face as she asked was impossible for me to refuse. "Of course I will, pet. And when you see it you'll remember that we're really attending for each other, even if no one else can know it."

# CHAPTER 19

A few days before prom I asked her, "What's your favorite flower?"

"My favorite flower?" She was genuinely baffled, like she'd never given it one thought in her life.

"Yes," I answered patiently. "Don't you like flowers?"

She thought about it. "Sure, I like them. No one's ever asked me that before."

That didn't surprise me. She'd been neglected in so many ways I'd lost track. "I'd like to get you flowers," I told her softly. "Would you like that?"

"I would," she answered. She didn't hesitate, but she still seemed unbalanced by the whole thing.

"What kind?" I asked her.

"You pick," she said slowly.

"You want me to pick your favorite flower for you?" I asked, bemused and beyond charmed by her, as usual.

"I'd love that," she said it and I thought she meant it.

"Pick whatever makes you think of me. That would make it my favorite."

I smiled at her warmly and kissed the top of her head. "I think I know just the thing.

I had to check several florists, but eventually I found one that put together both a large bouquet and a delicate corsage of peach Persian buttercups on short notice.

She cried when I gave them to her, and I kissed the tears away, moving my mouth tenderly over her fine cheeks.

And that tender spot in my chest, the one with her name on it, grew still bigger.

I'd presented the flowers to her early on as she was planning to leave ahead of time to get ready over at Michelle's. I didn't like it, but I couldn't tell her who she could hang out with. I really had no rights at all where she was concerned and it began to occur to me rather persistently that I would've liked it to have been otherwise.

The prom was held in the school's largest gymnasium.

I'd been required to attend for the whole event from start to finish though most of the students didn't show up on time. My presence was usually greatly requested and appreciated as I was the biggest male on staff and a coach, so when things got rowdy the football players actually listened to me.

I was chatting with some of the other chaperoning teachers, bored out of my mind. I tugged impatiently at my tie. We were near the entrance of the event, taking turns checking tickets and patrolling the room to make sure nothing too dumb was going on with the kids.

As chance would have it, or perhaps I'd been looking for her for hours, I caught sight of Nova right as she entered the room.

She was so beautiful it made my eyes sting a bit. A perfect dream girl.

The dress was worth all the effort she'd taken to find it. A shade of soft peach that set of her golden skin in a dizzying way—it was a long, gauzy, off the shoulder dress that hugged her curves perfectly.

She looked elegant and beautiful and so sexy it made my teeth ache.

It was a lovely princess dress, and I was happy I could help give that moment to her.

All of her thick black hair was pulled up into a complicated mass. I studied it, wondering how hard it would be to take it all down and bury my hands in it while I fucked us both raw.

"I think I see a flask," one of the other teachers pointed out.

I glanced where she was indicating. It was one of the football players. Typical.

All of the other chaperones looked at me, and I didn't blame them. I was the best candidate to confront drunk teenage guys, to make them submit rather than escalating the nonsense. Being bigger than most of them helped.

I sighed. At least I hadn't missed her grand entrance.

I went and took care of it.

It was a good twenty minutes later, five kids ejected from the dance, before I was able to scan the room for her again.

I caught sight of her quickly. She was in the middle of the dance floor, dancing with a bunch of giggling girls.

I was instantly relieved. I didn't want to know what I'd do if I saw her dancing with, or getting close to, some punk teenage boy.

I was standing behind one of our APs, Ms. Stanford, as she manned the refreshment table, basically giving her backup in case someone wanted to spike the drinks.

Nova and her all girl posse approached, and I couldn't take my eyes off her. She kept stealing shy little adoring glances at me and it took all I had not to jump her right there. I had to straight up stop looking at her, but looking at her friends was worse. They were sending me similar, smitten stares, which were not welcome as I was *emphatically* not interested.

I did wonder with a touch of hostility which one was Michelle, but they all sort of looked the same to me.

No student had ever caught my eye even slightly before Nova.

I was heading back from the restroom sometime later when Nova walked past me in the hallway. She didn't even look at me, just passed me a note as we walked by each other.

I stopped in my tracks, watching her retreating back, but she didn't look at me.

I glanced at the note.

*Meet me in the coach's office in 30 minutes. I want you to mess me up. Make sure the door is unlocked for me.*

It flipped a switch in me. I found myself instantly getting hard. It was *such* a bad idea, but I didn't even consider turning her down.

Who the fuck would?

Instead, I made plans. Very specific ones.

I went back to the gymnasium, timed out thirty minutes by counting each one, made the most half-assed of excuses, and left again.

I jumped her the second she walked into the office, pinning her facedown on my desk. I pulled up the layers of her dress, fingers seeking her, finding her cunt. The moment I confirmed she was wet, it was game on.

I didn't undress either of us, just took out my dick and pushed her panties to the side.

She was soft and compliant, utterly submissive as I held her down and fed my cock into her. I'd been breaking her in good, but she was still tight as ever and entering her was an overwhelming, bracing, glorious stretch. It was almost too much and *precisely* enough.

I punched deep and pulled out to the very tip without pausing, again and again, giving it to her as hard and deep and no holds barred as I needed it.

I was fucking the brains out of a perfect teenage princess. It was lurid. Tasteless. Out of line. And I couldn't get enough.

I also couldn't keep my mouth shut, couldn't keep in all the filthy things that I knew would get her off the fastest. "You little cum slut. You love this, don't you? Giving it up on prom night like the little fuck toy you are. Just don't forget, you're *my* fuck toy."

She really got off on that. Literally. She came, and I kept going in a perfect tireless tempo of flesh pounding flesh.

I had her shoulder pinned down with one hand, the other buried in her hair, pulling it as roughly as I was fucking her. Her perfect prom hair was unsalvageable, and I couldn't make myself stop.

It was so good and I didn't last long past that. A heavy, pressurized tide inside of me was set free, and I came like a furious wave breaking. I held her down and clinched tight inside of her as I let go.

I kissed her neck and stayed on top of her back, her cunt milking my dick, every last jerk. I stayed like that for a long time as I recovered from one of the most powerful orgasms of my life.

It was alarming, but all of the top ones were unquestionably with her, inside of this specific, gorgeous girl. In spite of my best efforts, I was getting too attached.

It was some time later and I hadn't moved, hadn't let her budge so much as an inch. Luckily she wasn't complaining. I decided to push my luck.

I was still punch-drunk from the last round as I dragged my wet, hard again dick up a few inches, pushing in. "You said you wanted me to mess you up," I rasped into her ear. "You want to be fucked *here*, prom princess?"

"Anything," she panted back quietly. "If you want to do it,

I want you to do it to me."

It was all the permission I needed. I worked my painstaking way into her virgin ass. Anal had never been my thing, but I wasn't strictly against it, particularly as it was another piece of her flesh I got to own first and exclusively, more territory I got to claim, just how I perversely needed it to be with her.

She whimpered and writhed underneath me, and I worried for a few excruciating moments whether I'd have to stop short here, if I was too much for her like this.

But then she said, "Please," and I was lost. In our own little intimate language I'd learned that when she begged me in just *that* exact way it meant only one thing, requesting a particular something from me that I was all too happy to give.

"Fucking take it, you little brat," I growled at her, sinking deeper. "I told you I was going to fill every hole of my little cum slut, and you're going to fucking take it." I pulled her hair hard and bottomed out.

I reached between her legs and pinched her clit with two fingers as I fucked her ass with no breaks. I gave it to her rough. She always said if I wanted to do it she wanted me to do it to her, and so far, she'd always meant it. This was no exception.

I felt like an animal. Uncivilized and thoroughly off my leash.

Her body was my territory, and I was proving that fact anywhere I could reach.

I would mark her everywhere.

"When we get home I'm going to stay inside of you till morning," I grunted at her as I pounded away. "I'm going to ride you all night like a dog. On your hands and knees until they're rug-burned and bruised. I'm going to fuck your cunt until you can't walk straight for days."

The noises she was making were soft, quiet, as she tended to be, but they still told me plenty, and just then she liked what she was hearing. "And you're going to *fucking take it*. You're going to *beg*."

I pounded in and out in a heavy drag and lunge, owning her asshole with brutal domination, one hand pinning her down, keeping her steady for the driving motion of my lower body.

The other was busy with sharp, delicate precision on her clit.

She came sobbing, and I followed a stuttering heartbeat later.

Afterward I became achingly tender because I just couldn't help myself. That's what she brought out in me: my most savage beast and my most caring lover. I'd been with more women than I'd ever bothered to count, but only she had ever gotten both and to this degree.

And perhaps more worrisome, the acute need for her—her body, her company—was not going away the more we carried on like this. I wasn't getting my fill so much as I was sowing the seeds of this obsession, not satiating it, instead making it *flourish*. And even knowing it was not sustainable, it was in fact a disastrously *bad* idea—she was too fucking young for something permanent; she didn't even know what all her options were yet—I still couldn't make myself withdraw, couldn't make myself resist her pull at all.

Some time later I was cleaning us both up with tissues as she tried to do something with her hair. She'd given up on putting it back up and was just trying to tame it into loose waves down her back. I wondered how she'd explain that to her friends.

I wondered if anyone had noticed that we'd both disappeared at roughly the same time, and she was about to come back looking thoroughly fucked.

I was tucking myself back into my slacks when I saw it.

We hadn't even closed the fucking door.

Jesus fucking Christ. Anyone could have seen us. We were in the same wing of the school as the packed gymnasium, just a few hallway turns away, and I hadn't even closed the door, let alone locked it.

What the hell was wrong with me?

She noticed the open door around the same time I did. She looked shocked and appalled. "I'm so sorry, Carter—"

I cut her off, "Do not apologize. This is not on you. I'm the adult here. You don't get to blame yourself for *any* of it."

Her eyes got a bit hard. It wasn't something I was used to seeing from her, had forgotten she even had that side to her in our recent delirium. "I'm an adult, too. We're both responsible for what we do together. Deny it all you want, but it's the truth."

"That wasn't my point." It was an argument for another day. "We're very lucky we weren't caught. We can't take risks like this, okay? From now on, I'm only fucking you at home."

"Yes, sir," she said, saluting me.

I pointed at her. "You're going to pay for that on your knees, you little brat."

"I can't fucking wait."

I softened. Every single thing inside of me—soft for her. "Don't stay out too late tonight, okay? And be careful."

"I'd go home with you right now if I could, but I promised my friends I'd stick with them until it's over."

She'd never sounded more like a teenager, but I didn't tell her that. She wouldn't like hearing it. I didn't particularly like that I'd noticed it.

She managed to make it home a few hours later, and I was true to my word.

I'd arrived at the house and showered as soon as it was

humanly possible and I was waiting for her.

I was on her the second she walked through the door.

I took her on hands and knees in the entryway, rutting in her for so long that her legs gave out, and I had to hold her up by the hips while I drove in and out tirelessly.

I opened her cheeks and studied her, pulled out, bent down and ate her ass. I could taste my seed still in her, and it drove me wild. As I straightened I spit on her there, pushing a finger in as my dick took her cunt again. I pulled her hair roughly while my finger fucked her ass and my cock fucked her pussy. The fact that both places were already full of my cum from earlier was really getting to me. I was so revved up that I barely got her off before I pulled out, ordered her to turn around, shoved into her mouth, and came deep down her throat.

"I filled every hole. Is that what you like, you little cum whore?" I asked her roughly, tone mean as I rooted so deep down her throat that I was impressed she wasn't gagging more. "You're a natural little cum guzzler. Most women take a lot of practice to get that good at deep throating, but you were born to suck my cock. Now fucking take it all. Lick my dick clean. That's right. Suck it all up, my dirty little whore."

Afterward I took care of her. I drew us a bath and washed every inch of her lithe, overused body. I fingered her tender sex as I cleaned her. "Are you sore?"

"Not too sore for you to do whatever you want to me." Her voice was quiet but sure.

"Don't say that," I said with a groan. She was going to get me going again. "It's too much."

"I love you," was her reply. That was too much, as well.

I got her ready for bed. I didn't even let her brush her own teeth. I took care of everything.

"Did you have a good night?" I asked her softly. "Was prom as good as you were hoping it would be?"

She was looking at me like I hung the moon. "It was so much better. Because of you."

I couldn't take her eyes for one more second. I pushed her face into my chest and kissed the top of her head.

I didn't take her again. She was already going to be sore tomorrow.

Instead, I put us both in soft T-shirts and loose boxers, and held her until she fell asleep, and eventually followed her.

# CHAPTER 20

The next few weeks passed in a dizzy, lust-hazed blur. We kept our distance from each other at school—the open door had been sobering—but at home I had my dick in her every second we could spare. Everything else became a distant priority in comparison to that.

I was behind on all my deadlines, but I did manage to keep her on track with her homework, mainly while I was recovering between bouts of fucking.

"Listen," I told her one afternoon as we worked out in my home gym. I lifted weights while she jogged on the treadmill and watched me with hungry eyes. "I have this monthly poker thing with some friends. It's supposed to be at my house this time. Do you mind?"

"Mind what? If you use your own house to play poker with your friends?"

The way she worded it made the question seem silly, but I just stared at her until she gave me a straight answer.

"Of course I don't mind," she finally said. "Want me to go somewhere else for the night, so they don't see me?"

"Of course not."

"Want me to stay in my room?"

"Stop that. You'll stay home and do whatever you want, you can meet everyone, whatever you prefer. They don't need to know all the details about us. Our business is our own."

"Sounds fun," she said cheerfully.

"One other thing," I said. I really didn't want to bring it up, but I knew it would be worse if she found out later.

"What?" she asked. She was studying my face. She already knew how to read me well, I thought.

"Two of the friends are sort of exes of mine," I told her.

She stared, her expression going stoic. I hated that. I liked to see what she was feeling and hated when she shut me out from reading her.

"Are all of your breakups friendly?" she eventually asked, tone neutral. Still hiding from me.

I tried to be straight with her. "If I have anything to say about it, yes. And they're not really even exes, but I hooked up with both of them several times. It's platonic now. I wanted to be upfront. I didn't want you to find out later and think I was hiding it from you."

"And they both know about each other?"

I flushed, a little embarrassed, I don't even know why. "They're with each other now. I set them up, actually."

She stared.

"They're both bi, and I thought they'd like each other. Turns out they hit it off and now they live together."

"And you're not jealous?"

The thought had never occurred to me. "Not at all."

"Did the three of you ever," she motioned vaguely with her hands, "like together?"

I was a bit perturbed and scandalized that she'd even thought of it.

"No," I said after a pause.

Her eyes narrowed. "Why'd you hesitate? Tell me."

I was outright blushing for the first time I could remember.

Only Nova did this to me. I couldn't be smooth for one second with her.

I really didn't want to talk about this with her anymore, but I thought if I walked away from the conversation now she'd take it worse than it actually was. "They offered a few times when they first started dating and weren't exclusive with each other yet. I said no."

She was studying my face like if she looked hard enough she'd see all my secrets. I wasn't sure she was wrong.

"Why'd you say no?"

"It's not my kind of thing. I like the intimacy of focusing on one person during sex. And I'm glad now that I didn't. I think it would have been awkward for the three of us since they ended up having a serious relationship soon after that."

"So you've never done a threesome at all?" she asked, and I saw then that she was teasing me.

"Now you're pushing it," I told her. "And I haven't. Can you stop now?"

"Only if you teach me how to play poker. I'd like to join in when your friends come over."

"Deal."

I was strangely nervous about the whole thing.

The real problem I was having was actually easy to pinpoint.

I was ashamed that I was living with and fucking one of my students. That was the absolute last thing I'd wanted to do when I became a teacher. The fact that I still thought it was wrong even while I continued doing it as much and as often as I possibly could didn't help at all.

The fact that I had no intention of stopping was worse even than that.

And several of my poker crew were longtime friends, not casual ones. I just couldn't imagine someone seeing Nova and I in a room together and not instantly knowing I spent half my day inside of that.

Poker night was kind of sexist, but only kind of. Most of my friends' wives were at a monthly girls' night thing called *fuck anonymous*, a sort of group therapy thing with alcohol, however *that* worked, and that was what had started the sexist tradition. Men weren't allowed to go to that, whereas poker night was at least partially coed.

It was one of the few social gatherings my friends' wives broke off for. In a random role reversal for one of the lesbian couples, we got Estella and *fuck anonymous* got her wife, Frankie, though going by their couple dynamic you'd think it might have gone the other way.

My friends Mark and Rod, old football buddies, showed up first. They were near carbon copies of each other, both blond and huge, built like football players that'd let themselves go a bit over the years.

I let them in and grabbed them both a drink. They'd be the only ones drinking beer. The rest were more of a wine or liquor crowd.

I'd opened a few nice bottles of Napa cab, my drink of choice, and poured them into carafes to decant. They were heavy wines and needed to aerate for a good hour before serving.

Nova drifted into the kitchen as I was prepping the charcuterie boards.

She was wearing little cheer shorts and a crop top. She was barefoot, hair loose around her hips.

I wanted to pin her face down on the kitchen floor and cram her full right that instant.

Both of the guys stopped talking mid-sentence, staring at her. She smiled at them.

God, she was stunning.

I glared. "Nova, go put some proper clothes on right now," I told her in my sternest teacher voice.

She shivered almost imperceptibly, shot me a sullen look, and left.

"Just who," Rod began slowly, "was that?"

"One of my students. A *high school* student. She needed a place to stay. Don't get any ideas. She's off-limits, *obviously*."

"Jesus fucking Christ," Mark muttered. "High school girls look different these days."

"No shit," Rod agreed.

"Not another word," I warned. I couldn't take one wrong thing said about her. Just could not tolerate it.

They both stared at me. I was normally an agreeable person, and I hadn't even bothered to use a pleasant tone there.

I stared right back. "Off-limits," I reiterated.

"How old is she?" Rod asked.

"Not your fucking concern," I said instantly. "Now have some fucking baked brie, you degenerates. It goes great with the fig jam."

They laughed and I tried to smile like I wasn't being deadly serious. Going by the looks they were shooting me, I didn't think I pulled it off.

Bella and Ariel, the couple I'd told Nova about, the ones I'd dated separately before setting them up, showed up next.

They were both pretty, leggy model types around my age.

Bella was pale, with blond hair and green eyes. Ariel had curly black hair, and a deep brown, lovely skin tone. They made a striking, beautiful couple. They'd joked more than once about fighting over which one got to have me as the best man at their wedding, so they were practically engaged at this point.

I was a bit relieved that Nova wasn't in the room by the way they both greeted me. They got a kick out of hugging me between them and kissing both of my cheeks at the same time.

"Our favorite sexy cupid," Bella said, giggling.

"Our number one fuckboy matchmaker," Ariel added.

"Hey, now," I protested. She always called me that, and I genuinely didn't like it. "Not a fuckboy here."

"My *favorite* fuckboy," Ariel shot back. By her warm smile she meant no offense, but I didn't want Nova to hear anything like that said about me.

It was harmless teasing, but I had no idea how Nova would see it.

I knew their preferences and poured them both a glass of the cab before they even asked. I also poured one for myself.

We were tapping glasses when Nova strutted back into the kitchen, looking good enough to eat.

She'd changed into a shirt that wasn't missing its lower half but kept the cheer shorts. It wasn't much of an improvement. The shirt was made of a thin, soft cotton that clung to every curve and the shorts showed off all of her legs and even a bit of her ass.

I didn't say a word, trying to pretend I didn't notice. There wasn't much I could do about it now without drawing more attention to her and her delectable body.

I introduced her to Bella and Ariel. If they had thoughts on her presence they were polite enough not to voice them aloud.

I caught a glimpse of Rod checking out Nova's ass and almost punched him. He saw me looking at him and pretended he hadn't been ogling her like a creep.

He might have let himself go since college, but I sure as hell hadn't and I knew I could still kick his ass.

The doorbell rang, distracting me from murdering him.

It was my friends Turner, Dair, Estella, and Heath. They'd carpooled together, their wives likely doing the same to their girls' night.

Dair and Turner were fellow authors. Dair was a reserved man in his forties, the type you'd go to for sensible advice. Turner was the opposite. In his late thirties, he couldn't have been less reserved if it was his goal in life. There was absolutely no filter between his brain and his mouth, and his thoughts were often irreverent and usually hilarious.

The three of us usually brainstormed together a few times a month, at least. We had writing patterns and extensive gym routines in common. It had been more than enough to form lasting friendships between us when I'd first moved to Vegas.

Heath was Dair's brother-in-law. I honestly didn't know what Heath did for a living. I'd never asked. He didn't like to answer questions about himself, and he wasn't the type of guy you riled on purpose. He might have been even bigger than me, and he had the scariest, stone-cold eyes I'd ever come across.

Estella was a friend I had met through the other authors, though she didn't work in the industry. Her job, as far as I knew, was to co-star on a reality TV show that centered on her wife's tattoo parlor.

She was pretty and petite with a mass of wild curly brown hair. She was from Brazil, had moved to the states years ago, but still maintained the sexy accent. She gave me a long, tight hug, kissing me on both cheeks.

Again, it was perfectly innocent, she was happily married to a very nice lady—a friend of mine—but I worried that Nova might take it the wrong way. I sincerely didn't want to upset her.

I poured Heath, Estella and Dair a glass of the cab, and made a neat glass of Scotch for Turner.

Turner took his drink straight to the poker table and started shuffling cards.

I decanted another two bottles of cab for later, put out more food, adding cheese to the charcuterie. I took Boursin stuffed, bacon wrapped jalapeños out of the oven and plated them. I laid out several types of chips and some from scratch dips I'd prepped earlier in the day.

I was hyper aware of Nova even as I put my efforts toward being a good host. She'd disappeared a while ago, and I was antsy to know what she was up to, exactly.

The last two to arrive were our friends Stephan and Javier. I poured them each a glass of wine. Everyone loaded up on snack plates and headed into my formal dining room turned temporary poker room.

"Where are dimples and pretty boy?" Turner asked the second he spotted Stephan and Javier as we walked into the room together. "What's their excuse for skipping out on poker this month?"

Stephan answered, as he was the one Turner had been addressing, though he'd spoken to the room at large. "James is in New York. Last minute business trip he couldn't avoid. Tristan is at an out of town football game for one of his sons."

"I guess those are good enough excuses. By the way," Turner was still talking. He rarely ever stopped. "Explain to me how this works. Is an all-male couple blocked out of *fuck anonymous* altogether? That's fucked up, no?"

"Here he goes again," Heath muttered darkly.

Javier laughed. "They've actually invited me. I just prefer poker."

Turner only looked slightly mollified by that. He was forever antagonized by the injustice of their all girls' night. He'd only gotten more vocal about it when he'd gotten married himself and his wife started attending it religiously.

"Iris actually isn't too pleased that our poker nights

always conflict with their girls' nights," Dair remarked blandly. Iris was his much younger wife.

I stifled a laugh. He was clearly messing with Turner.

"The poker started initially because all your wives were going to that thing, if you'll recall," Turner shot back instantly. "And your wife is banned from playing with us anyway," Turner continued without stopping for a breath as he shuffled cards. "Did she forget?"

"She cheats," Estella added dramatically. Iris was one of her closest friends.

"She just never loses," Heath, Iris' brother, defended, though his tone was expressionless, just stating facts. He wasn't much of a talker. "There's a difference."

"Even I won't play with her," Dair said. He paused. "Poker, that is."

"We don't need to know any more of your kinky bedroom shit, man," Turner told Dair, shooting him a disgruntled look. "We've seen and heard enough. Think of your poor brother-in-law." Turner shot Heath a sympathetic look that bounced off the other man like a rubber bullet.

I refreshed everyone's drinks, and we took our seats around the table.

Just as we were settling in to play, Nova walked into the room, looking unsure of herself.

Everyone stopped and stared.

I sighed. "Everyone, this is Nova. She's one of my students, and she's staying with me." I went around the room, introducing her to everyone she hadn't already met.

I wished I'd planned it better, but I hadn't noticed that the last empty seat at the table was between Rod and Mark, the only other single men here.

I gritted my teeth as she sat between them.

The first thing Rob fucking did was offer her a beer.

"No. No. *No,*" I said, voice raised a bit and hard with

anger. "She can't drink. She's a high school student. Use your head."

"Stern Dad Carter," Bella said with a grin. "I like it."

"Stop that," I said instantly. "That's not even funny to joke about."

"Okay, Daddy," Ariel jumped in. "I think it has a nice ring to it. How about a teeny tiny glass of wine? Can Nova have that? We don't want her to feel left out."

"Absolutely fucking not. She's underage," I told them sternly.

Just about everyone in the room did a double take at me. I was usually affable to a fault.

"Isn't she eighteen?" Bella butted in again for no fucking reason.

"She's still in high school, *my student*, and under my direct care," I said, trying to sound calm and reasonable but knowing I was coming off a bit deranged. "She's *not* drinking. And in case anyone forgot, *twenty-one* is the legal drinking age."

Everyone was staring at me, some of them looking a little shocked.

Not Turner. He was shaking his head and starting to smile. "Haven't seen the teacher side of you before," he noted. "You're like an overprotective dad. Maybe it's time for you to settle down and have kids. Baby fever's in the air, if you haven't heard."

"Nope, not on my radar," I said instantly, not even thinking about it. It was the automatic response and always had been. "Maybe in ten years," I added. "No, more. Fifteen."

Nova stood suddenly, not looking at anyone. "I'm just going to the restroom," she said quietly and darted off.

**NOVA**

I didn't go to the bathroom. At least not right away. Instead I left the room, lingered just around the corner, and listened in.

What I heard made my shoulders fold forward in defeat. Everything that was said was something I'd already feared, which was why I'd left the room. I hadn't wanted to betray my reaction when I heard it.

Whatever silly dreams I'd had that we were building something lasting disappeared in a little puff of smoke.

I went and splashed water on my face and took a breather.

I tried a trick I'd learned when my parents died and I had to go back to school almost immediately. I gave myself five minutes. To cry. To grieve.

After that I shut it all way and mentally locked it up.

I was walking out when I noticed a beautiful man with wavy dark hair leaning against the wall across from the bathroom.

He smiled. "I'm Javier. Is everything all right?

"Oh yeah," I said automatically. "I just got something in my eye."

"You can talk to me," he said easily. "I won't share, and I won't judge."

There was something about him, the way he wasn't outgoing but was so obviously being open with me, had me wanting to spill my guts to him in a way I never did. I felt tears welling up again.

I shook my head. "I really am okay. I just didn't know all that stuff about Carter. . . about him being, well ya know. . ."

Javier's brows shot up, but it was in amusement not judgement. "A fuckboy? I wouldn't worry about it. He's a really nice guy."

I appreciated his efforts, but I was *very* worried about it. In fact, I knew the idea would consume my thoughts for the foreseeable future.

"I take it you have a crush on him," he said blandly.

I shrugged, watched his face, then nodded. "It can't go anywhere," I stated the obvious. "He's my teacher."

He shrugged back like he didn't care either way. "You're eighteen, right? And you graduate soon?"

"Well, yeah. That doesn't matter, though. Carter thinks I'm too young to make any long-term decisions about my life."

Javier shrugged again, sharing an infectious smile with me. "That's not really up to him, now, is it?"

"I guess not. I'd be living at a shelter if it wasn't for him. I try to take his advice. And he doesn't want a relationship with someone like me."

"Did he say that?"

"Pretty much."

"Interesting. Well, let's exchange numbers. You can call me if you need anything or if you just want to chat."

I did, a little dazzled by someone like him taking notice of me, obviously going out of his way to befriend me. "I'd love that," I said and gave him my number.

"Do you have plans tomorrow?" he asked. Are you up for a pool day?"

"I'd like that," I said. "Carter has a pool."

"I had something else in mind." He gave me a wide smile.

When I went back to the poker table, Javier had cheered me up enough that I was able to act convincingly like nothing was wrong.

# CHAPTER 21

**CARTER**

"Mr. Corn fed fuckboy extraordinaire *would* make a good daddy," Ariel put in unhelpfully.

"Corn fed fuckboy extraordinaire?" Estella asked, giggling.

Bella answered, "It's his nickname in some of our group chats. The fact that so many of his hookups talk to each other and none of us have one bad thing to say about him is pretty impressive if you think about it."

"Calling me a fuckboy feels like an insult," I pointed out. It was a longstanding argument.

I didn't even want to *know* what Nova would think of this conversation. I was more than a little irritated and mortified that if she hadn't just left she'd be hearing all this.

"It's a term of endearment when we say it about *you*," Ariel jumped in.

"Daddy fuckboy Carter," Turner added and laughed.

"Do you have to make every single thing sound like absolute filth?" I asked him.

Javier excused himself from the table and I barely noticed.

"Ariel started it," Turner said defensively. "And no. Not *everything*." He paused. "Maybe. Probably. Who knows? Not the point. We all know you'll be a great father, so why not start soon? Our kids could be the same age." He wiggled his eyebrows at me.

His wife was currently pregnant, and apparently baby fever really was a thing.

"Not happening," I said with no hesitation. "Does not appeal. First of all, last time I checked it takes two people to have a baby, and if you hadn't noticed, I'm very much single." It wasn't strictly the truth, but for this crowd I was sticking to it. "And I'm too young to settle down. Maybe when I'm forty or older it will appeal to me, but right now it emphatically doesn't, and that's enough about the subject." I paused. "Now let's play," I added for good measure.

Everyone finally dropped it, thank God, Nova came back in, and we got down to poker.

I'd gone over the game previously with Nova so she had a good notion of the rules, but Rod and Mark were hell-bent on helping her learn, leaning close and speaking to her quietly, pointing things out, clearly instructing her as we played.

It was distracting me.

And making me feel violent. I wanted to fight them both for leaning too close to her, for looking at her like that.

At one point Rod put his arm around her, touching her shoulder as he explained something about her hand of cards to her.

I stood abruptly. "I'm going to get a bottle of water? Anyone else need anything?"

A few requests were thrown out. Perfect.

"Nova," I said sharply. "Come help me carry the drinks."

She blinked up at me innocently and obeyed.

The second we were in the kitchen I pushed her into the walk-in pantry, shut us in, and pinned her hard to the wall, our chests flush. "Are you flirting with Rod?" I asked her harshly.

Her eyes were wide. She shook her head instantly and the way she was looking at me as she did it made me realize I was being a maniac.

I rubbed my body against hers. "Well, stay away from him." I grabbed her cunt. "Don't forget this is my fucking territory." I gripped a tit roughly. "All of it. Say it."

"My body is your territory," she said, no hesitation.

It was gratifying, but I needed more. "And who do you belong to?"

"You."

I took a deep breath, feeling instant relief. That's what I'd needed from her.

I gave her what she needed right back.

"After everyone leaves I'm going to fuck you like I hate you," I told her roughly. "And then I'm going to make you crawl on the floor on all fours and take my cock all the way down your throat, you little cocksleeve. I'm going to face fuck you. You're going to suck my dick while it's still dripping from your pussy and my cum. You're going to lick it clean."

She shivered in delight.

I pulled her shirt up and stuffed it in her mouth. "Be quiet," I told her harshly, pulling the cup of her bra down to pinch her nipple *hard*.

I placed a hand around her throat.

She whimpered. I choked her with one hand, reaching the other into her shorts, and got her off.

It was agony, but I peeled myself away from her and grabbed the requested drinks.

When we returned to the room I made Rod switch seats with me, not bothering to come up with a good reason for it, just glaring at him until he complied. I'd had enough of him being near her, looking at her like that, and I simply wasn't going to put up with it anymore.

I moved Nova's seat too, so she was sitting next to Stephan instead of Mark. The single guys of the group could stay a football field away from her as far as I was concerned.

We were a few more hands in, everyone laughing about a hilarious bluff Javier had pulled off when my palm went to the back of her head, fingers stroking her silky hair, gripping it lightly, even pulling a bit just how she liked. It was an unconscious, natural motion. Muscle memory that was set off before my brain even registered what I was doing.

I snatched my hand away just as soon as my mind caught on to what I'd done, looking around the table to see who'd noticed.

Turner caught my eye, giving me a long, pointed look. He'd seen the accidental tell and was judging me for it.

A few minutes later Nova left to grab a plate of food between hands.

"What the fuck?" Turner asked me the moment she left. "What are even you doing, man?"

He was right, but I didn't want to hear it. "Just fucking drop it," I warned him.

Of course that didn't stop him. It would take more than that—possibly the earth opening to swallow him whole—to shut Turner up. "As much as I love general disruption, anarchy, and misbehavior in general," he told me pointedly, "you *do* know you absolutely should not hit that, right?

"Of course I fucking do," I growled back.

He just kept going. "Eighteen is too young for you." He

paused. He looked at Dair, smirked. "No offense."

Dair had been forty, his wife eighteen, when they met.

"None taken," Dair said wryly, not even looking up from his phone. He was checking in with his kids every time we had a break.

"But eighteen isn't even the biggest problem," Turner continued his rant at me. "The homeless high school student thing is downright sordid, especially since she's *your* student. If nothing else, it will ruin your teaching career."

"There's absolutely nothing you could say that I haven't told myself," I told him tersely. "Just drop it."

He shook his head, outright laughing now. "I always knew when you broke bad it would be fucking out of line, but you've outdone even my wild imagination, man."

# CHAPTER 22

Turner had been right about everything he'd said about Nova, but I was too far gone for right.

I'd swerved off into wrong with her some time ago, and I didn't stop speeding in that direction exactly the second everyone left that night.

I tore her clothes off and fucked her face down on the poker table. It was a rough, angry fuck, just the thought of other men looking at her making me mad with rage.

She was so delicate, so helpless, so utterly submissive under my huge hands. I couldn't get enough of it.

Practically everyone was small compared to me, but with her I found it irresistible to dominate her vulnerable self with my overpowering self.

She came so hard her core choked my cock as I shot my load in her. I stayed rooted deep inside of her for a long time, savoring the feel of her milking my dick.

Eventually I pulled out of her in a long, delicious drag of slick flesh on flesh, turned her, and perched her butt on the edge of the table. I buried my hands in her hair and kissed her with deep passion for long minutes. I got her off with soft fingers pinching her clit, telling her all the sweet things I just couldn't keep in sometimes. "You're so beautiful," I told her. "I can hardly stand it. Being near you for even a *second* without putting my hands on you is unbearable to me, you know that?"

I left her perched there abruptly, a cry still leaving her lips from her last orgasm.

I set a chair across the room and sat down.

"Crawl to me," I ordered her. My sex coated dick was still hanging out of my pants and hard again. Watching her crawl naked was a sight to behold. I couldn't help it, I started stroking myself as I watched her. When she got to me, I made her take me down her throat, shoving deep. "Eat it up," I told her, tone cold with command. "Fucking take it, you little whore," I said, jamming my dick as far down her throat as she could take it, farther, unstoppably, mercilessly.

I fucked her face, both hands gripped in her hair as I thrust my hips, fists pushing and pulling her fast and mean as my heavy cock moved in and out furiously. She was getting good at taking me deeper but I pushed it enough to make her gag a few times in my fervor, churning my hips to push deeper even then. And then I made her lick every long inch of me clean.

I took it so far that I felt bad afterward, like I'd crossed a line even beyond the degradation play she begged for.

I found myself apologizing to her. I'd said some pretty messed up shit in the heat of the moment.

She didn't miss a beat, her soulful eyes pulling me in deep as she said, "If you want to do it, I want you to do it to me.

"Are you absolutely sure about that?" I asked her gently.

She smiled a siren's smile. "You can make it up to me by fucking me like you hate me again."

She was still on her knees in front of me. I pushed my thumb in her mouth, making her suck it, and said, "You know you're my perfect dream girl, right? Best I've ever had."

She just nodded, my thumb still in her mouth, her eyes shining up at me with rapt devotion.

My perfect fucking dream girl.

What on earth was I going to do with her?

**NOVA**

I should have slept like the dead after Carter was done with me for the night, but I didn't.

He was spooning me from behind. He had me cradled in his big arms even in sleep. That usually calmed me past all my usual worries, but that night even his comforting, affectionate embrace didn't work.

I just lay there against him in the dark, eyes aimed straight ahead, and processed everything I'd learned that night.

All of Carter's friends were nice, and I'd enjoyed meeting them, but some of the things they were saying about him, the little tidbits that came out throughout the night, were almost too much for me to take.

Them calling him a fuckboy, but moreover, the idea that he might be one, that what we shared he'd shared indiscriminately and would continue to do so, disturbed me greatly.

Worse than that, it hurt me, a deep, throbbing ache in my chest.

Also, the way he'd acted when they brought up him being a father, like he was nowhere near ready for it.

What had he said? In ten to fifteen years he'd consider it. That was troubling. I hadn't known he saw it that way, as something for the distant future, nowhere close to where he was now.

He'd also said he was single, that he wasn't ready to settle down, and he'd said it with *such* conviction. That worried me most of all.

It had been a silly, desperate dream of mine, but some part me had been hoping he'd want to settle down with *me*. That we'd already been headed in that direction.

It was a deeper wound than I'd ever admit out loud and as the night wore on I couldn't sleep, couldn't stop agonizing over the small death of my dream, of the idea that I could have Carter, that he could be mine for good, that he could even want that with someone like me.

Tears were running down my cheeks and onto the arm he had cushioned under my cheek, but it didn't disturb his sleep, thank God.

I'd never tell him, never burden him with the notion that I'd wanted more from him than I deserved. He'd been nothing but good to me, given me everything I could've asked for and more.

Some part of me knew, had always known, that I could take advantage of that, that he'd do anything for me, if not out of love then obligation.

But I couldn't do that, couldn't anchor him to me out of duty, out of pity, even if in my darkest moments I'd entertained the idea rather earnestly.

# CHAPTER 23

**CARTER**

"Anything you want to do today?" I asked her the next morning over breakfast. It was a Saturday and she was almost caught up in most of her classes. Maybe we'd watch a movie or something when I wasn't actively rutting inside of her.

"I'd like to go swimming," said Nova.

"Okay," I agreed. That one was easy. I had a pool, and I'd seen to buying her several bikinis when I'd done all my online shopping for her. I'd been looking forward to seeing her in them ever since.

"At the Cavendish resort," she added.

I stared at her.

"Javier said he could get us into the rooftop VIP pool area easily, even get us a cabana. Those reservations are booked out by like six months to a year. Did you know he and Stephan own a bar inside the casino there?"

"I did," I said evenly. What she was asking for was ridiculous. We shouldn't be seen in public together, period, let alone with her in a swimsuit of any kind. And I certainly hadn't picked her bikinis out thinking anyone would see her in them but me.

"Isn't it twenty-one and over?" I asked pointedly. Finding a flaw in the plan was easier than point blank telling her no. I hated refusing her anything. It went against the grain, in fact I found it deeply unpleasant to do so.

"The casino is," she said cheerfully, and I knew a *but* was coming, "and the bar, but not most of the pool areas. We could even have some privacy, with the cabana and all."

"You know we can't be seen together," I told her gently. "Nothing's changed. We can't go on a date."

"It doesn't have to be a date. It could be perfectly innocent. On the slim chance we see anyone we know, we'll just say it's a coincidence, that we both just happen to be at the same pool. We bumped into each other and started talking. Something like that. It's not like we'll be having sex in public. No one can prove anything just by us being in the same place at the same time."

It was a terrible idea. And completely unreasonable for her to suggest it.

But she was so earnest about it, so hopeful and happy, and I was so sated, feeling benevolent from the night before, and I found myself considering it.

"No touching," I told her.

"No touching," she agreed, grinning like I'd just made her day.

"No hand holding. We can't so much as even touch pinkies. In fact, you have to stay at least one foot away from me at all times."

"Yes, Mr. North."

I glared. "And none of that."

I changed into swim trunks and a lightweight T-shirt and packed a change of clothes.

I walked into Nova's room without knocking. She was tying herself into one of the bikinis I'd picked out for her, and I gave her a hand. I even behaved myself, mostly.

I picked out a change of clothes for her myself, adding it to the bag with mine. I didn't trust her to pick out an outfit. Even as I had the thought I knew it was pointless and ridiculous. It wasn't the clothes she wore that were driving me crazy. It was what was inside of them.

It was *who* was inside of them.

We left for the strip not long after that.

Nova was in a white bikini that set off her dusky golden skin. She was within reach in the passenger seat, and it was driving me nuts.

She was wearing the most pointless matching cover-up; it was just a sheer skirt that left nothing to the imagination.

It was possibly the worst one she could have picked, the tiniest one, and this was the first time I'd seen her wear it. I had a pool, but we'd been too busy to go swimming.

I kept stealing glances at her. I couldn't help it.

I was so wrapped up in the sight of her that it took me a minute to realize she'd asked me a question. A troubling one.

"Are you really a fuckboy?"

There was no judgment in her voice, but there was something worse, a weak sort of vulnerability that made me feel helpless.

I sighed, hand going to the back of her head to rub it affectionately. "You heard that, huh? My friends were just messing around. Please don't take anything they said last night too seriously."

It wasn't exactly an answer, but she processed it quietly,

and I hoped that was the end of it.

It wasn't, of course.

"But you've been with a lot of women?" she finally asked in a rush like it was a tide she'd been holding in. "Like, you've slept around?"

My free hand moved from the back of her head to grip her nape.

I tried to choose my words carefully. This was a touchy subject with *any* sexual partner, let alone one you'd taken the innocence of. "I haven't been a fuckboy," I began. "That really was a joke. I don't lie to anyone. I don't play games. I've never led anyone on or treated them badly. But I've only been in a few long-term relationships, and the rest of the time I've been single. I have a very healthy sex drive, and when I'm single I still. . . need a lot of sex."

Fuck. I could tell with the way she was stiffening under my hand, and the arrested expression on her face that I was fucking up badly.

Brutal honesty was not the way to handle this, I realized.

Perhaps another flavor of honesty was.

"Listen, I can't do anything about my past," I tried again. "Yes, I've slept around. I've had a lot of casual sex, but none of that has anything to do with you and me."

"But am I—are *we* having casual sex?"

I was massaging her nape almost roughly now, bending her forward with the force of it. "No," I said sharply. "That's not what I was saying. I've never been like this with anyone else. Never been able to express my best and worst, to be both tender and also play out every dark fantasy like this. I've never felt this free sexually with anyone but you, okay? You're the best I've ever had. Like no one else. Does that answer your question?"

Her eyes were warm on me, and she was practically crawling into my lap.

"I think so," she said quietly. "Does that mean you're not sleeping with anyone else?"

That got a reaction out of me. I wanted to shake her. "Of course not. How exactly do you think I could pull that off? My dick's inside of you practically every waking hour."

"So we're exclusive," she said, rubbing my dick through my swim shorts.

I realized she'd been leading me in that direction rather skillfully.

"I'm not sleeping with anyone else," I reiterated stubbornly. "And this is not a good time," I warned her sternly. "It's going to be hours before I can do anything about a hard-on so I'd appreciate you not making it worse."

"How about I make it better then?"

"No," I said firmly. I really didn't want to, but I made myself force the word out and her hand away. "We can go a few hours without getting off. Until we get back home, we're going to keep this strictly platonic. No touching, remember?"

We did fine with the no touching rule for the first half hour. We drank virgin piña coladas and waded in the ritzy rooftop pool.

The second we'd been led to our cabana and I got a good look at it, I'd headed straight for the water. If I got inside of that thing with her and took the curtain down, we were going to fuck. The only solution was to avoid it altogether.

Nova had followed me without complaining. In fact, she rarely complained. I knew that was because she'd had no one for so long that she expected nothing, and *that* opened the soft spot in my heart for her even wider. As unfair as it was, I wanted her to expect things from me. Above all, I never wanted to let her down.

We were standing a foot apart, out of earshot of anyone else. There was no homework around to worry about, no manuscript within reach, and I couldn't put my dick in her for at least a few hours.

I took the rare opportunity to try to get some new information out of her. "So your aunt and uncle are really your only living family?"

I had a huge, loud, wonderful family, so this fact seemed particularly tragic to me.

She shrugged, not looking at me. I could tell she didn't like the question but she answered me. "I have a grandma, aunt, and some cousins in Columbia, but I don't hear from them much. I know they'd take me in, but I'm not moving there. I'm not even fluent in Spanish, much to my abuela's disappointment."

"So your mother was Columbian?" I gave her an encouraging smile. She was so closed off that anything she shared about herself was a treat that I gobbled up.

"Yes," she answered, not elaborating.

"What about your dad?" I tried, hoping she stayed in a sharing mood.

"Scottish and Dutch, I think, and some other stuff. Just white, ya know, like you."

I laughed. "Well my origins are English and Italian, to be precise, if that was your way of asking."

She gave me her sweet smile, the one I couldn't get enough of. She didn't look at anyone else the way she looked at me, and I never wanted that to change, though of course that was unlikely, to say the least. "It kind of was," she admitted. "Do you have a big family?" she asked.

"Yes. Massive. Two brothers and two sisters, though none of them live close, unfortunately. We're all kind of scattered around the country at the moment."

"And your parents? Are they alive and still together?"

I found the question to be sad, like she assumed all families were broken or gone like hers. It brought out the protective side of me—even more than usual. I wanted to fold her into my own family, to make sure she was never alone again. "They are. They live in Florida."

"And do you get along with them?"

"I do. They're wonderful."

"And all your siblings? You get along with them too?"

"Most of the time. With siblings it can be complicated, but for the most part we're all pretty close.

"It sounds like a really nice family. You're lucky."

She sounded so forlorn and wishful then that it was a struggle not to move close and touch her. My hands flexed with the effort not to grab handfuls of her.

I wanted to tell her she could meet them, that I would share my big family with her, that they'd welcome her with open arms, but I couldn't.

They wouldn't. They'd all be horrified by what I was doing with a student.

And worse than that, none of it was really on the table. Our status was so in the now, no future in sight. It was a long shot at best to think I'd be introducing her to my family.

I wanted her to think about what *she* wanted to do with *her* life, not lose herself in mine. Anything else would be unfair to her.

"In the sun, your eyes look liquid like honey," she surprised me by blurting out.

I don't know why, but that put me at my limit. I excused myself.

I used the restroom, taking the time to collect myself. She was temptation incarnate, but that was nothing new. There was a reason I'd long since lost the battle against my obsession for her.

I grabbed a stiff drink at the nearest bar and knocked it back. It was going to be a long day with her looking like that and me unable to partake. Liquor it was.

When I came back to where she waded in the pool I found

some middle-aged man talking to her, standing way too fucking close.

I couldn't help myself. I moved behind her, rubbing my chest into her. I stroked her stomach underwater, nuzzling the top of her head. I threw my free arm over the front of her collarbone, gripping her shoulder possessively.

I met the man's gaze boldly. "Who is this, pet? Made a new friend?" Even as I spoke I was rubbing her tummy, pushing her back firmly until her ass was flush with my groin.

I smiled unpleasantly at him.

He paled. I was twice his size.

"Excuse me," he choked out, "I see someone I know." He practically ran away.

I watched him go, hands still full of her delicious skin. I put my mouth against her ear and said softly, "You're going to get it for that."

She shivered. "For what, exactly?" she gasped.

I couldn't see her face but I could read her mind or at the very least her body. She was deeply turned on.

"For talking to strangers," I growled into her ear.

"I wasn't talking to him. He approached me. I barely said a word."

"It doesn't matter. Nothing you can say will erase the way he was looking at you out of my brain. It's not fair, but neither is life, and you're going to pay for that look. I'm going to have to fuck my aggression out on you now, and soon. Frankly, I'm having a hard time remembering why I shouldn't fuck you right where we stand."

"Probably because it's against the law," she said archly.

"I bet I could nut before any police intervene," I mused.

"But then they'd put their hands on me as they were arresting us," she pointed out.

"Fair point. Nearest wall it is."

"What about the cabana?"

An hour ago I wouldn't have considered it, but I was so far gone I just didn't care anymore.

"Fine," I bit out. "Get moving. A cabana fuck it is, but you better keep your filthy little mouth shut."

"I don't think *I'm* the one we have to worry about," she said sassily as she started walking.

Just for that I grabbed her wrists, pulled them up and behind her head, and pushed her in front of me with one hand in a perp walk all the way from the middle of the pool to our cabana.

We got some strange looks, and I still just didn't care.

We got to the cabana and dismissed the attendant. "We're taking a nap," I told her, practically shutting the curtain in her face.

I pushed Nova hard enough that she fell on her back on the lounger, legs sprawling apart. Perfect.

I didn't undress either of us, just took my cock out, shoved her bikini bottoms to the side, covered her mouth with mine in a heated kiss, and had at it.

I fucked her, quick and mean, coming deep inside, furiously and selfishly.

To make up for it I moved down her body, pulled off her bikini bottoms, and stuffed them in her mouth. I tugged the triangles of her top to the side until her nipples were exposed, perky flesh spilling out.

I stared at her for a long moment, pleased with the picture she made like that, then returned to my goal, moving down her body. I tongued her to completion with my semen still hot and seeping out of her, one hand busy on her clit, the other kneading at her luscious tits.

Some time later we were back in the pool, and I wasn't even trying to keep my hands off her.

Clarity used to come a bit after an orgasm, sanity after the storm, but we seemed to be past that these days.

And fuck it, I was just too far gone to care.

The urgency of touching her beat out any concerns I had that were less urgent, which at that moment was *all* of them.

What were the chances we'd run into anyone from school, anyway? I'd never been much of a gambler, but Vegas was big, and I was playing the odds.

I had both of my hands on her butt and I was whispering some pretty filthy stuff into her ear when I realized we had company.

I pulled away far enough to meet Javier's smiling eyes and Stephan's wary, judging ones.

"We took a few hours off from running the bar to join you for a swim," Javier said cheerfully, brushing his wavy black hair out of his face. "There are perks to owning the joint."

"Isn't she in high school? And aren't you her teacher?" Stephan asked coldly. He just kept looking back and forth between Nova and I like he wasn't quite sure if he should intervene. I understood what he was thinking all too well. We'd painted a very different picture of our relationship the last time he'd seen us at my house.

I reluctantly took my hands off her ass and moved a small step away.

I had a brief, awkward, borderline hostile stare down with Stephan. He was a big guy, we were of a height, but I had some weight on him, and it wasn't idle weight. I had heard, though, that he was a talented fighter. Still, I figured I could take him.

Javier elbowed him, then slipped under his arm to hug him around the ribs.

Javier wasn't short, but he looked it next to Stephan. That and almost delicately beautiful, particularly next to his husband's big, blond, buff form.

He kissed along the larger man's clenched jawline and said

quietly, "She's eighteen, she's clearly in love with him, and it's *not* our business. Stand down."

Some of the tension left Stephan's body at that, and some of the hostility left his eyes. He dragged his hand through the other man's hair almost absently, then gripped his nape firmly, unconsciously dominating him. "If he gives you any problems, call us, and we'll fix it," Stephan told Nova. He met my eyes again. "If you hurt her, I'll hurt you worse. A lot worse. You've got a few pounds on me, but trust me, I know how to fight dirtier than you can imagine."

I wasn't offended by his speech. In fact, it made me like him more. "Understood," I said simply. "If I ever hurt her, I'd welcome a beating, trust me."

That seemed to settle it. Nova slipped under my arm, hugging my waist, a near mirror pose to what Stephan and Javier were doing.

I glanced down at her. She was looking up at me with that deep, soulful stare that got to me every time. She was so young, but those beautiful eyes of hers were ageless.

"Can I have one little drink?" she asked me in her sweetest voice, the one she used when she begged me for the things I rarely denied her. "I don't think they'll give us any problems if I don't go up to the bar directly, you know, like if someone just brings one to me."

I gave her a disapproving look. "No. I'm not letting you have alcohol. You're underage."

She pouted, but I wasn't budging on this.

Javier snorted so loudly I looked at him.

He was laughing at me. "She's not old enough for a drink, but she's old enough for whatever this is?" He waved a hand in our direction.

I flushed, but I wasn't surprised. I figured it was pretty obvious to anyone with eyes that I was fucking her. Even now I had handfuls of her, one gripping low on her hip, the other cupping the back of her head, and I hadn't even realized I was reaching for her. My hands acted on their own at this point.

It was just that innate now—my sense of ownership for her.

But all that was beside the point. "It's a no," I stated firmly. "I know it's fucked up that I'm her teacher, but that's also *exactly* why I won't be a party to her drinking when she's underage and in my direct care."

Javier shrugged, but he looked more amused than ever. "Whatever, man. Want to play some pool volleyball?"

# CHAPTER 24

**NOVA**

After spending hours at the pool, Stephan and Javier invited us to join them for dinner and I was surprised when Carter actually agreed.

I showered in the large locker room attached to the resort's many pools and changed into dry clothes.

Carter had packed them for me, and I found myself in sweat pants and an oversized UCLA sweatshirt. My hair was still wet as I slipped my feet back into the slides I'd worn to the pool.

I wasn't sure where we were going for dinner, but I was positive this wasn't the dress code for it.

I stepped out of the changing room, expecting to be the last one ready as the rest of them were guys, but only Javier was waiting for me.

Javier took one look at me and started shaking his head. "Carter packed my clothes," I explained. "Normally he's surprisingly good at choosing outfits for me, but I think he was just trying to cover up as much skin as possible here."

Javier laughed. "A bit pointless at this point, no? That cat's out of the bag."

I shrugged and tried my best not to blush.

Just then Stephan and Carter joined us, both newly changed into dry clothes. Stephan and Javier were wearing nice slacks and dress shirts, looking put together down to their still wet but still styled hair, but Carter was wearing an outfit nearly identical to mine. He was even wearing a similar college sweatshirt.

I indicated the front of my shirt. "I take it you went to UCLA?" I asked Carter. I gobbled up every little tidbit I learned about him.

He looked sheepish. "I did."

His eyes were running over me, taking me in in *his* clothes from *his* school, and I could tell by his heavy eyelids that it really did something to him.

I loved it, loved that he'd wanted to put a stamp of ownership on me in public even as he'd tried to cover up every inch of my skin. In spite of his protestations, our bedroom inclinations were starting to spill over into other parts of life, and though it may have been wishful thinking on my part, I couldn't help but be encouraged by it.

"I'll push the reservation back an hour," Javier said decisively. He pointed at Carter. "Stephan, take him to find something more appropriate to wear to a Michelin star restaurant. I've got Nova."

We started to walk away when Javier stopped suddenly. He strode back to Carter and held out his hand.

Carter stared at him, raising a brow. "What?"

"Your credit card," Javier said, a world of sass in it.

Carter smirked. He didn't look at me as he said, "She already has it."

We were walking away from them a beat later when Javier took my arm with a delicate touch and said loudly, "That's my girl."

Both men chuckled at our retreating backs.

For some reason I wasn't offended by the implication. The way he teased about it made it feel so unserious, and I found that empowering.

"I know you're only eighteen," Javier said in a casual tone as we walked, "but that man is going to marry you. It's what you want, right?"

I blushed profusely at that, feeling unaccountably sad. "You have that all wrong. He doesn't even want to have a relationship with me at all. I think I embarrass him. And us sleeping together. . . it was my idea. I seduced him. He still hates that he couldn't resist me."

Javier seemed unfazed by everything I'd said. "That man is whipped. Anything you want him to do for you, he will. If that's not a relationship, I can't tell you what is."

I didn't try to explain it to him any more than that. Instead I let myself wish for the short duration of our stroll that he was right and I was wrong, though I knew it was a delusion. Carter would do anything for me, but it was out of obligation, out of his own innate goodness, not because he was in love with me.

He was deeply in lust with me, though, and I was going to let that be enough. It was still the best thing that had ever happened to me.

The boutique Javier brought me to was intimidating, to say the least. It was small and exclusive, the walls lined with beautiful lingerie, the racks full of expensive designer clothing. The tall blond woman that approached us the second we walked into the store looked like the type that wouldn't even let someone like me in the door.

However, she got one look at Javier and squealed with

delight. "Javier! Who's this? Where's Bianca? I don't believe I've ever seen you in here without her."

"That's because I'm her honorary stylist when she's in town. But this week she's in New York with James and the kids. And this is my lovely friend Nova. Nova, this delightful woman is Adele. Nova needs something gorgeous to wear on short notice. Like, we have less than an hour, and I still have to drag her to the salon for quick hair and makeup."

Adele eyed me top to bottom but not in a bad way. It was more a pleased, measuring look. She crooked a finger at me. "Nova, we're on too much of a time crunch to be shy with each other, so come with me."

I followed her into the dressing room, the sound of Javier on his phone booking me last minute salon treatments echoing behind me.

"Strip," Adele said with a smile, "I'll be right back," she added and left me in the dressing room.

I was down to my sports bra and panties when she strode back in with an armful of clothes.

"Can I assume you're dressing with a particular special someone in mind?" she asked, thrusting a slinky black dress at me.

I couldn't exactly deny it. "Yes."

She smiled a Cheshire cat smile and handed me a hanger with almost nothing on it, just a series of small silk ribbons and three delicate, beautifully embroidered roses.

I held the two items in my hands and stared back and forth between them.

"I'll need a real bra," I pointed out. My breasts were too large to go without in public and not have it be obscene.

"Just put it all on," she said without missing a beat. "You're going to love it, I promise. You're busty, but you're also young and perky. The dress has built in bust support so the lingerie is all you need. While you do that I'll go next door and grab your shoes."

She didn't need an answer as she was already gone before I could open my mouth. I wrapped myself into the lingerie with some difficulty but as soon as I saw my reflection in it I knew I'd be wearing it tonight.

I was almost naked in it aside from the lovely floating roses placed over my nipples and one just above my sex, not hiding it but accentuating it.

Carter was going to lose his mind when he saw it.

I pulled the little black dress on over it and fell instantly in love. Adele knew what she was doing.

It was sexy but classy, the neckline sweetheart style and not too low, but the slit in the thigh high enough to be daring. And sure enough, my chest was even supported by a hidden shelf bra in the clever getup.

The back was nearly bare, pairing perfectly with my nearly nonexistent underthings.

I didn't look like a teenager anymore. I looked like a femme fatale seductress and I loved it.

Adele sailed back into the dressing room with a pair of shiny, blood red, spiked heels. "These aren't comfortable but they're worth the pain," she said, setting them in front of me.

She was right about both.

Javier got one look at me and grinned. "Perfect," he said, then whisked me off to the next stop.

At the resort's posh salon he'd set me up with two quick, simultaneous services. A stylist blew out my hair while a makeup artist gave me a quick, glam makeup job.

We were behind Stephan and Carter getting to the restaurant but not by much.

All the effort was well worth it when I saw Carter's reaction to my express makeover.

His eyes ran over me like a caress, and I read something

there, some new piece of approval that made me think he'd noticed what I did, that I looked more like an adult and less like a teenager like this, and he very much approved.

Which was good considering he'd spent a small fortune for it all.

For his part, he looked so good in light gray slacks, shiny matching shoes, and a crisp white dress shirt that I wanted to drop to my knees and show him how much I liked it right there. Of course, I felt that way when he was wearing sweats.

I had it so bad.

The dinner reservations were at an expensive French restaurant next to Stephan and Javier's bar.

I ordered something I could barely pronounce, not wanting to ask what anything was since no one else seemed to be having trouble. I'd suffer through a lot before illustrating how unsophisticated I was in front of Carter, though of course he already knew.

Stephan and Javier made good company for dinner and in general. I really liked them both, and especially appreciated how Javier had taken the time to befriend and hang out with me.

"So you're James Cavendish's wife's best friend?" I asked Stephan, referring to the billionaire that this very casino was named after.

"Closer to family," Javier corrected. "We're their children's godparents. We're family," he reiterated. "Close family."

"That's cool," I said, smiling. "What's he like?"

I thought it was a pretty easy question but both men thought it over for several moments before I got an answer.

"He's a good man," Stephan finally said. "A family man. I couldn't ask for someone better for my best friend to be married to."

"Is he fun though?" I asked. I'd never met a billionaire before and James Cavendish was a particularly interesting one.

"In a way," Javier mused, a twist to his mouth. "He can be rather serious, but he has a good sense of humor. He's great with his kids, as well."

Carter laughed, stroking a hand over my hair. When I wore it down he couldn't stop touching it so of course I wore it down all the time now. "I don't think you'll get an answer from them that James's PR wouldn't come up with personally, pet."

"What about his wife?" I tried. I'd seen pictures of her. The impression I'd gotten was that she was beautiful, blond but sort of aloof looking. "Is she nice?"

Stephan didn't have to think about it. "She's the nicest. I'm sure you'll meet her sometime. People are intimidated by her, because of how she looks and because she's quiet, but don't be. You won't meet a kinder soul."

Carter laughed again, his hand gripping my nape now. I loved his hand there. It felt like he was claiming me when he grabbed me just like that. "I don't think you'll get anything but a best friend answer to that. But I've met them too. James comes to poker occasionally. They're both very nice."

We were eating dessert by that point, a crème brûlée that Javier insisted we had to try, and I was pushing the last bit of it around in the dish, too full to take another bite.

"On that note," Stephan said, sitting up straight, "we're calling it a night. But we have a surprise for you, if you want it." He glanced at Carter, then back at me. "Have you heard of Tristan Vega?"

I stared at him. "The rock star? Of course I've heard of him. He has a residency in this casino. He's on the billboard out front."

"He alternates shows every six months," Stephan explained. "He performs with his band for half the year, and then he also has a magic show that he likes to constantly switch up for the other half. Anyway, he's in the rock star phase of his year."

"He's sold out for months ahead of time," Carter pointed out. "He's been harassing James to build him a larger theatre."

I glanced at him.

"He comes to poker night sometimes, too," he explained to me.

"Well, anyway, it's a great show, and I have seats for it tonight for you if you want them," Stephan finished.

I looked up at Carter. "Please, please, please, can we go?"

He gave me a certain look he had, one that told me he was about to give in even though he didn't really want to. "Okay," he said with a sigh.

I hugged Javier and Stephan goodbye. I was amused to watch Javier give Carter a hug as well. Carter was fist bumping Stephan as the other man pulled away.

I watched them go with a smile. "They're really nice," I said, a little dazzled by it all.

"They are," Carter agreed, guiding me in the opposite direction with a hand at the small of my back.

I was so excited suddenly I could hardly contain myself. "I've always wanted to see this show! They really hooked us up with this."

"They did," Carter agreed, unfazed.

"Have you ever seen it before? I guess you know him so you can probably go any time."

"I've seen it, but it's the sort of thing that you want to see again. The band plays different set lists all the time."

I did wonder how many other women he'd taken to this exact show.

I managed not to ask him, though. It was a near perfect day for us and I didn't want to ruin it for any reason.

Whatever our tickets were they let us enter the theatre

early, leading us to box seats with a perfect view of the stage.

"These seats are amazing," I said with wonder.

"They are," Carter agreed. "This is actually the family box, shared with only his closest friends. Sometimes his wife and kids come to watch the show, and when they do these are their seats."

"Will they be here tonight?"

"I don't think so. They have a ton of kids, so there's usually something going on every Saturday. Also, I think Stephan would have said so."

I glanced around, wanting to rub my hands together with glee. I'd never done VIP anything but from the pool, to the boutique, to the salon, to this, it'd been a lifetime's worth of special treatment for me.

We were the only ones there, but the box was big enough to fit dozens. We even had our own bartender—though of course Carter wouldn't let me have a drink.

"Will more join us in the box? Are we just the first ones?"

"I really don't know for sure. I haven't heard about anyone else coming, so I'm thinking we might have it all to ourselves."

I gazed at him meaningfully. "Privacy."

He gave me a stern professor look and I shivered.

"Tell me about your aunt and uncle," he said, catching me off guard. "I know there's more to the story. You didn't just leave because they ran out of room."

I considered that for a long time, debating what to tell him.

I decided to be open with him. If not him, who else? "That really was a big part of it," I told him, because it was true. "But you're right. There was more to it. Things were getting . . . bad."

"Tell me what bad means," he said, a world of understanding in his voice.

It was very hard not to pour my whole heart out to him

when he sounded like that, when he looked at me with such soft eyes.

"My aunt's brother, the one that moved in with his family, is a bit of a creep."

Something interesting happened to his face, but I couldn't put my finger on quite what it meant.

"A bit?" he asked in a perfectly blank voice.

I shrugged and grimaced. "He didn't do anything to me, but he said some gross stuff. And I had to sleep on the couch in the living room once he and his family moved in, and a few times I woke up with him lying next to me, like spooning me when I was asleep."

"I'll kill him," Carter said, his voice so bleached of emotion that it scared me. Not for myself, but for what kind of trouble he could get himself into.

"Not necessary. That was the extent of the creepiness. It only happened three times before I left. Anyway, I told my uncle about it. My aunt heard me telling him and slapped me around. She never beat me or anything, but she's always been a fan of slapping. The things she said were worse, though. She has a way of tearing people down that always hits its mark. Anyway, I wasn't welcome to stay there after that."

"No one defended you? Not even your uncle? Your father's brother, right?"

I was impressed he'd remembered something like that, something that I'd only mentioned to him once in passing. "That's right. And no, he didn't. I think he might have been more scared of his wife than I was."

"Well, it's good you got out of that hellhole. They didn't deserve you. Sometimes it's better to make your own family."

My heart stuttered in my chest, impossible hope blooming. The way I wanted to take that and the way he probably meant it couldn’t match up, but it was my dearest wish that it would. That it could.

# CHAPTER 25

We did end up being the only ones in the family box. It was a surreal experience since the rest of the large theatre was packed to a seat.

The show was amazing. I'd heard about Tristan Vega's magic shows. They were elaborate and show stopping, but if anything the rock concert was understated, show wise. It was just the band on the stage, music perfectly amplified, sounding as good if not better live as they did recorded. The lead singer's voice was weathered in the best way—deep, but emotional, beautiful.

It was a wonderful experience, and more wonderful was Carter hugging me from behind throughout most of it. I couldn't stay in my seat, instead stood at the rail, and he was right there with me, kissing my neck, the top of my head, lacing his fingers with mine.

We got home late, but I was anything but tired.

I was the opposite. Restless and wired. Being out with him, not hiding anything had been a heady experience, a sharp glimpse into how I wanted things to be.

He led me straight to his bedroom with a firm hand at my nape. I'd taken to staying in there every night, though I kept all my things across the house in my room. I didn't want to push my luck.

I was constantly in a state of worry that he'd realize he was too good for me and kick me out of his bed or even his house.

When I was being logical I knew that wasn't something he'd do, but my whole life had taught me not to trust any feelings of safety, that they were always temporary and usually ended with me being worse off than I'd started. It was hard to reprogram a gut instinct that ran so deep inside of you that it had helped form most of your core belief system.

I shook off the dark thoughts. I was good at that and being anywhere near Carter made it easy. He was my very favorite distraction.

We got to his room, and he kept walking until we stood directly next to his bed. One of his hands gripped my hair, angling my head for better access. He kissed the side of my neck, his other hand on my belly, rubbing low.

"Let me show you something," I said, and it came out as a pant. He knew how to get me going with a few simple touches now. He'd somehow learned my body better than I could ever hope to.

He bit the lobe of my ear oh so softly and I shivered, head to toe.

When he didn't say anything, I made myself take a few steps away from him. I kicked off my shoes.

He just watched me, quirking a brow.

Never breaking eye contact, I peeled myself out of my dress slowly, seductively, until all I was left in was the wicked little piece of lingerie. I fingered one of the little flowers that barely covered my nipple. "Do you like it?"

He was silent for a time, but that didn't mean he wasn't communicating.

He had a half-mad look in his eyes. They were alive and alight with a deep need that told me everything I wanted to know.

He moved behind me again.

His voice was hot velvet on my nape. "I like it so much that I think I'll tear it to pieces while I'm fucking you and then buy you a dozen more."

I shut my eyes, leaning back against him. "I wish you would," I breathed.

His hand was on my hip, a possessive grip. "I told myself all night that I was going to make love to you slowly for once, but I don't think it's going to be like that. You're irresistible, you know that?"

I opened my mouth to answer, but my breath was stolen from me as he whipped me around by the shoulders, picked me up, and threw me roughly onto the bed.

I hadn't caught my breath yet when he was on me and over me, his big hands parting my legs, his hips fitting between.

"You're wet," he said thickly. He reached a hand down, his fingers stroking over me, gathering the moisture. He held it where I could see. "You're ready for my cock. Is this all for me?"

"Yes," I breathed.

"You're always wet for me, aren't you?" his words were more of a statement in the form of a question.

I looked down. His dick was already out of his slacks, pushing against my entrance.

"Yes," I gasped. The wide crest of his cock pushed into me with that slow, slick, sweet, thick glide I'd become addicted to.

Our eyes locked and he started to move, pumping in and

out of me in heavy punches of his hips, his balls slapping loudly against my ass.

He never looked away from me, not for an instant.

It felt so intimate, it made my eyes sting with tears. I loved him so much, and somehow everything he did to me, even if it had nothing to do with love, only made that love grow.

"Please," I whimpered at him.

He knew what I was asking for.

It flipped a switch in him. A switch he'd only ever switched for me.

His thrusts stuttered for a moment, the skin around his cheekbones taut with strain.

His fists had been on either side of my head as he braced himself over me. Now one reached down and ripped one of the roses off my nipple, then pinched me roughly.

His thrusts went from a smooth pump into a hard jounce that made my whole body jerk with each motion. My breasts bounced with every measured jolt.

He spoke all the while, rough filth pouring out of his mouth, bathing me—my preferred aphrodisiac.

"Fucking take it," he grunted. Thrust. "Fuck toy." Thrust. "My perfect little whore." Thrust. "Cum vacuum." Thrust. "Mine." Thrust. Only mine." Thrust. *"Fucking mine.* Say it."

I came with a hoarse cry. Nothing got to me faster than his words, and moreover, his rough demands of ownership.

He wasn't finished, didn't even pause. He brought my arms above my head, holding my wrists.

I loved it when he did that, trapping and subjugating me to his ruthless will, then eventually, his generous mercy.

His other hand ripped the other embroidered rose off my nipple, hand gripping the soft flesh roughly.

His strokes never slowed, but got harder, more frenzied.

He stamped his pleasure into me, stirring my insides into his shape in a harsh, relentless tempo as he grew close to his own release.

*"Fucking say it,"* he growled.

"Yours," I cried, and toes curling, I came again.

He followed with a tormented groan.

He stayed on top of me and in me after. It was a habit of his that I loved, as though, even spent, he couldn't bear to tear himself away.

Eventually he bent and kissed me as he dragged himself out.

"I'll draw us a bath, pet," he murmured and went into the other room.

This was possibly my favorite part of it all, when he tended to me with tender focus after we finished.

I loved the attention. No one ever took care of me like he did. No one else took care of me at all since my parents passed.

He was stripped bare when he came back in the room.

I didn't bother to move. I let him carry my limp self into the bathroom and lower me slowly into the hot water.

He joined me, sliding in behind me. It was a big tub, but he dominated it to the point I was always surprised we both fit.

He washed me, and I didn't lift a finger to help. I could fall asleep right here and I knew he'd get me to bed with no trouble. Another pattern we'd fallen into.

He stroked my breasts, nibbling at my neck. I wasn't sure I could stay awake for another round, but for him I'd try.

I don't know why I said it, why I thought of it then. I think it was just what came out when I was trying my hardest not to say *I love you* to him yet again, and instead managed to say something even worse.

"It's alright if you hurt me," I told him, voice catching. "I'm figuring on it. It's worth it—the pain—to feel like this."

He hummed out a little distressed noise into my ear.

"Don't say that, pet. I have no intention of hurting you. Don't you know I'd never do that?"

I didn't tell him he wouldn't do it on purpose.

Pain was just the natural conclusion to any relationship where only one of you was in love.

# CHAPTER 26

**CARTER**

There was only two weeks until the school year ended. It couldn't come soon enough to suit me. Once Nova graduated so much would become simpler.

She had a lot to figure out about her future, but at least we wouldn't have to hide anything. We wouldn't be student/teacher anymore.

We'd just be two lovers shacking up. It sounded delightful.

It was my free period, and I was behind my desk grading assignments on my computer. Nova's work was conspicuously missing from this round. She owed me a few things, in fact, but I was still making her catch up on all of her other classes first. I would never fail her, and as a sop to my conscience I figured I could always have her make up for it after school was finished for the year.

Suddenly the door flew open and someone strode aggressively into my classroom.

"Carter, I need you to come with me," one of the APs said to me the second she walked into my classroom.

No greeting, just that foreboding sentence out of her mouth.

"Is something the matter, Sharon?" I asked slowly.

But I knew.

I knew from the tone of her voice that something was terribly wrong.

The first and only thing my mind went to was Nova. I knew, with lancing certainty that we'd been found out. Nothing else could account for that tone from a usually warm, friendly colleague.

"Just come with me," she said stiffly.

She didn't even let me follow her, as though she was afraid I'd try to make a break for it. Instead she instructed me where to go, following closely behind.

I thought that part was more than a little ridiculous. If I wanted to go somewhere, to try to run, to avoid this, there was no way she could have stopped me, but I just went where she instructed on leaden feet.

We went to some sort of conference room I'd never seen before, deep behind the principal's office. The principal, Anna Green, waited inside, standing beside an empty chair in front of an open laptop.

*What the fuck was all this?*

"Have a seat, Carter," Anna instructed me tonelessly. Anna was a kindly woman in her fifties. She had a smile for everyone and rarely a harsh word. She left that sort of thing to her APs, usually playing the good cop herself, but not now.

Now she was eyeing me in a way I'd never experienced before.

Like I was the scum of the earth.

I didn't see another option, so I sat in front of the open laptop.

"You probably know why you're here," Anna began.

It felt suddenly like a police interview. "You're going to have to tell me," I returned, pleased that my voice was bland in spite of my pounding heart.

"Nova Monroe," she said succinctly. "And your conduct in regards to her. Your *sexual relations* with a *student*."

I shut my eyes tightly, wanting to deny the entire thing, to pretend even to myself that I hadn't done what I'd done, but there was no escaping it now. I wouldn't be here if they didn't already know.

"Obviously, your contract with the school district will be terminated," she continued mercilessly. She didn't sound pleased with it though, instead she sounded like a disappointed parent and somehow that was worse. "And frankly, you should not even think of trying to apply anywhere else. This is going to follow you, Carter. Your teaching career is over. But I'm afraid that's not your biggest problem."

My eyes opened and just because my gaze was pointed at it, what was paused on the computer caught my eye. I knew from that one still shot what it was, and I was instantly nauseous.

"What's my biggest problem?" I asked blankly. I had a thought. "She's eighteen," I said, and hated myself for how it sounded.

"Yes, we know, but—" Sharon began.

Anna held up a hand, silencing the other woman. "Age of consent is not the issue today. We're actually concerned about a different type of consent altogether."

I gave her a hard look. That was a bit much. "What are you trying to say?" I asked sharply.

She nodded at the laptop. "Why don't you watch this and

ask me that again?"

They didn't say another word, just played the video for me, watching me and not the screen as they did so.

I watched the whole thing, my skin crawling with shame.

Someone had captured a video of us, of me and Nova in the coach's office the night of the prom. The angle came from the hallway.

That fucking open door.

The footage was shaky enough that I could tell it wasn't surveillance footage. A person had been holding the camera.

Someone had been watching us, not ten feet away. I was disgusted and furious.

And beyond that, I was horrified.

I could see why it looked worse than it even was, and what it was was bad enough by a mile.

In the video I had her pinned face down on the desk. I was pulling her hair with one hand, the other holding her shoulder to pin her in place while I drilled into her.

I was huge as it was and with the angle, me closer to the camera, she was particularly small in comparison to my oversized self.

At least we hadn't undressed completely. We were both in our prom clothes, and I'd just taken my dick out and buried it in her.

And at least you could barely see her in the shot, her voluminous gown was covering her, and my massive thrusting back was taking up most of it.

She hadn't been silent while I fucked her brains out, it's just that I was much louder, filth spewing out of my mouth in a constant stream through the entire thing

Some of it was rough to hear, especially out of context.

I was being a bit rough with her, aggressive, dominating her, and she tended to get really soft and cooperative when I fucked her like that, which was part of the heaven of it all.

It didn't look good here, though, and while I knew she'd been quite willing it was not immediately apparent in the video.

I flinched because it didn't end there, and I knew what was coming next. It was the time I'd taken her in the ass, and some creep had captured it all from just a few feet away.

Our faces and our privates were blocked from view throughout because of where the camera was angled, thank God, it was mostly a shot of my bare ass thrusting like a jackhammer, but the whole thing was still completely lurid, and by the awful things I was saying it was impossible to mistake what I was doing to her.

It was horrifying and humiliating, but more than anything in that moment, I was worried about Nova.

"This is online?" I asked, feeling just sick about it.

"Yes. Steps are being taken to remove it as much as possible, but I'm sure you know how it works. Once it's out there, there's no getting it back, not really."

I did know that, and a wave of self-disgust moved over me.

It was so powerful I felt ill with it.

I'd done this to her, my carelessness had landed her on the internet in a seedy sex tape for any random pervert to get off on. I hated it. More even than what was coming to me personally, all the various consequences for what I'd done, I hated the fact that I hadn't protected her properly, when that was my fucking job.

"You see the problem," Anna said when the awful video finally finished.

I shut the laptop, exerting some effort not to slam it closed, not to punch a hole through the nearest wall. "I think so," I said tonelessly.

"It's not immediately apparent that Nova is a willing participant there," Sharon added sharply.

I just stared her down. I had a lot to answer for here, but that was going too far. "Has Nova seen this?" I asked.

"She has. We're holding her in another room. Some of the other APs are still getting her side of things."

I hated that, hated so much that she was probably scared right then, and I couldn't be with her to comfort her at the very least. "And what has she said? About whether she was a willing participant?" I asked.

I hated to play that card but I just knew, there was absolutely no doubt in my mind that Nova wouldn't do that to me, wouldn't for one *second* infer that I had forced her.

"That's part of the problem. She's barely talking. She won't even corroborate that it's you in the video. She insists you've never laid a finger on her.

In spite of the hell I currently found myself in, I felt something warm roll around in my chest. That was my perfect girl.

"Let me talk to her," I said.

They both stared at me like I'd lost my mind.

"You won't go near that girl," Sharon almost snarled, "*ever* again."

I didn't like that. They could fire me, there's nowhere else this could go, but they couldn't keep her away from me outside of school.

Could they?

A new type of sickness was creeping up on me, this one heavy with the weight of my fear.

"Let me call her," I said, trying to sound reasonable. From their faces they weren't buying it. "If I can talk to her for thirty seconds, she'll cooperate more, okay?"

After a brief stare down Anna said, "Fine. Call her. But you have thirty seconds exactly, and you better not say one threatening word to her."

I glared. "I would *never—*"

"We heard you on the video, Carter. Never is a strong word. Now watch what you say. Sharon, go tell Stevie and Marian to let Nova take his call."

Sharon looked like she badly wanted to refuse, but she left in a huff.

"Nova," I said gently when I finally got her on the line.

"Mr. North," she said stiffly.

I shut my eyes. "You can tell them, Nova. They know about us. The damage is done. What they're worried about is whether . . . " I had a hard time even saying the words to her. "Whether you were a willing participant. They're worried I was forcing you in that video."

She made a little noise on the other end, a sound of distress, and Anna snatched the phone out of my hand. "That's thirty seconds," she told me sharply.

She was striding from the room when she barked at me, "Don't move."

I waited alone in that room for hours. I'd never felt more helpless in my life.

I felt a brief punch of panic in my gut when Anna finally came back, this time with two LEOs in tow.

The principal lectured and berated me for a good twenty minutes before I realized I wasn't being charged with anything.

Just fired and humiliated.

I knew I was getting off light.

Sharon and the silent two LEOs walked me out all the way to my car but at least they didn't arrest me.

When I got to the house it was more torturous waiting. Nova didn't come home when she should have after school, and she wasn't taking any calls.

She was hours late, but she did come home eventually.

I snatched her up and gathered her to me in a bear hug the second she walked in the door. I ran my hands over her back and kissed the side of her head. "Thank God. It felt like they were going to keep you indefinitely. They even claimed I couldn't see you again."

She was nuzzling into my chest. "I'm so sorry, Carter. This is all my fault—"

"Don't say that. Of course it isn't."

I was holding her as the relief of having her home wore off, and suddenly, jarringly, I felt a sense of distinct discomfort.

She tried to kiss me. I turned my head away. "Not now. We need to take a break . . . from this. Just for now. It's not your fault. It's not you at all, it's me." I knew how it sounded, so pat and cliché, and I could tell by her arrested expression what I was doing to her, but it was still necessary. "I need some space. Just some time to think, okay? We'll stay in our own sides of the house, out of each other's way, while I sort things out."

She looked crestfallen but I didn't know how to comfort her just then. I was just so disappointed in myself and still coming to terms with how much my life had just been turned upside down.

No more teaching. No more coaching. Ever again. It was sobering and frankly gutting. I hadn't thought I'd teach for the long haul, but I'd never planned to let go of coaching.

That night she ignored what I'd said and crawled into bed with me.

For the first time ever she touched me, and I didn't get hard. I felt no desire at all, in fact. I had too much inner turmoil going on to think with my dick, for once.

I kissed the top of her head and pushed her away. "I meant it. I need some time."

She hadn't spoken since she'd entered the room, and she left without a word, her posture dejected.

I didn't even feel bad. I felt numb. I simply knew I couldn't go there now, not for a few days at least, while I processed all that had happened.

# CHAPTER 27

**NOVA**

I'd known the instant I was pulled into the office at school that everything was going to change for us, but even so it felt like I watched us end in slow motion.

The whole mess felt like all too many patterns in my life so far.

It felt like things were breaking, coming apart, like my foundation, never steady, was disintegrating into barest crumbs once more.

This was not the first time or even the second the rug had been pulled out from under me.

I hadn't been through what I'd been through without learning one most basic fact: When it was time to move on.

I loved being with Carter. Every second of it. But my feelings were not his feelings, and he'd been reluctant from the start.

This had all been my idea, at my insistence. He'd really just given in. Who knew why?

Simple but powerful lust. Pity. An irresistible combination of the two was my best guess.

And now I'd ruined his life and even that uncomplicated lust was gone in an instant, only barest traces of pity left in his hollow gaze.

He didn't want me anymore, hadn't touched me since we'd been caught and he'd been fired, in fact he could barely look at me.

He didn't outright kick me out of his house, and that was something.

However, I knew I'd have to leave and soon. I could only see it going a few ways, and none of them were good. Either he'd eventually get up the nerve to ask me to leave, and that would break me, or he never would, instead letting me stay with him for good but only out of his own innate core of decency. That would break me too, just more slowly.

I couldn't use his pity to trap him, couldn't take advantage of his sense of obligation.

I used to think that I could, but I loved him too much not to want him to have exactly the life he wanted, not a life I thrust upon him.

It was agony, but I started making plans for the future. Plans that didn't include Carter.

My friend Maddie wanted to get a place close to UNLV and needed a roommate. I jumped on the chance. I wouldn't be attending college in the near future, but the location was good for all kinds of other reasons, not the least of which was that a free clinic was right there and a lot of places were always hiring within easy distance.

Also, I didn't want to be alone. I'd discovered by then just how much money Carter had deposited into my bank account and even though I knew I could afford my own place that was the last thing I wanted now.

I went apartment shopping for weeks with Maddie. I

began packing. I knew what I was going to do, but I dragged my feet for every bit of it.

We eventually settled on a place.

I moved my things from the house to the apartment one carload at a time.

Carter didn't notice any of it. Or maybe he did, but he just didn't care. I figured I'd never know.

I didn't say goodbye to him in person.

I didn't tell him anything.

Not that I was heartbroken.

Not that I was pregnant.

I kept it all to myself. For him, not for me.

Instead, I left a note.

*Carter,*

*Thank you for everything. I've decided it's better for both of us if I move out and move on. I'm starting the next chapter of my life, and I know you would approve. I'm taking the car because I have no other way to get around and and you said it was mine, but if you change your mind about that, just tell me, and I'll return it. Otherwise, please don't call or text me. A clean break is what I need.*

*With love,*

*Nova*

I knew if I told him face to face he'd protest and talk me out of it.

He wouldn't even have to mean it.

And so I set the note on the kitchen counter and walked out his door for the last time.

I wondered how long it would take him to realize I was gone. If he didn't notice the note, it could take weeks that was how dedicated he'd been to avoiding me by that point.

I got a job at a café near campus. I started working full-time.

I was only a few weeks into the job when I was late for a shift because of morning sickness. The manager wasn't pleased, but it took two more offenses before she fired me.

I found a twenty-four hour diner and requested the night shift. I wasn't as sick at night, or so I thought.

That turned into me being sick *at* work, which was worse than being late.

I started to expect it, to prepare for it, and I managed to hold onto that job longer.

I was starting to show before Maddie caught on.

"Is that Coach North's baby?" she finally asked me one day, her eyes wide.

Maddie had been a cheerleader back in school, and I'd forgotten that was how she thought of him.

Recalling that was a sore spot, reminding me of the fact he couldn't be a coach now, either. I'd robbed him of so many things.

"Yes," I answered.

"Does he know?" she asked

"No."

"You have to tell him. He would help you, don't you think? He'd step up."

"He's already helped me enough. Besides that, I know he doesn't want any kids yet. He said he doesn't want to settle down for a long time. If I told him, it would be trapping him. Even though he doesn't want me or a baby, he's too decent not to take care of his own kid."

"Well, maybe for the baby's sake, that's how it needs to be."

"I won't keep it from him forever, but there's no reason to tell him now. After the baby's born, maybe I'll do it."

*"Maybe?"*

"I know what it's like to be unwanted. Trust me when I

say having just one parent is better than that. I'm sorry I didn't tell you sooner," I said, changing the subject. "You had a right to know before we moved in together. I'll understand if you want me to find another place to stay. Having a baby around will be a lot different than what you were expecting when we did this."

"Stop that. Of course you don't need to find another place. I'm busy most of the time with school and work right now, but when I'm not, I do love babies. How far along are you?"

"Almost five months." I hadn't gotten very big yet, and I blamed that on being constantly sick.

"Wow. Your belly's still so small. Is it a boy or a girl?"

I shrugged. "I'll know at my five month appointment."

"Do you have any gut feeling? My mom always said she knew if she was having a boy or a girl instinctively."

I thought about it. "I don't have a preference, I just want them to be healthy, but when I dream about the baby, it's always a boy."

"So you're keeping up with all your checkups?" she asked.

She was my age exactly, but she sounded suddenly like a mother hen. I loved it, loved any sign that another human cared about me.

"Yes, it took a while, but I finally got my health insurance figured out and I've made every appointment since then."

"At least you're being responsible."

"I am," I said solemnly. "I'm taking it very seriously."

"I still think you should tell the coach about this."

"Listen, if I can't cut it on my own, I'll call Carter."

I had the five month appointment and cried when I found out it was a boy. All I could picture was a miniature Carter, and it broke my heart all over again.

It was around then I found out Carter had deposited another fifty grand into my bank account. I was elated at first, but the more I thought about it, the worse it felt.

Was this him writing me off for good?

Or worse. I felt sick suddenly. Had he somehow figured out about the pregnancy? Was this his way taking care of it without having to deal with me or the baby? A payoff? Or some sort of a sop to his conscience?

I almost contacted him then. To do what, I wasn't sure. Maybe to ask him what the money was for, or even to turn it down. But I knew I couldn't do that. I didn't only have myself to think about now. I couldn't turn down help for my son. I had to think of him first. I was all he had.

# CHAPTER 28

**CARTER**

Having to tell my whole family what had happened was its own special little slice of hell. I did it fast, like ripping off a Band-Aid.

Their reactions were all exactly what I'd expected and still it was a blow. My mother was shocked. My father was deeply disappointed. My siblings were as judgmental as I knew they'd be. I told them all myself, figuring it was the better option than having it come from someone else, as it inevitably would.

I knew it was the better option, but that didn't mean it didn't send me into an even darker spiral of depression.

Days went by. Then weeks. I slept a lot, watched a lot of

nonsense television in my room.

I knew Nova graduated. She approached me briefly to tell me she'd passed all her classes.

I was relieved, but my reaction was an absent-mended, "Oh, that's good."

I knew time passed, knew there were things I needed to do, but I felt a little anesthetized to life, and eventually I realized I was depressed.

At some point Nova told me, "I found out who made the video and released it." Her voice was dead. Gaze flinty. It was troubling to see her eyes go hard like that. I was only used to them soft, but I realized then, in a disjointed sort of way, that her soft side was all for me.

I was sitting at the desk in my office, and she hovered in the doorway as though even walking in the room was off-limits to her now.

I studied her, tried to see for a moment what she was going through, but her face was closed off to me by that point, utterly stoic.

"Who?" I eventually asked, only mildly curious about it.

"It was Michelle. She confessed to me, said she was sorry, that she only did it out of jealousy."

I just stared at her. "Jealousy?"

"She always had a crush on you, too. She said she'd called dibs. She said I violated girl code."

I didn't even know who the fuck Michelle was aside from Nova's worst friend. "That's insane," I said, but there was no heat in it. I was barely in the conversation, as significant as it was.

Nova nodded and I realized tears were running down her face, though her expression was still holding. "I told her I would never forgive her," she said emotionally, a break in her composure. "I'm never speaking to her again. I can take when she does awful things to me, but what she did to you. . .

that I can't take, can't forget."

"That's good," I said, not so much feeling that way as knowing if I were in my normal mindset that I would. "You shouldn't be friends with people that don't treat you well. You gave her enough chances."

She was sniffling now, barely keeping herself from openly sobbing.

I should have gotten up to comfort her, but I just . . . didn't.

"I should have listened to you the first time you said that. Carter, I'm *so* sorry."

"Don't apologize," I said automatically. "None of this is your fault."

"Of course it is. It's completely my fault. All of it was my *idea*." With that she practically ran out of the room, sobbing.

I was troubled by her pain, but it was like there was a wall between me and that feeling. Between me and any feeling.

I didn't follow her. I would come to regret that deeply.

When I found the note on the counter, I wasn't sure how long she'd been gone.

With the realization of her absence, the fog of numbness lifted for a time replaced by pain and more than a touch of anger.

She couldn't do this. I'd bring her back. I could talk her out of this. I knew it.

But what right did I have? She'd said in the note that she didn't even want me to contact her. There was no way to twist or misinterpret that. She wanted a clean break. She wanted to move on. And she was *so young*. She had her whole life ahead of her. Who was I to decide what she should do with it? To make her spend it with me?

When she'd clearly made another choice.

That's when it hit me. She was *gone*. She'd left me.

I was filled with sorrow. Dejection.

Resignation.

She was gone and there was nothing I could do, or should do, about it.

That was when the real depression set in, and it was worse than all the darkness that came before it.

A few more months passed by in a blur. I missed a few deadlines and didn't even feel bad about it when my work ethic was normally impeccable.

Turner caught wind that something was up and eventually talked me into a brainstorming session at his house with him and Dair.

I knew a half hour into it that it was a good idea, though I didn't contribute much to the conversation, the distraction of it was good for me, and Turner was always that.

An hour in and Dair and Turner were prying the details out of me relentlessly.

I spilled my guts.

Dair was suitably sympathetic.

Turner was howling with laughter by the end, the bastard.

"Ro, did you hear this?" he called out loudly.

Turner's cute little, pregnant wife peeked her head into the office like she'd been waiting for a bat signal. "What's that?" she asked him.

"Carter banged a student, had a sex tape made out of it against their wishes—revenge porn, if you think about it—got fired, and lost her. Literally *lost* her. Like he has no idea where she is." Turner raised his brows at me and made an I told you so face. "I knew when you broke bad it'd be a doozy, but damn, man."

"Iris could find her," Ro pointed out. She bustled in and set a few books on his desk. The second she was in reach, his hand shot out, pulled a few pins out of her hair with precise darting motions.

Her long hair uncoiled from its bun until it was hanging down to her hips in thick dark waves.

I barely noticed their endearing little interaction, intent on rolling Ro's suggestion around in my mind.

I considered it. I really did. But I had no right to stalk Nova. I'd already taken advantage of her. She had a right to leave me, a right to move on. I *hated* it, but that didn't change what was right.

Ro shot Turner a half-hearted glare, batting her hair out of her face. "Don't mess with me. I'm pregnant and ready to rumble."

He gave her a besotted look. "You complete me."

"Like a ball and chain," she shot back, deadpan.

He stared at her. He looked like he was trying to pull off judgmental but came across more doting than anything else. "A little on the nose with that one, don't you think?"

"Don't knock a classic."

"Come over here, and I'll show you just how much I can knock."

"Reprobate."

"*Reformed* reprobate, you little hoyden."

She bustled off.

"Get back here!" he called at her back.

"Get back to work!" she called back.

He was so happy I could barely look at him.

Could that have been Nova and I? I was at the point in my life where I knew exactly what I wanted, but how could she?

I glanced at Dair. It was no better. He always oozed a certain air of subtle contentment that had the same effect on my miserable self.

"So let's work this out," Turner said to me. "She's too young for you, but you clearly don't care, so let's find her. Dair, put your government plant of a wife on the case."

Dair studied me. "If that's what you want, Carter, I can ask her. I'm sure she wouldn't mind."

"She *loves* to meddle," Turner said, and there was affection in it.

"So do you, apparently," I pointed out.

When I left Turner's house that day, nothing was solved, but I did feel marginally better. I started meeting up with them again weekly to brainstorm, started getting back into routines, started writing again.

I almost texted Nova a dozen times, more. Just to ask how she was doing, a few times to pathetically tell her I missed her, but I made myself stop short each time. She'd been clear enough that I couldn't misunderstand what she wanted. Reaching out to her was for me, not for her, and I figured I'd been selfish enough where she was concerned.

In my more hopeful moments, I fantasized about a future where we met up again, where she came back to me, and we were together again, but that's all those thoughts were. Fantasies. She'd moved on without looking back.

# CHAPTER 29

I was on a date. A hot one. I fully expected to get laid tonight, to stick my dick in a new, gorgeous woman.

I felt a little nauseous at the thought, but I planned to push through that. I'd let myself wallow in misery for months. Nova had clearly moved on, and I needed to do the same.

It was that or track her down and drag her back to my house like a caveman.

My date was named Jovie, and she was a model. A real one, with all the credentials. Runway walk, magazine covers, legs for days, stunning face, and a perfect, lithe body.

I knew in a dispassionate sort of way that she had to be one of the most beautiful women on the planet. Her curly dark blond hair just brushed her shoulders and was styled artlessly. She had striking blue eyes that contrasted in a traffic stopping way with her honey brown, perfectly even skin.

Also she was nice, funny even. Just my type. Anyone with a pulse's type, to be fair.

I was trying to rouse up the will to fuck her at the end of the night. I was way overdue.

We were at the Fashion Show Mall. Not my first choice, but I'd left it up to her. Mall dates were beyond tedious but even tedious distractions were welcome these days.

I needed to move the fuck on and if someone like Jovie couldn't help me with that I had no earthly clue what could.

She'd slipped into my DMs pretty recently. At first I'd half assumed I was being catfished when I saw her supermodel timeline.

Still, I'd dated models before, even met them in similar ways, so I gave it a shot. She traveled constantly for work and when her schedule brought her through town, we'd set up a date.

And here we were.

The fact that she was even more gorgeous in person had been as unexpected as the rest of it.

I was unmoved by it, but that was my issue, not hers. Again, I needed to move the fuck on.

I figured a mall date with a model of her caliber would cost a pretty penny. This was not going to be a cheap day. Every shop we passed, I offered to buy her whatever she was looking at, but she surprised me by refusing everything.

In fact, she was treating me more like a friend than a hookup or even a date, and that was so much more natural to me that it took me a good hour to realize she was doing it.

I tried to care, but I just didn't.

"So what kind of modeling work brings you through Vegas?" I asked her, just trying to make conversation.

She was easy to talk to, and we were both well-mannered

to a fault, so things were going fine, but I struggled to stay interested in what she was saying.

I was still trying to get through the rather powerful depression that had me in its grip, though, so I knew it was that rather than the date itself that had me so disconnected.

"LV is opening a new shop in one of the casinos. I've been doing campaigns with them for most of my career so they brought me in for the photo ops. Only a few hours of work, really."

"Doesn't sound like a bad gig," I remarked politely.

"Not at all. My job is wonderful. It's not perfect, it has its cons, but what job doesn't?"

"That's a great attitude."

"It's hard to have a bad one when you've been as lucky as I have. Hey, want to stop for a cup of coffee at this café?"

I looked up, only then noticing where she'd led us. "Sure," I agreed readily.

It was a sit down place and a hostess led us to a booth. I was surprised when Jovie slid in next to me instead of sitting across, but I made room for her without a word. She moved closer until I had to throw my arm over the back of her seat to make space. Strangely as she did this she wasn't even looking at me, her eyes scanning the café, aimed toward the back, I thought.

"I made dinner reservations at—" I began but was interrupted when her mouth suddenly covered mine.

There'd been no warning, but I let it happen readily enough.

She started kissing me right there at the table, and I tried my best to match her with interest.

Maybe she'd do the trick. She was a great kisser. It wasn't stirring me yet, but sometimes these things took time.

She pulled back suddenly, looking around again.

I studied her with some bemusement. "What are you

looking for?" I finally asked her. If nothing else, she was entertaining.

"I think that waitress knows you," she said, not looking at me.

I followed her eyes and couldn't figure out who she meant.

"She just went in the back," Jovie explained. "But she was definitely giving you a certain look."

I shrugged. Who the fuck cared? "I couldn't tell you how or why."

Jovie held up a hand. "Wait. Just wait until she comes back and then tell me that."

I humored her, watching the *Employees Only* door along with her.

I stopped humoring her about five seconds later.

I forgot she was even there.

Through that door came a sight that froze the blood in my veins.

A sight that stopped my heart in its tracks.

A million powerful emotions swept me, and even I couldn't have said which was the most dominant.

Relief. Anger. Horror. Hurt. Elation.

Lust. Yes, that. Rage. So much of that. Raw pain, *that* most of all.

It was Nova, wearing a little café apron and staring at me with something awful in her eyes.

But even that arresting, dreadful look on her face didn't grab my full attention. My eyes were on her belly. Her obviously pregnant belly.

I'm not even sure what I said to Jovie, how I dismissed her, but whatever it was, she took it well, even giving me a rather sympathetic, "Good luck, Carter," as she left.

It was curious, but I was too distracted by my own personal train wreck of a life to care about Jovie's strange attitude.

I have no idea how long Nova and I stared at each other before she turned around and went back through the door.

I didn't move a muscle for who knows how long, and she didn't come back out.

Another waitress came by and I ordered a coffee, still staring at the door.

I drank three cups black before I realized I'd been sitting there for hours and Nova hadn't come back out.

It didn't matter, I thought at first. I'd wait all fucking day. I was going to stalk her until she went into fucking labor.

It sank in somewhat more slowly that the café probably had an exit in the back for employees, and she might have actually slipped away.

I felt true panic then. I waved down my waitress and asked, "Is that pregnant waitress still here?"

She glanced toward the back of the store, then to me, looking distinctly uncomfortable. "I'm sorry, sir. She went home sick. Is there anything I can help you with?"

I knew there was nothing I wanted to ask her that she could actually answer so I left without another word.

Before the day was over, I'd hired a private investigator. I spent the night sitting in my car in the underground Fashion Show Mall parking lot, staked out at a spot I'd figured out she'd have to pass to get back to her job, but even that was no guarantee. It may well have been her day off.

Or hell, for all I knew, she might not even come back now that I knew how to find her.

I lucked out when she passed by my car around noon.

I didn't even consciously decide to move, I hadn't figured out what I'd do with her once I found her, but with no planning and no permission from my brain, I had her backed into the concrete wall and caged in with both arms.

She was trembling and looking at me like I was a stranger. Just then I felt like one. I'd never been so furious in my life.

Or so hurt. I felt like a wounded animal.

I could practically feel her neck in my hands, though I didn't lay one finger on her.

I didn't even know what to say to her. It was just a stare down for quite some time.

Finally I said, "You're coming with me."

I hadn't realized that was going to come out of my mouth, but I didn't take it back.

Abduction it was.

"Get in my car," I added in a growl.

"I have to work," she said in a small voice. "I can't lose this job."

My breathing was ragged. It had been that way for a while. "Yes, you can. You fucking can. Are you kidding me?" I tried to calm myself. Failed utterly. "Get in my fucking car *now*," I said through my teeth.

I was parked close, and she knew which car was mine, so she simply moved toward it without another word. I opened the passenger door and handed her in.

I was able to take a deep breath then. She was in my hands again, at least.

I got into the driver's seat, grabbing the steering wheel so I wouldn't touch her. I didn't look at her as I spoke, "Anything to say for yourself?"

She didn't even bother to answer, her gaze aimed out the window.

I started to drive. It was simple. I was going to drag her to my house like a caveman.

We drove most of the way in heavy silence.

Finally I spoke. I couldn't keep it in one *second* longer.

It wasn't pretty.

"You'd rather our child had *no* father than—" my voice choked on the words, and I couldn't continue for a moment. I made myself finish the sentence, but it was an effort, "*—me*?"

She still didn't look at me, but she did answer me. "I knew it wasn't what you wanted. I'd rather he had no father than one that hadn't wanted him. I know what it's like to be unwanted. There's nothing worse."

I couldn't speak for a long time. Even when I'd composed myself enough to say something, the tears in my voice were evident. *"He?"*

She had both her hands on her belly, and it was covetous. I could tell she thought this baby was hers alone. Not fucking likely. Not anymore. "It's a boy," she confirmed quietly.

"And I never would have known," I was choking out each word, "about my *son* if I hadn't run across you at the mall by *chance.*"

"With your hot date," she said dully.

I ignored that. It was the least significant thing that was happening here. My pain receded just enough for the rage to take over. "Did you know you were pregnant when you left me?" I asked her.

She didn't hesitate. "Yes."

It was like she was a stranger. "You fucking bitch."

She didn't even flinch.

"Did you think I'd react poorly?" I asked her, trying to make sense of it. Trying to find some reason behind her doing something so senseless and frankly cruel.

I'd never been as angry and disappointed in someone as I was with her in that moment, but in spite of that, I pushed those feelings to the side and stuck to the point. To the only thing that mattered now.

"Did you think that I'd pressure you to do something you didn't want to? I don't understand," my voice was trembling with fury, "I cannot even *fathom* how you could have thought I wouldn't take responsibility for this. You fucking knew better."

"I knew better," she agreed quietly.

"So why?" I asked, voice agonized in spite of my efforts at composure. "How? How could you leave me when you *knew*?"

"I thought it was for the best. I'd already ruined your life enough."

"Because I had to stop teaching? You think *that* ruined my life? That was nothing, *absolutely nothing* compared to you trying to take my son away from me, to *erase* me as his father. *How dare you?"*

# CHAPTER 30

**NOVA**

My mind was scrabbling, trying to keep up with what was happening, all of the changes that were coming at me so fast it felt like whiplash.

I'd thought about what it would be like if I ever saw him again, of course, but never had I pictured a scenario like this.

"I was doing you a favor," I finally told him. "I knew you'd do the right thing, but for the wrong reasons, and I simply couldn't *take* your pity, not more than I already have, not over something like this. I figured if you still wanted me, you'd have followed me, baby or no."

He looked furious, so unhinged in a way I never thought to see him. If anyone else this huge had been this angry with me, I'd have been scared to be alone with him.

"Well, your plan didn't work out," he told me, tone deeply unpleasant. "Tough luck for you. How far along are you?"

"Six months," I answered automatically, thought about it, then corrected, "Wait, almost seven now."

"You're moving back in," he began.

"I'm no—" I interrupted.

He held up a hand. "Shut the fuck up and listen," he said through gritted teeth. "I tried to let you have your freedom, since it was so fucking important to you, but that's off the table now. Your motives don't really matter at this point, and how I feel about you," he paused, took a few deep breaths, continued, "and how you feel about *me* is irrelevant. We're having a child together and that is absolutely the *only* thing that matters."

I opened my mouth to speak.

"Don't," he warned me. "You will let me finish. You can hate me for the rest of your life. I might just hate you back. I don't ever need to touch you again, but you will be moving in with me, and I will be helping you with this child. I'll support you both, of course. We'll be raising him together."

Part of me was relieved that this choice had been taken out of my hands now that he was here to help, but it was a small part in the face of all the other emotions battling within me.

Everything he was saying hurt, deep wounds, but it also made me angry. I glared at him.

He wasn't finished. "And we're getting married. I'm old-fashioned. My son will carry my name, and so will his spiteful mother."

The married part had my breath catching in my throat—with hope, with anguish that it was happening like this—but the spiteful charge was an accusation I could not take in silence. "I'm not spiteful," I said firmly. "I told you. I was doing you a favor. You clearly had no problems moving on from me."

He was pulling into his garage at this point. He was around the car to help me out before I could even open my door, but he didn't touch me more than absolutely necessary.

"You're quitting your job," he told me, clearly not remotely done raging at me. "You don't need to be on your feet all day this far along."

I didn't respond and it seemed to calm him a bit.

"This isn't just *your* child," he started lecturing me in his darkest teacher tone, "and you need to make peace with the fact that everything is not going to go your way on this."

When we got into the house we both just stopped and stared at each other. His eyes were on my hands clutching my belly.

"What now?" I asked. I felt suddenly resigned, just too exhausted to fight him.

"You agree, then?" he asked, clearly nowhere near done. He didn't wait for me to answer. "We'll get you settled into my room and make a list of all the things you need—for the baby, for the pregnancy."

"*Your* room?" I asked, studying his face. He was so hostile, and he'd said a few things that made me think he wasn't interested in *that* anymore. Also, my body had changed so much I didn't assume he could want me like this.

"You're pretty heavily pregnant. If something happens and you need me, I'm not going to be across the house from you. Don't worry, I'm not planning on laying a fucking finger on you."

I felt like he'd slapped me, and it was a real effort not to burst into tears right in front of him.

"Where were you living?" he asked, his tone gentling all of a sudden. "I'll get all your stuff moved back here. Today."

"I had an apartment with my friend Maddie. I can't just desert her. She can't make rent on her own."

"That's not an issue. I'll pay your half of the rent. Text me the address and her number. I'll take care of everything."

"I should give Maddie a call before you do anything."

"That would be best, if you're up for it. You can let her know what's happening."

"I'm not sure what to tell her," I confessed honestly.

"It's quite simple," he said bitingly. "Tell her you're marrying the father of your child."

I stared at him for a beat, studying his expression, not quite believing him, nowhere near understanding him. Whatever he was thinking, I was finding nothing I could read.

Finally I got out my phone and called my roommate.

"Hey," I said when Maddie answered.

"Hey," she responded. "Everything okay? Aren't you at work?" It was unusual for me to have free time, let alone my phone on hand, while on the job.

I was instantly stumped on where to start. "I ran into Coach North," I finally settled on.

I heard her gasp on the other end. "What did he say about the pregnancy?" she finally asked.

"He wants me to move back in with him," I continued, "but he'll still cover my half of the rent."

"Okay," she said slowly. "That would be nice. I'll look for someone else, but while I'm looking, I'd appreciate that. So, are you guys like back together?"

I looked at Carter. He was just staring at me, arms crossed over his chest.

"We were never really together," I explained, because it was the truth, "but now that he knows about the baby, he wants to help out with him."

"Is that what *you* want?" Maddie asked.

"If it's what he wants," I responded.

Carter was glaring at me. "Tell her I'll be coming by to get your stuff today," he said, voice stern and leaning into mean.

Maddie heard him. "He sounds angry. I'll pack your stuff up for you, if this is really what you want. Are you okay?"

"I'm okay," I said, trying to sound convincing. "Just a little shocked and tired."

"How did you just happen to run into him?" Maddie asked. She was having as hard of a time taking this all in as I was.

"He was on a date at the mall, and they came into the café together."

"He was on a *date*?" She sounded scandalized.

I was a bit gratified that she was stuck on this fact, because I sure as hell was. "He was."

"Was it like his girlfriend? Is he even *single* now?"

"I don't know. They were pretty hot and heavy." Now it was me glaring back at Carter as I spoke.

He took the phone out of my hand and put it to his ear. "She's getting off track. We're getting married today or tomorrow. I'll be there in a few hours to get all her things. She'll call you back later."

He put my phone in his pocket. I don't even think he realized he hadn't handed it back. He was already on his own phone.

"I'm looking into what we need and how soon we can be married," he said without looking up. "It's Vegas, so I assume I can arrange it all quickly, though obviously I've never done this before, never even thought about it, so we'll have to figure it out as we go along."

"Can I have my phone back?" I asked him, tone careful. He was just so volatile in his current mood. "I need to call work. My boss is really nice. It's rude to just not show up."

He handed it to me. "As long as you calling them involves you quitting that job. I saw the size of some of the trays the waitresses were carrying around there. I can't believe you thought that was a good idea when you're *seven months pregnant*."

I was back to glaring at him. "What else could I do? I'm

not exactly qualified for anything else."

"You weren't supposed to get a fucking job at all, not in your condition. You were supposed to tell the *rich* father of your child that you were pregnant. I know you fucking know I always would have supported you."

I didn't say anything.

"Tell me you knew that," he prompted.

"I knew that," I repeated back dully.

He was shaking his head, still looking at his phone. "I can't believe you. I still can't believe what you tried to do. You knew better."

He was repeating himself at this point, and I knew he was just venting now.

"Okay, I found it, here it is," he said, "We just need our IDs to go fill out the applications for the license in person. There's no waiting period. We can be married at the courthouse by this afternoon.

# CHAPTER 31

**CARTER**

She paled suddenly. "I think I need to lie down."

My heart seized up in trepidation but I didn't hesitate. I'd picked her up and had her halfway to my bed before she was done speaking.

I had her spread out comfortably, shoes off when I realized she was already sleeping.

I was concerned. Was this normal?

I sat at her hip and stared at her for a long time. Eventually I couldn't help myself I laid a heavy hand on her belly.

It *moved* under my hand. Startled at first, I snatched my hand away, then tried again. Another movement and I knew it was my child in there, reacting to my touch.

It was barbaric and far from what I'd promised her mere

minutes before, but I just sort of lost it. I have no excuse, aside from an overwhelming sense of ownership and *need*.

I started stripping her out of her work clothes while she slept on. I got her bare and laid both hands and my cheek softly against her belly. I stayed like that for a long time, tears running unchecked down my face and onto her warm, soft skin.

I was only roused out of my strange spell of comfort and grief when I felt her hand touch my hair softly.

"I thought you weren't interested in laying a finger on me," she spoke in a quiet voice that I couldn't read.

"Apparently, I lied," I said, sitting up. "I didn't know that when I said it, but there it is."

I stared down at her, swallowing a heavy lump in my throat. I couldn't read her face either, but she wasn't saying no.

I stroked her breasts. "Your body's changed," I told her in a thick voice.

"I'm fat," she said, and looked suddenly like she wanted to cry.

I bent down and sucked a plump nipple into my mouth, one hand going down to finger her slick folds. "You're beautiful," I said against her skin and went back to sucking.

I straightened to meet her eyes again. "I want you," I said thickly and pushed a finger inside of her.

"Why?" she asked on a gasp.

That stopped me. "I don't understand the question."

"Why do you want *me*? I've seen your type."

I stared at her, finally getting the picture she'd been trying to show me since I'd picked her up. "You're jealous of Jovie," I accused, far from displeased with the notion.

I played with her clit.

"Is *that* her name?" she asked in a pant. "That woman you were with? Is she your girlfriend?"

"You left me, if you'll recall," I said mercilessly. It was all her fucking fault. "You *wanted* me to move on."

"Clearly that's what *you* wanted," she shot back. "She's really beautiful. I can't compete with that."

"Sure you can," I couldn't help pointing out. "She can't compete with *you*. You're the mother of my child. And she's not my girlfriend. That was our first date, and I don't know if you saw, but it didn't end well. There's no question there won't be another one. I'm getting married in a few hours."

I pushed two fingers into her, my other hand tugging at her nipple almost roughly.

Her reaction was gratifying. She was crying out and moving her hips against me. I pinched her nipple harder.

"It's too much," she sobbed. I twisted it and pinched her clit and she sobbed harder and came.

I snapped, stripping down and mounting her before my brain caught up to my body.

I had to get creative with her big belly. I put her on her side, straddled one leg, the other pulled up as I pushed into her. She was slick, she had been from the moment I'd touched her, and I shoved in smoothly. Two strokes in, my finger on her clit, and she came so hard she screamed with it.

It was enough to stop me even at my most unstoppable. I froze mid-stroke and stared. "You okay?" I asked her, feeling my old tenderness for her sweep through my whole body, head to toe.

She just nodded and I started fucking her again in earnest, her cunt still spasming around me. "Is it too much, too deep, with the baby?" I asked her. I'd never fucked a pregnant woman before, obviously.

"Don't stop," was all she said, and promptly came again, screaming.

I froze mid-stroke again. I was throbbing inside of her, had been ready to come from the second my tip touched her entrance, but even with all that I managed to say roughly, "I think I'll keep you pregnant, if this is what it's like," and started ramming into her again, humping in and out in fast, heaving pumps. She came again, and I didn't stop that time, couldn't have if my life depended on it. I rooted deep and came so hard I had to fight not to black out on top of her.

That broke the longest bout of abstinence I'd suffered in my adult life.

Of course once wasn't enough.

She'd always been beautifully responsive in bed, but the pregnancy took it to lavish, decadent, multi-orgasmic proportions. She was a hair trigger like this and I couldn't stop getting her off, playing with her like a favorite toy.

I got a little carried away.

I alternated between sucking on her clit, working her with my hands, and rooting my dick inside her as much and as often as possible.

She'd come so many times and so intensely that she was begging me to stop.

I had her hips pulled to the edge of the mattress, her legs over my shoulders. I was rooting around, mashing the tip of my dick into a spot deep inside that was making her scream and come with every blunt impact, like pushing a button. A pregnancy come button. It was divine.

I couldn't stop pushing it.

My impulse control had utterly deserted me. "You're my own personal sex toy. I'm going to do whatever I want with you, do you understand? Because you're my property. Say it. Say I'm your toy, your property."

Even as I was coming yet again, stuffing her compulsively and overwhelmingly with my seed, I still kept moving, jarring into that sweet spot.

And again, I got carried away. I only realized it when she passed out cold with me still inside of her.

I felt like an absolute bastard, overcome with instant and powerful remorse.

Thank God she roused from it easily enough, and I made myself stop playing with her body, even folding her into one of my T-shirts and tucking her in.

Even then I was over her, kissing her mouth, her face cupped in my hands. "I'm sorry," I told her between kisses. "I went too far."

Her hand went to my dick, stroking me. I pulled it away.

"I can do something else for you, if it wasn't enough," she told me sweetly.

It was like the old Nova was back, the one from before all the hell she'd put me through for no good reason, and some part of me was ready to forgive her for *all* of it, if only to have her back as I knew her.

"It was enough," I told her finally, though it wasn't what I wanted to say. I'd come three times in the last two hours but I still wanted more and I knew that wasn't reasonable, especially considering her condition.

"I could sit up and you could titty fuck me," she suggested. "Or I could suck you off."

I was already standing. "What about both?" I asked, grinning at her.

It was a bit of a contortion, but we carefully avoided jostling her belly as she managed to hold her heavy tits around my shaft, her head bent down to suck the tip with every thrust as I pumped against her as gently as I could manage.

"Is that good?" she asked me as she slurped at the head of my ramming cock.

I gripped her hair in one hand, the other holding a tit as I fucked up her chest and into her mouth. "It's so good. I'm gonna come so hard. So fast. Don't swallow. I want to mess you up."

"Do it. I want it. Make a mess of me," she said between sucking thrusts of my dick.

That did the trick. I came in a torrent, coating everything within dick's reach: her tits, her neck, her clavicle. That gorgeous face, those pouty lips, her cheekbones, her jaw.

I even got some in her eye, which was just rude. There was no excuse for it. I was out of control, marking my territory beyond all sense or reason.

I was washing her in the shower, my hands cleaning her breasts for so long they were past squeaky clean and straight back to filth again.

"If you're up for it, if you're not too worn out, we'll go get married after we get dressed," I said into her ear.

"You don't have to do that," she told me weakly.

"Don't start with that. Just prepare yourself for it. It's happening, and soon."

"I don't have any clothing, so that might be a problem. I'd prefer not to get married in my café uniform."

I hadn't thought of that. "You left a closet full of clothing but I don't suppose any of that fits you right now?"

"I could look for something really baggy, but I doubt it."

I dried us both off and folded her into one of my robes that dwarfed her. It was an effort to stop touching her, but I made myself do it. "Why don't you go to your old room and see if you can find anything to wear while I start making the arrangements. If you can't find anything we'll stop at your apartment on our way to the courthouse.

# CHAPTER 32

**NOVA**

I couldn't find anything in my closet to wear. Finally, Carter put me into one of his big T-shirts and a pair of boxers and we headed to my old apartment to grab something.

I still couldn't believe he'd said he wanted to get married today, and he really seemed to mean it.

"Do you still hate me?" I asked him after a long stretch of silence in the car.

He'd been much calmer after coming several times, but he was still acting much differently, more coldly, than his old self.

"Don't use that tone with me," he finally answered.

"What tone?" I asked, honestly baffled.

"That wounded, wary tone, like I'm some ogre. You know

I could never hate you. I was just very, very angry at you.

"Are you still angry at me?" I asked in a small voice.

"I'm getting over it," he said, but each word was clipped. "The wedding will help."

"Are you sure you really want to marry me?" I asked. More than anything I didn't want him to regret such a big step.

He didn't even seem to hear the question. "If I just don't think about what would have happened if I hadn't run into you, I can start to move past it," he told me, "but the thought of you going through all of this alone with no help. *That's* what drives me mad. The idea of you needing me and not letting me take care of you. I can't stand that. I need you to swear you'll never do anything like that to me again."

I didn't realize he was demanding an immediate response until he added tersely, "Fucking swear it, Nova."

"I left because you didn't want me anymore," I explained to him. It hadn't been some whim on my part, some desire *I* had. Just the opposite. I'd done it *for* him, because he'd shown me quite clearly that he hadn't wanted me around anymore, and I didn't think he should have to spell it out, not to mention how much more unbearable that would have been for me. "I couldn't stay where I wasn't wanted," I continued firmly. "I've had enough of that. The last four years of my life have been that.

"What the fuck are you talking about?" he burst out.

It shocked me a bit, his renewed fury, and it took me a moment to regain enough composure to elaborate. "After all that stuff happened, with school, with the video," I told him as calmly as I could. "You were done with me after that."

"When did I ever say that?" he bit the question out severely.

"You didn't have to spell it out. It was obvious. I could *feel* it. Everything bad that had happened was my fault, and you were done with me."

"Well, you suck at reading my mind," he said harshly. "I was upset and depressed about some of the things that happened, yes, but I didn't blame you for any of it, and I never stopped wanting you. It was exactly what I told you it was. I needed some time. Now, swear it. Swear you won't pull any shit like that on me again."

"I swear it," I said solemnly. Not leaving him again sounded heavenly. Leaving had been the unnatural thing. It had been hard as hell to go against all my natural inclinations, which were always to stay close to him.

Another stretch of silence took us, and I was the one that broke it again, "Do you plan to be faithful?" I asked him tonelessly. What he was proposing here was in every sense a forced marriage of convenience for the baby. I just needed to know what that meant to him. "I know you didn't choose this that *I* wasn't your choice," my voice cracked in spite of my attempt at composure, "but I'd like to know."

We were at a stop light, and he turned his head to stare at me. He looked like he'd never been so offended in his entire life. Like the very question had made him ill. "What kind of a guy do you think I am?" he asked, tone filled with disgust. "I've slept around before when I was *single*, but I've never cheated on even a *casual* girlfriend in my entire life, but you think I'd screw around on my *wife*? On the *mother of my child*?"

He seemed to be growing more upset with every word, but they were having the opposite effect on me.

This was going to be a real marriage. My chest filled with warmth, with elation.

Even if he never grew to love me, I thought this could be enough. No one that spent five minutes with Carter could doubt he'd be a good husband and father. It was more than I'd ever even let myself hope for. Wanting more was just greedy, I told myself.

We arrived at my apartment building.

Of course Carter didn't like the neighborhood.

Our place was three stories up with no elevator, and Carter started cursing darkly as soon as he realized it.

"You've got to be fucking kidding me," he muttered from behind me on the stairs. "Heavily pregnant and going up and down these stairs."

"Top floor apartments are a bit cheaper," I said defensively.

I could feel him glaring at my back.

Maddie was home and packing my things. She ran to me and hugged me the second I walked through the door. "Are you really okay?" she asked into my ear.

I just nodded. Honestly I was getting more okay by the minute.

She pulled back, looking behind me. "Uh, hey, Coach North," she said awkwardly. "Long time no see."

He nodded at her, shutting the door behind him. "Thank you for helping her pack up, for helping her in general," he said, though his tone was at odds with the words. He was in full cold teacher mode.

He pointed behind her. "This was her room?" he asked her.

Maddie nodded.

He shot me an unreadable look, stroked a hand over my hair as he passed by me, and pointed at the sofa. "Sit down and rest," he told me.

I obeyed. Maddie watched us both with wide eyes.

"I'll grab some things and take inventory, see how many boxes we'll need to move you," Carter continued. "You two can have a moment to say goodbye."

He walked into my room. I opened my mouth to tell him I didn't have much to move, but closed it. He'd see soon enough.

Maddie sat down next to me, staring after him even when he'd shut the door behind him.

"I never remember him being *this* intense," she said with awe.

"It's been an intense day," I said ruefully.

"He's so hot," she added. I didn't like that, but she distracted me by adding, "He's like *really* into you."

I stared at her, trying to figure out how she'd gotten that out of our brief and tense interaction. "He takes being a father very seriously," I finally settled on saying. It sort of explained everything.

"I knew you had an affair with him and all," she continued like I hadn't spoken, "but I didn't think it was like *that*. He's, like, obsessed with you."

Again, I didn't see how she got that out of a few seconds of him ordering me to sit down. "It's just because of the baby," I explained. "He might be obsessed with the baby."

She shot me a look like I was the crazy one. "Why on earth would you leave him when you were pregnant and he's like in *love* with you?"

"He was never in love with me," I said firmly. "Not even a little bit. Trust me."

"Nova," Carter's voice barked out.

I jumped in my seat. I hadn't even noticed the door to my bedroom opening again. "Yes?" I answered.

His jaw was clenched so hard it looked like it was a struggle for him to open it up to speak, "You don't have anything to wear for the wedding. We'll have to make a quick stop somewhere. Why don't you map out a maternity store you like while I work on this?"

He looked at my friend. "Maddie, will you get her a glass of water?" He glanced back at me. "This is going to take a minute, but I think I can get most of your stuff packed into my car now. Just give me thirty minutes." He disappeared again.

"Can I be like a witness at your wedding?" Maddie asked as she handed me a glass of water a minute later.

I beamed at her. "I love that idea."

"That's fine," Carter called from the bedroom. He had unholy hearing, I was learning. "As long as you don't mind taking your own car. Ours is going to be a bit stuffed."

"You could fill up my car too," she called back to him helpfully. "After you get hitched, I can follow you back to your place, save you a trip."

He appeared in the doorway with an armful of my clothing. He seemed to think about it. "No, that's all right. We'll have to come back again to get her car tomorrow anyway."

"I could get my car now and just meet you at the courthouse," I suggested.

He stared at me and it didn't feel friendly. "No, that's all right," he said shortly, and went back into my room.

"I don't think he's going to let you out of his sight any time soon," Maddie noted a bit gleefully.

Clearly she found us both entertaining.

In less than thirty minutes we were driving again, Maddie following, as we headed to a maternity store. "I don't know what to wear to something like this," I said somewhat absently. I was mostly thinking out loud.

"Something like *this*?" he asked acerbically. "You mean a wedding? I'd recommend a dress, preferably a white one."

I looked down at my big belly, amused. "I don't think white is quite the right color."

He put a warm hand on my belly, eyes still aimed straight ahead at the road. "Yes, it is. You're marrying the man that took your virtue. The *only* man you'll be with for the rest of your life. For *that*, you wear white."

I was trembling, tears running down my face. I covered

his hand with both of my own. I loved him so much and it was an effort not to say it out loud. "Okay," I finally managed to get out. "I'll wear white."

I thought he'd let Maddie and I handle it, but Carter didn't stay in the car when we got to the maternity boutique. He followed me in and started going through racks of pregnancy dresses like it was the most natural thing in the world.

Maddie and I watched him, both a little thunderstruck, I think.

He held up a gauzy white dress before I even started looking. "Will you try this one on?"

"Okay," I said, moving to take the dress without even thinking about it.

"Why don't you go to the dressing room and we'll bring you what we find?" he suggested, going through dresses again.

I obeyed automatically, still shell-shocked by the strange, eventful day.

I was half undressed when Carter stepped into the dressing room with an armful of dresses to join me. He hung them on the rack on the wall.

"I thought you might need help," he said, all business.

I didn't respond and he finished undressing me. He fingered the material of my bra, a near caress, and I couldn't tell what he was thinking, whether he wanted me or was just this impatient to find me the right clothes.

"You need more maternity bras," he said and cupped my breasts with both hands. "Some nursing ones, too. What size is this one? I'll go pick some out.

"Thirty-four G," I told him, breath unsteady.

"Jesus, they're glorious. You are." With a heavy sigh, he let go of my flesh and reached for the first dress, pulling it over my head.

I wanted him. Right this second, *wanted him*, but he

seemed to have other plans.

I didn't have to do a thing but stand there as he dressed and undressed me. I barely had to form an opinion, though he did ask my preference.

We settled on the first dress he'd picked out. It was by far the best fitting and most flattering.

"Just leave it on," he told me. "I'll take the tag and pay for it. Grab anything else you see that you like. I'm going to grab those bras. Also, you need shoes."

He started to step away, but I grabbed his hand. He froze, an arrested look on his face, and started shaking his head. "Not here, not now" he said tersely. "I'm not going to fuck you again until you're my wife."

While I loved the sound of that, I was in a state, all the little touches as he'd dressed and undressed me building me up into a bonfire of need.

I moved his hand down my body, closing my eyes. "Can you do something else then?" I asked him tremulously. "Please. I need it."

He loved that, his voice in my ear telling me just how much as he finger fucked me, his other hand covering my mouth. He found just the right spot to pound his fist against me as he worked two fingers in and out.

Once wasn't enough, for him, for me, and he got me off a quick-fire three times before tearing himself away unsteadily.

By the time we left the store, I was wearing my wedding dress with some comfortable white matching sandals, and I had more maternity gear than I thought I could even wear in the next few months, but I wasn't complaining.

He barely fit the bags into what little space was left in his car, but he managed.

There was a florist along the drive and I was confused when he pulled in to park in front of it.

"Stay here," he told me, and got out of the car. He went

inside and Maddie, who was still following us, got out of her car and came to my window. I rolled it down.

"What's he doing?" she asked.

"I have no idea."

"Did you guys have sex in the dressing room?" she asked, smirking.

"Not exactly," I hedged, blushing profusely.

She shook her head. "I still can't believe you left him. You two as a couple are not at all what you led me to believe."

"We're very . . . sexually compatible, I think, if that's what you mean."

"No, Nova, that is not what I mean. What I mean is I think you're delusional where he's concerned. You're so certain no one could love you that you've done some pretty heavy mental gymnastics to convince yourself of it, but that man has it bad, at least as bad as you have it for him."

"Stop," I said weakly. I just couldn't take it. "Don't give me hope. Hope hurts, and it's certainly never worked out for me before."

She put her hands up. "Fine. I'll drop it, but someday I get to say I told you so, and it's going to be a lot of fun for me."

Carter walked out of the florist shop right then. He had something in his hands and he was smiling.

He unwrapped it and it was a crown of peach Persian buttercups.

"How did they make that so fast?" I asked him, stunned. There was no way they just had something so specific on hand.

"I called ahead and talked them into a rush order. One more stop and we'll be good to go."

"One more stop?" I asked, dazed.

Maddie was still standing by my open window and now she was rubbing her hands together and grinning. "A jewelry store, I bet."

Carter nodded, handing me the crown through my window and heading around to the driver's side. "That's right. You can pick out a proper diamond later, but for now I've found a place that has wedding bands ready for us."

Wedding bands in hand, white dress, and beautiful crown on my head, we made it to the courthouse in time to fill out the paperwork and get a wedding license. Ten minutes after that we were married in front of a bored judge and a gleeful, teary Maddie.

I cried too, happy, relieved tears. No matter what, I had a real family now. There was nothing I needed or wanted more than that.

Carter kissed me deeply to seal the vows and all that stopped him from getting completely carried away was Maddie giggling loudly in the background.

We were walking out of the courthouse when Maddie told Carter boldly, "I believe it's a tradition to take your witness out to a fancy dinner."

He glanced at her, clearly amused. "You're not friends with Michelle, are you?"

Maddie looked taken about, but she answered easily, "Not after what she did to Nova."

He smiled at her and it was much warmer. "You'll do. And how about I make you both a fancy dinner instead of going out for one?"

"Deal," Maddie said instantly. "I've always wanted to see your house."

I shook my head, laughing at her. "Don't be weird about it."

Carter made us a creamy sun dried tomato and chicken pasta dish that was the best thing I'd had since I'd left him.

He didn't seem to care that Maddie was right across the table, after he served me he sat down close beside me, rubbed my belly with one hand and started feeding me each bite with the other.

I waved him off when I was full. "You need to eat, too."

"I've been eating between your bites," he said, and as if to prove the point, put another forkful in his mouth. "Dessert?" he asked me after swallowing.

I shook my head. "I'm too stuffed. And sleepy. Something about the pregnancy makes me need to sleep almost the instant I stop eating."

"I guess I'll go," Maddie said with a sigh. "You forgot I was even here. And here I didn't even get a tour of the house."

Carter laughed. "Nova will give you a tour the next time you visit," he told her.

Maddie hugged me goodbye without making me stand and promptly left.

"Do you need me to carry you to bed?" Carter asked me.

I laughed. "No! My legs work." I stood, and he stood with me. "Actually I think I'll go drift off on the couch watching anime, if you don't mind."

"Whatever you want, pet."

# EPILOGUE

I fell asleep watching Jujutsu Kaisen while Carter rubbed my feet. I barely stirred later as he carried me to bed, undressed me, and tucked me in tenderly, hugging my back as I drifted back to sleep.

I was swiftly getting my old Carter back. Everything felt too good to be true, especially considering how things usually went for me.

We'd just finished breakfast and were sitting at the kitchen table the next day when I brought it up.

"Aren't you the least bit mad about this?" I asked him.

"About what, exactly?" he asked me in a careful tone.

"That I got pregnant. That I wasn't on birth control. Didn't you assume that I was?"

"I was mad about a lot of things, mad at *you*, at what you did, leaving like that, then finding out you were pregnant when you did, but I'm not angry with you for *that*. You can't be blamed for that. And I certainly shouldn't be surprised. Yes, I assumed you were on something since I never used a condom and you never brought it up, but I never even asked you about birth control. This is on me. I fucked you bareback too many times to count because it felt good and I couldn't get enough of it. *God*, just talking about it makes me want to get inside of you again." He paused, collected himself. "I can't tell you what I was thinking, except to say that mostly I wasn't, and whatever part of me was clearly had no problem getting you pregnant. But I have no regrets and I'm sorry if you do."

"Really?" I asked tremulously. Big tears were running down my cheeks.

"Get over here," he told me gruffly. "I can't take you like this for another second without my hands on you. Now come sit on my lap and let me bounce you on my dick."

I ignored that, though it wasn't easy. I was squirming in my seat. "You said you didn't want kids for another ten years."

"I didn't mean it," he said, no hesitation. "I was barely paying attention to what I was saying when I did. I was just talking. It's just something you say when your married friends are ribbing you about starting a family. Believe me, if I'd known you'd take it to heart, that you'd do what you did because you heard that, I'd have kept my fucking mouth shut. Now come here."

He had his dick out now, and this time I obeyed. He was unwrapping me like a present when he asked, "How many kids do you want? I'd like more than one."

He seated me on him, impaling me slowly.

"One at a time," I said on a gasp.

He started fucking me, holding me above him and thrusting in and out, bouncing me on him, an uneven, addictive ride. Eventually he said, "You robbed me of *months* of this pregnancy. I'd like at least one extra child to make up for that."

It took me a long time to answer. I only spoke after I'd come, and he was holding me still on top of him as I recovered. "I've been no fun for most of this one. I kept getting sick."

"When did the multi-orgasmic phase start?"

"When you had me naked in your bed again."

He liked that. He really liked it. He started fucking me again in earnest. He got me off again before he seated me balls deep and came hard. His hips churned as I milked out every bit of it. He made me come again just with his aftershocks.

"You're too much like this," he said into my ear, fondling my heavy breasts. "I love it. What having my baby is doing to your body, to my property. It belongs to me more than ever. You're my creature now, completely. I own you, pet. Say it."

I was squirming on his dick, and I was one little flick of the clit away from coming again. "You own me," I said.

He got me off again then let me loose.

"I'm still worried after that passing out incident," he told me. "Otherwise I'd stay inside of you all day."

We watched anime for most of the day while I half-napped on the couch. I laid back against the arm of the sofa while he rubbed my legs, my feet. Eventually he got behind me and massaged my back and shoulders, my head and neck. When he started kneading at my breasts, I knew it was game over. He was so obsessed with them at this point I thought he could have come just from fondling me.

He devoted as much time as I'd let him taking care of my every need for the next few days. He was obsessed with the idea. He didn't like for me to lift a finger.

He worked on his laptop next to me while I caught up on all my favorite shows. He told me that everything he wrote, everything he thought about involved my pregnant, voluptuous self.

"I'd like to keep you pregnant for the next decade," he told me later as he was pumping into me. "How does five sound?

Is that too many?"

I didn't answer, but my screaming orgasm surely told him something.

"What would the mother of my children like for dinner today?" he asked me later.

I was smiling at that, just beaming at him. "It's just one child so far."

"That's a technicality," he told me. "You've pretty much agreed to at least one more. Five if I'm actively making you come."

"I'd like a small break after this one, to adjust, to maybe take a few college classes."

That pleased him greatly. He gave me that particular approving teacher look that I loved. "Of course, pet. I'll help you get registered whenever you're ready."

Eventually I worked up the nerve to ask him a question I didn't necessarily want the answer to. "Were you with a lot of women . . . after I left?"

"You shouldn't have left," he pointed out instantly. It was still a sore subject.

And that wasn't an answer. I tried again. "You were kissing Jovie the first time I saw you again. Clearly you'd moved on."

"She kissed me," he shot back. "I was rather surprised, to be honest. It came out of nowhere."

"You were kissing her back," I pointed out.

"I was *trying* to move on," he told me in a voice that ached. "I wasn't successful, but I was trying. It was the first and *only* date I'd been on since you left. Don't you understand? You broke my heart."

My heart stopped. I was afraid to take that how I yearned to.

"I did?" I asked slowly.

"Of course you did. You left me. I'm madly in love with

you, and you just left. I was depressed and going through a rough time and you disappeared. Don't you think that hurt? You didn't even talk to me first. And you told me not to so much as contact you. Yes, *of course,* you broke my heart."

"You're in love with me?" My voice broke on the question.

"Of course I am."

"You never told me. Not once. I said it a lot, and you never said it back."

"I didn't want to trap you, but now you're trapped with me forever, so I'm not holding anything back. Not ever again."

"I love you too," I told him, crying now.

He moved to me, his soft lips on my cheeks, kissing away the tears. "I know, pet. You have such a beautiful heart, and I'm *so* lucky it's mine. I'll take good care of it, I promise."

Not even a week later, his large family descended on the house.

The *entire* family.

It was overwhelming. And nice.

I knew I was a surprise to all of them, the pregnancy even more so, but they took it with grace.

His parents were wonderful, warm, and welcoming, and everything I'd missed and more since my own passed. I'm not sure I was who they'd have chosen for their son, but since he'd chosen me they seemed determined to back him up with extra credit.

His mother, Caroline, was rubbing my belly while we sat side by side on the sofa one afternoon when she said, "This will be my fifth grandchild and my first grandson. I can't tell you how happy this makes me. Thank you for joining our family. We'll make sure you never regret it. I'm sure you know this, but you won't find a better man than Carter. I promise he'll make you happy."

"I know," I said, and I was sobbing. In my whole life I'd

never met anyone as instantly loving toward me as his mother, and I didn't know if it was just her or the pregnancy or both, but her sweet little speeches made me cry every time.

No one said one word about the fact that we'd clearly gotten married after I was heavily pregnant, and I appreciated that.

There were a few awkward moments, mostly when anyone was reminded of my age or the fact that Carter and I had met because he was my high school teacher, which was particularly scandalous for his traditional-minded family, but the moments passed quickly.

I didn't realize until a few days into the little family reunion that Carter was the youngest of the five kids. The oldest was his sister Constance and she had him by twelve years. The table went speechless during dinner when the math was done and everyone realized she was beyond old enough to be my mother, but even that was laughed away good-naturedly.

All of his siblings stayed a solid two weeks just to get to know me better, and his parents stayed another week.

By the time we had the house all to ourselves again, I felt thoroughly ensconced in his wonderful family. It was everything I'd ever wanted.

**CARTER**

We were at Dair's house for a brainstorming session a few weeks later when we put all the pieces together.

I'd just finished updating the guys on all the details of my impromptu wedding and my impending fatherhood when Turner got the ball rolling.

"Wait," Turner said slowly, like something was dawning on him. He was looking at Dair, but speaking to me. "Whose idea was the mall date?"

"Jovie's," I answered. I'd told them every little detail of

our reunion, even down to my strange date.

Turner had a talent for dragging that sort of thing out of a person.

"Does she know Iris?" Turner asked, his eyes narrowed in thought.

"Iris?" I asked, confused. "Of course not. I met Jovie on Instagram. Wait, what are you implying here?"

"Ro!" he shouted. Iris, his wife, and Nova were baking cupcakes together with Iris and Dair's kids while we brainstormed in Dair's office.

Ro appeared impressively fast, sassy hands on hips. She was heavily pregnant, due any day, any minute now. "Yes, milord!" she said, smirking at him.

Turner beamed at her like her sass was his own personal ray of sunshine.

"Dair, Ro," Turner addressed them both, holding his palms out and speaking slowly like he was making a big reveal. "Tell me this doesn't smack of Iris fuckery."

"You're crazy," Ro stated flatly.

"So?" he shot back at her. "You haven't even heard what I'm talking about yet."

He explained it all to her, the quick, crude, Turner version of events.

"Now answer the question," he told her. "Does this smack of Iris fuckery?"

"Paranoid weirdo," Ro muttered.

"Pregnant shrew," he returned, then, "Dair, you're awfully quiet."

Dair opened his mouth to say something when Iris appeared in the doorway, smiling.

Turner pointed at her. "Do you *have* to appear when we say your name three times? Did we summon you out of the depths? Is it some kind of witchcraft?"

She giggled and went to sit beside her husband, patting his

knee and winking at him.

"Hear me out," Turner continued his tirade. "Iris found your pregnant girl and led you to her." As he spoke he was on his phone. A minute passed.

I did find it curious how smug Iris looked.

"Aha!" Turner exclaimed. "Here it is. Iris and Jovie in a picture together at some party in L.A. Care to explain yourself?"

He was looking at Iris. We all were.

*Seriously*? I thought. I hadn't for a *second* believed he could be onto something, but that right there was very suspicious.

Iris just shrugged and said, "To be clear: I did not set you up with your student. Even *I'm* not that twisted. I only involved myself when you fucked up and lost her."

I was stunned. Maybe Iris really *had* done all the crazy stuff Turner thought she had. It was mind-boggling. "You set me up with Jovie so I would run into Nova while we were on our date?

"Yes. Don't worry, Jovie knew it was all fake, and she was game. She's a doll."

"Do you think *that's* what I was worried about?"

She giggled. "You're welcome."

"Admit it, you and Heath are both spooks," Turner accused her.

She didn't bat an eye. "Whatever work we have or have not done for the government is confidential, but I will say, whatever it was, I'm mostly retired and so is Heath."

Turner was like a dog with a bone. "*Mostly*?"

She shrugged. "Mostly."

"I knew it!" Turner said triumphantly. He'd been trying to get her to admit that for *years*.

Nova appeared in the doorway. "What's going on?"

"Nova, how do you know Iris?" Turner asked her. "Like,

before today, you've met her before, right?"

"She was a customer at the café several times," Nova said easily. "She was always nice and she tipped well.

Iris winked at her. "I found her, scoped her out, brought you to her, and gave you both a push toward getting back together by way of supermodel. Like I said, you're welcome."

**NOVA**

I went into labor three weeks early. My water broke but I never dilated, and Carter just about lost his mind when we got to the hospital and my labor seemed to freeze in place.

Eight hours in the doctor gave me Pitocin to bring on full labor, theorizing that I'd have to start dilating then.

It went on long enough that his parents were able to catch a flight and make it into town before our son made his first appearance.

Every single one of Carter's siblings tried to make it in time too, and though they didn't quite manage it, they all made it into town soon after the birth.

Twelve hours in I still hadn't dilated an inch but the contractions were coming fast and hard and they started prepping for an emergency C-section.

I found myself holding Carter's hand and comforting him. He took me being in pain much worse than I did. "I'm fine. Everything is fine. He was just waiting for your parents."

"Are you in pain?" he asked, his eyes wet and intent on mine.

"No," I lied. "Have you thought of a name yet?"

"I think his name is Paxton. What do you think?"

"I love it," I told him. "Let's see what your parents think. How close are they?"

"Ten minutes out. Are you sure you're not in pain?"

"I'm fine," I said. I was actively having an impotent

contraction, all pain and no production without dilation, but I'd be damned before I made him feel it with me. "How far out is the anesthesiologist?" I asked in as stoic of a tone as I could manage.

He did a double take, studying me. His hand in mine started trembling. "You are in pain," he accused.

I smiled as serenely as I could manage. "How far out?" I repeated.

"They said five minutes thirty minutes ago. Let me go get him myself. I'll fucking wring his neck."

I wouldn't let go of his hand. "I'll take the pain over you leaving. It's fine. I can wait five minutes."

It was less than that before I was prepped for surgery and finally given an epidural. It was all easy after that as far as I was concerned.

Even three weeks early, baby Paxton weighed in at nine pounds even. My future football player baby.

Carter cut the umbilical cord and cried as he held our son first. I got him second, his mother third, his father William, fourth.

We all cried happy tears together, all with hands on Paxton while I held him against my chest.

My son would never go through what I'd had to endure. Even if the worst happened, he would never be alone, not with a family like this.

I'd never felt more safe, more loved.

## OTHER BOOKS BY R.K. LILLEY

### STANDALONES

*ARRANGED*

### THE LOVE IS WAR SAGA

*BREAKING HIM*
*BREAKING HER*
*SAVAGES - COMING SOON*

### THE WILD SIDE SERIES

*THE WILD SIDE -IRIS-DAIR*
*THE OTHER MAN*
*TYRANT*
*TEACHER'S PET*

### THE UP IN THE AIR SERIES

*IN FLIGHT*
*MILE HIGH*
*GROUNDED*
*MR. BEAUTIFUL*
*LANA*

### THE TRISTAN & DANIKA SERIES

*BAD THINGS*
*ROCK BOTTOM*
*LOVELY TRIGGER*

### THE HERETIC DAUGHTERS SERIES

*BREATHING FIRE*
*CROSSING FIRE*